SONG

OF THE

WILD

Melissa Matos

MOMTOAST

PUBLISHING

Song of the Wild

Copyright © 2021 by Momtoast Publishing

This is a work of fiction. Any characters, names, places, or likenesses are purely fictional. Resemblances to any of the items listed above are merely coincidental.

For permission requests, please contact the publisher, Momtoast Publishing via e-mail, at the e-mail address below:

melissa@momtoast.com

ISBN
Paperback: 978-1-7364970-0-5
eBook: 978-1-7364970-1-2

Cover design by Crystal L. Kirkham
Interior design by B.K. Bass
Editing by Crystal L. Kirkham

melissamatosauthor.com

To my dad, who knew I could do this, and my brother, who pushed me to finish. I miss you both. This is for you.

ACKNOWLEDGEMENTS

It is impossible to thank everyone who had a hand in making this book happen. A thousand little influences every day have gone into creating this story, many probably without my noticing. But I do have to thank my mom for putting up with a fantasy geek and a moody writer for a daughter, my grammy for enjoying fantasy with me, my nieces for reminding me of the joy of life and magical wonder, and my critique partners Michael Bujtas and Catherine Slamka for a lot of great advice for keeping my writing on track.

I also want to give a huge thank you to B.K. Bass, Sam Hendricks, Crystal L. Kirkham, and the whole team at Kyanite Publishing for choosing this book to be part of their catalog. They do a lot of work over there, and are wonderful to work with, and I am grateful to be part of such a team for my debut novel.

SONG

OF THE

WILD

CHAPTER ONE

I swung open the door of the Wyvern's Den eager to eat a good meal, sleep in my own bed, and get out of my disguise. Instead a chorus of voices shouted, "Welcome home, Warden." A banner with the same words in big red letters hung from the ceiling, and the gray stone walls were covered with tapestries featuring armored figures fighting dragons. I sidestepped out of the doorway as a large woman in yards of pink silk rushed forward, her arms open wide.

"Harkor, welcome home." She threw her arms around the young man who hadn't made it inside yet. "We were so pleased to hear you were accepted we couldn't wait to celebrate." She dragged Harkor into the Den and over to a seat beneath the banner.

Loria peered into the doorway, the tip of the longbow she carried on her back bumping the top of the door frame. She looked left and right. "Is it safe to come in?" she asked. I smirked and waved her inside.

"I'm sure it's fine. No one's here to hug us." I didn't recognize any of the crowd pressing in to shake Harkor's hand. I looked around the tavern, hoping to spot a familiar face, but not even the regulars were warming their seats at the bar.

"I can't believe he made Warden already," Loria said. "I mean, is that all it takes now? If you can read a spell broadside and stomach a rotation at a Tower, you're in?"

"He isn't half bad with a rapier," I said. I stayed by the door, not wanting to push into the room stuffy from too many bodies and too much perfume. Harkor disappeared into a crowd of his family and friends, getting claps on the back from uncles and kisses on the cheek from cousins.

"We could always go to Heddle's," Loria suggested. I nodded and we reversed course, hoping to slip away.

"Glade!" I stopped in the doorway, but Loria hurried on, waving over her shoulder as she disappeared into the dark street outside. I turned to see Jinelle, the owner of the Den, waving to me from behind the bar. I shut the door and shuffled over, adjusting my own traveling pack to keep my guitar from bumping anyone in the crowded room.

"You rent the place out for parties now?" I asked. She was directing two servers to set their food laden trays out on the bar. Her eyes glimmered when she looked at me, and her smile was sharp. Everything about her face was sharp; her eyes, her cheekbones, the points on her ears.

4

"If they're willing to pay, I'm willing to rent." She inspected the food trays, straightening a skewered bit of meat here and there. "People will pay top prices for a place with atmosphere." She stopped and looked directly at me. "You know, atmosphere. They paid for the whole package."

I chewed my lip, and nodded, putting on my best imitation of a smile. "Right, of course, atmosphere. Do you think I should change first? Make myself a little more presentable?"

"I think the traveling clothes make you look more authentic."

"Right." That was me, classic tavern bard. "Well. Any special requests?"

"Just start with some dance music. The mother's opinionated enough she'll let you know if she wants something different." She looked over the trays again, and then headed back into the kitchen shouting something about soup.

I took a deep breath. It would only be a few more hours. I could hold on to my disguise for a few more hours. It had only been three weeks, and an easy three weeks at that. What were a few more hours? Harkor was sitting on the small platform that passed for a stage at the Wyvern's Den, but if all they wanted was atmosphere, I wouldn't want to be center stage. I pulled a stool away from the bar to an out of the way corner of the room. There were several nooks in the natural stone walls of the Den where I could tuck myself away. I slapped a quick beat on the face of my guitar and started a jaunty dance tune.

Another cheer erupted from the crowd, and several couples peeled away from the group and proceeded around the room with skipping steps. Others turned to watch and keep time, clapping their hands together or against their hips. I regretted not changing. As more couples started to dance, the temperature rose.. I couldn't stop to scratch at the trickles of sweat under my leather armor, so I made do with rubbing my back against the wall behind me like a bear.

Harkor hadn't spoken about his family much while at the Tower. It had been his first border job, and he'd had a thousand questions, most of them about useless superstitions of the Wild and what we would have to face. The family were much like I imagined they would be, merchants or lawyers or bankers, not wealthy enough to own a palazzo on the top level but with enough money to finance their son as a Warden and rent out a tavern to congratulate him.

I watched the dancers swirl in their bright, high waisted gowns and fashionable short tunics as I sweat through my linens, wondering how they weren't all wilting like flowers. Most were elves or humans, or a mix of the two, lithe, sun-bronzed and lively. They danced and ate and danced some more. They were generous with their drinks, and their tips. Once they found I could play the newer, more risque songs from back east they started throwing coins at me to play faster and rowdier as the night went on.

At the finale of one of these robust dances, Harkor and his current partner ended up leaning against the wall beside the nook I was tucked into. The spell that had made her dress vary in color from deep sea green to midnight blue had worn off an hour ago. Now it was only a creamy white against her glistening dark skin. She sidled up against Harkor and whispered something in his ear that made him blush.

"Congratulations on making Warden," I said, to be sure they noticed I was there. My words startled them, and it was the woman's turn to blush.

"Thanks Glade." Harkor tucked his arm around the waist of the woman.

"Sorry about the Mazza." The only Wild creature that had shown up in the whole three weeks was a short, hairy Mazza who had stumbled out of the forest accidentally. He'd lost his red hat, and had come running towards the Tower after it.

"Oh, don't even think about it," he said. He waved his other arm and wobbled. The woman managed to keep him steady. "Loria shouldn't have been up on that log to begin with. She could have aimed at it from the ground. Then you wouldn't have knocked her down, and she wouldn't have fallen into me before I could stab it. No one got hurt, it went back into the Wild, that's what matters, right? Besides, I managed to get a different souvenir. Something pretty for my mom."

"Oh, how sweet," his dance partner cooed. "What did you get her? Did you find some of that Wild silk? I hear it sparkles in the moonlight." She looked down at her own faded gown and frowned.

"No, even better." Harkor crouched closer to me, bringing the woman along with him, but was too tipsy to actually lower his voice. "I caught an Aletta."

I ground my teeth together, and my skin grew tingly. I locked myself in my seat, and counted to keep my breathing even. In, two, three, four. Out, two, three, four. It wouldn't help matters to lose my disguise here. The woman's eyes grew round and shiny.

"How did you do that?" she asked.

"Easy enough. You put out a tray of milk just before twilight and drop an iron cage on them. They're so distracted by eating they don't even see you coming." He stood up tall and puffed his chest out as though he had vanquished an ogre instead of catching the Wild equivalent of a firefly. "I left it in our cart." He frowned. "Do you think it will be all right out there for the night? Maybe I should check on it."

"No, let me." I jumped out of my stool, setting the strings on my guitar ringing. I leaned it against the wall. "You have your guests. And you don't want to spoil the surprise for your mother." I backed towards the door. "I need a break anyway. Your family is hard to keep up with." I shook my hand out as though it had cramped from the rowdy playing. Harkor grinned and bobbed his head up and down.

"Thanks, Glade, I really appreciate it. Maybe you could sneak it in the back? Then I can give it to my mother before we leave."

"Sure thing," I said, and ducked out the door.

Outside everything was cool and quiet. The canal's steady flow kept a few small boats bobbing and creaking at their moors. Torchlight glimmered on the marble columns across the canal and was swallowed by the darkness that cloaked the South Piazza. Everything was wrapped in the scent of clean water and damp stone.

Our small cart was parked against the rough rock wall of the Den, the pony that had pulled it home stabled on the level below us. A wooden sign creaked over my head bearing a faded red wyvern. The Den stood out on the walk, otherwise lined with marble facades, but that was part of its appeal. Under the wyvern the sign proclaimed, 'historic charm in a modern district.' I strained to hear anything out of the ordinary, and wondered how I hadn't known, why I hadn't felt, that Harkor had brought something back with us.

I caught a brief hint of crying. It was a tiny sound, but it made the hairs on my neck stand up, and my skin felt suddenly hot as though I were standing in full blazing sunlight. Harkor must have drugged it, put some poppy juice in the milk or something, and it was only now awake enough to set off the familiar warning sign that a creature of the Wild was nearby. It sounded like a child crying into a wad of cotton.

I rushed to the cart and began tugging at the canvas covering that Harkor had secured over top of it, until I found a tie that wasn't so secure. A few more tugs and it was loosened. I eased it up over the edge of the cart. The bed was a jumble of clothes, boxes, bags, loose cups and pans. I rummaged frantically under the canvas as far as my arm would stretch, alternating glances between the walk and the tavern. I could hear footsteps, but they could be coming from any direction and echoing between the stone walk and the marble arches above.

My arm brushed something icy cold. I grit my teeth and grasped it, pulling it from the cart and hurrying to get out of the torch light. I found a shadowy spot under a nearby staircase, and nearly dropped the small cage, my hand was so numb. It was a delicate, swirly thing made of wrought iron. Inside it was a tiny person about three inches tall with dragonfly wings, a shock of white fuzzy hair, and a faint green glow to its skin. Its sobs were musical, like bells being rung by falling water.

I set the cage on the ground and opened the tiny door. The Aletta was paralyzed inside, staring up at me with tiny blue lights for eyes. The elves call the little winged ones Alettas. They had faithfully cataloged and described every form of Wild creature they had seen. That is not what the Alettas called themselves. I was lucky I had learned how to pronounce anything in their tongue, but pronouncing their name still eluded me.

"I am setting you free," I said as best I could in their tinkling language. It didn't move. I tore off a scrap of fabric from my shirt and tucked it around the door of the cage so it could climb out without having to touch the iron. Anything forged by fire would wound Wild creatures, freezing them so harshly it would burn through their flesh. Even with the fabric, it refused to move, hunched on a wooden perch in the center of the cage. I kept still, ignoring the rising heat on my skin as the effects of whatever

Harkor had given it continued wearing off, and the green glow of its skin grew brighter.

After a breathless minute, the Aletta made a move toward the cage door, then froze again, never taking its eyes off me. Its little chest was rising and falling impossibly fast. Its wings shivered, and then it dashed for the door, climbing along the fabric and out. It took flight, making a tight happy loop, and stopped an inch from my nose. I had to hold my breath to keep from sneezing as little wisps of sparkling dust floated out from it.

It bobbed its head, thanking me in its little ringing bell voice. Then, of course, it offered me a boon. I wanted to let it go with no obligations, but it would not have understood that, and would have hung around me waiting for an opportunity to pay me back and get itself captured again.

"Do you know the Golden One?" I asked, pronouncing the name carefully. At the sound of her name its wings shivered, and it floated back an inch as though I had blown on it. "Would you take her a message from me?"

The tiny head nodded, and it struck a brave pose. It was foolish to send a message. There would be no answer. But it would give the Aletta something to do, and at least I would know that I'd tried.

"Tell her I saved you," I whispered.

The Aletta spun in a perfect pirouette and shot out over the canal and into the piazza. I watched until it disappeared into the darkness, and looked around again. The footsteps were gone, and no one had appeared either on the walk or on the water. I tossed the cage into the canal and headed back into the Wyvern's Den.

The trick to looking normal when you've just done something wrong was not to act normal. People acting normal look awkward and out of place. Or so Drinn always told me, and she taught me everything I knew about grifting. All you had to do was choose the part you needed to play and throw yourself into it. I arranged my face in an expression of deep disappointment and shock, and slumped back into the Den. Harkor noticed my face and hurried over.

"What happened?"

"I'm so sorry, it looks like, well, I think it was stolen."

Harkor stomped his foot. "Fires above, I knew I shouldn't have left it out there. Now I don't have a gift for Mother."

"You'll have other chances," I said. It made my stomach lurch, but I patted his arm in consolation. "Besides, she's so happy right now that you're a Warden I don't think any gift could make her happier."

He sullenly made his way to the bar to eat a bit more and get another glass of whatever he was drinking. I headed for my spot, picked up my guitar, and started tuning it again. Jinelle was making her rounds, picking up empty plates or discarded napkins, and assessing the contentment of her patrons.

"Oh, before I forget," she said, pausing near me. "Roya was looking for you while you were gone."

"You know Roya Sontuoso?" Harkor had heard her from the bar and his head snapped around, all thoughts of his lost prize gone.

"No," I answered. "Why was he looking for me?"

"Maybe he's throwing a party too," Harkor offered.

"He said he had a job offer for you," Jinelle said.

I shook my head. "He has house musicians. In fact, I think his servants have their own musicians."

"I don't think it was that kind of job," Jinelle said. "He was asking specifics, like what rank Warden you are and when exactly you'd be back."

Harkor whistled. "You know, Glade, you do one job for Roya you can retire."

"If you survive one job for Roya," I corrected. "I'm no thrill seeker."

"It's not good business, skirting Roya," Jinelle said. She took an empty plate from someone passing by and added it to her pile. "Looks like things are winding down." That was Jinelle's way of telling me to start adding magic to my songs, the kind that made customers drowsy and sent them home. I began strumming an easy tune, *Long Away Home*, that I played along the road to help companions sleep on the way out or back from a Tower. It was the sort of magic I enjoyed, requiring subtlety and skill. Too much and the crowd would fall asleep in the bar. Too clumsy and they would know they were being influenced by magic and be insulted.

"She's right, you know." Harkor settled into his seat and yawned. "You should at least hear what he has to say."

"The last story I heard about one of his quests, only one Warden made it back, and she still hasn't spoken a word to anyone."

"It's all just stories, to drive the prices up," he said, waving his glass at me. "We were just at the border. The worst thing that happened to me was poison ivy. "

One of his cousins interrupted to shake his hand and say goodbye. I took the opportunity to start singing. Harkor thought three weeks at the border made him an expert on the dangers of the Wild. I knew what kinds of things lurked out there, and what happened when they crossed that border, and I wasn't eager to go looking for it, no matter what Roya would pay.

My mood was reflected in my song choices. After a few more sleepy campfire songs, I launched into an old and long ballad, *The*

Lost Prince. It was a story from before the Fairy Wars, about the first and only prince of the elves. The melody was slow and haunting, allowing for a lot of improvisation so the elements of the story could be emphasized. The chorus sometimes floated through my mind, especially as Midsummer drew closer.

> *Kings may come and kings may go,*
> *Sang the maid so fair and clever.*
> *The rose it blooms for but a day,*
> *But thorns leave scars forever.*

Even more than the Prince, or the Wild Queen of Winter, the character from the song that fascinated me the most was simply called the Lady. In the song she was called to judge the Prince, and after judging him to be innocent, disobeyed the Queen's order to kill him, saving him from the Wild and restoring him to his family. There was no other story or song I had ever heard where a Wild creature was able to disobey a Queen, but every version of this tale included that fact.

When I finished the song, only Harkor, his mother, and three others were left, gathering up their decorations. Jinelle nodded to me and waved towards the door, and that was all the encouragement I needed. I headed out the door and up the stairs to my room on the second floor. Doing night work at the Den earned me free room and board. It was tiring, but a room here beat the cramped and fallow rooms I had stayed in when I first moved to Cyfar in the original, bottom level of the city.

I made sure my door was locked behind me, set my guitar down on its stand, and collapsed onto my bed. It was just a straw mattress on the floor, piled high with pillows, but it was more than I'd had the past three weeks. I didn't even bother to stand up to pull off my armor and rolled from side to side to reach the laces or pull the pieces off. I tossed the whole smelly mess into a pile next to me, and stretched out, letting the cool air draw the sweat off my body.

I took a long deep breath in, and let it out slowly. The illusion that I wore every day slipped away. Dark reddish-brown skin brightened and took on a more golden hue like wild honey. Straight black hair grew light and frizzier, floating up around my head like silk on a corn stalk. My ears became pointier and my eyes changed from dark brown to bright, luminescent green.

Every day and night for the past three weeks I had held that illusion in place, appearing to everyone like just one more half-elf bard earning some coin as a Warden. Half-elf was acceptable. Half-Wild, well, at best I would still be living in the ancient, crumbling bottom layer of Cyfar. At worst... I thought of the Aletta in its ornate iron cage. I didn't want to think about the worst possibilities.

Now that it was gone, I felt like I could breathe again. I felt my mind unwind, untangling the strict concentration that had kept the illusion in place for so long. The pillows grew soft around me, and I was asleep in minutes.

Chapter Two

"Fresh trout! Get your fresh trout!" I rolled over and covered my ears with a pillow. My stiff muscles protested and I groaned. I hadn't moved all night. It was useless to try and get back to sleep. The South Piazza housed the main market for Cyfar. As soon as there was light, the fishmonger started, his booming voice echoing through the streets. The fruit and vegetable stall across the way opened next, a shrill set of women's voices countering the fishmonger's bass. Then the town crier delighted in starting the news at our end of the market. Then the full symphony of the market would crescendo and drown out any hope of peace and quiet. I dragged myself out of bed, defeated.

I washed, dressed, and braided my hair into one long rope. Dropping the illusion that disguised my Wild features was a letting go, a relaxing. Putting the illusion back on was a regimented practice. I opened the case on my dresser and laid out several pots of powder and a vial of liquid. It had taken years to get the combination of ingredients right, and I still tweaked it now and then when a new formula came out. I blended the powders into different piles, one brown for my skin, one black for my hair, and then added some of the liquid to make a paste. I rubbed the mixtures into my skin and hair, careful to cover as much as I could. Then I sang the tune that had given me the ability to activate it for long periods of time. It was a plain tune, long and monotonous, and each time I reiterated the main melody, the illusion became firmer. After singing through it about twenty times, I moved over to the mirror to examine the illusion.

The rest of my room was simple, a dresser, a chair, the straw mattress, and my shelves of sheet music. The mirror was my one luxury item, the clearest and largest one I could afford with three panels. I had to be able to see every angle of myself to be sure that my illusion was complete.

When I had first learned how to disguise myself, I had tried many different looks, mostly variations of voluptuous beauty. But I quickly learned the best use of the illusion was to blend in, to get away from being the Changeling girl and from home. I would stand out for my voice, and for my playing, not for my appearance. So when I checked my illusion in the mirror, an average half-elf woman, brown skinned, brown eyes, straight black hair and plain features looked back at me.

The next priority, or course, was coffee. The Den served something that could be called coffee, sort of. Rather than suffer through a cup of that, I strolled down to a coffee cart that was always parked at the end of the walk beside the foot bridge over the canal. The dwarves that ran the Fire Peak Coffee Cart knew my order so well I didn't even have to speak. I would show up and in a few minutes, I'd have a cup of my favorite brew. An invaluable system on days when I had to be up earlier than my words.

Once I was properly fueled, I headed across the bridge and into the market. The South Piazza was crowded with wooden stalls and the lanes between them were already thick with people. Rather than fight my way through the crowd, I ducked into a narrow side lane. The stalls were so close together here that the roofs nearly met overhead. I didn't take a lot of time to peruse the stalls, or I would be late to the shop for my shift. But I had taken the lane that passed The Silver Bell, and I couldn't resist looking over the sparkly treasures on display.

I didn't recognize the young elf behind the counter. She was pale and wispy, what most people called a 'winter daughter', not as common on this side of the river. She waved nervously.

"Good morning," she said, her voice fluttering with nerves. "Let me know if I can help you find something."

"Good morning." I smiled at her, and looked over the stall, trying to spot the new pieces. There were a few pendants that caught my eye. I lingered over a tiny sword wrapped with a thorny vine. The sword hung point downward, and at the tip the vine held a bright red gem shaped like a rose in bloom.

"What kind of stone is this?" I let the admiration shine in my voice.

"It's a garnet," she said. "You can pick it up to look more closely." I heard the pride in her voice, and knew I had found one of her creations. "And that's pure Lumina silver." Silver from the river west of us was considered the purest available, better even than what the dwarves carted east from the mountains.

"Where did you get the idea for the design?" I plucked it from the black velvet tray.

"I saw it on a statue when I was young," she said with a shrug. "I've always thought it was pretty."

17

I fought the urge to interrogate her about the statue and where she had seen it. A sword and a rose could mean anything. Just because the Lady was often pictured with a sword and a rose didn't mean the girl had seen a statue of her. There were very few of the classic statues left in or near Cyfar, and if there had been one of the Lady, I'm sure I would have found it. But winter elves were usually from the west, and there would be more statues left there. Hopefully the girl would be around for some time, and I could bring it up later.

"This is an amazing piece," I said, turning it over in my palm.

"Thank you." She blushed.

"Did you just start here?" I had meant to put the pendant down after a short look, but I kept turning it over and over in my hand. There were little tinges of cold prickling my skin where the pendant landed. "I haven't seen you before."

"Yes. My name is Niev, and I just started this week. I didn't think they would let me show my own pieces yet, but Hala insisted."

"I can see why. This really is lovely." I hesitated a moment, thinking over how much money I had. I had just finished my last Tower rotation before Midsummer, and the payment for that was a boost, but there would be no more income until that had passed. Reluctantly, I set the pendant down. "I hope you do well, Niev."

Her smile was bright. "Thank you."

I headed on my way, casting a glance over my shoulder at the stall, and trying to rush the rest of the way to work. It was not the best time to be in the mood for sparklies.

Potions and Powders is a necessary stop for any Warden passing through Cyfar. They always have the purest healing potions and the latest spell broadsides. It's the first place the ministry sends you to when you get your Warden's license, and we all knew to stay on Netty's good side. She ran her shop with pride and care, and expected her patrons to behave accordingly. The shop was built into the base of the central column of Cyfar, under the first leg of winding stairs that led to the upper levels.

My first task was to carry in the bundle of that day's broadsides and sort them into their bins around the counter. There were shops above that still carried hand copied spell scrolls for those who could afford them, but printed sheets were cheaper and easier to read. The more popular spells were illusions that could change the color or texture of their target and sleeping spells. I hefted the bundle over my shoulder and reached for the door. It was still locked.

Netty always opened and closed the shop. She had even dragged herself out of bed one morning when she'd lost her voice to let me in, her tiny body racked with coughs. I looked around the door for a note, but nothing looked out of place. I backed into the walkway and looked up at the stairs but nothing stood out.

"Netty?" I made my way around the corner and found her shaking the handle of the side door and muttering under her breath. "Netty are you all right?"

She sighed and looked up at me, setting her bony hands on her hips. Even at three feet tall the look on her face made me want to head back to the door and wait for instructions.

"You don't know how to pick a lock, do you?"

I looked away, and down, clearing my throat. "What? Why?"

"So I went into the back aisles to get some more sulfur for the jar on the counter, and when I get back two boys were picking at the broadsides, hoping to sneak a few away while I wasn't looking. So I grabbed a broom and chased after them, making sure they

19

knew not to target my store again." She gestured down at a broom lying on the walk in two pieces. "But I left my keys inside and the door blew shut behind me." The fire in her tale dimmed as she finished, and she ran her hand through her shock of blue hair.

"I'm sorry, Netty, I'm not so good at picking locks." I set the bundle down and looked up at the building. "But I could probably lift you into that window." The window on the second story was open, and a set of dark gray curtains was sticking out.

"I guess that will have to do." She motioned for me to move against the wall. "I'll just climb up." She scrabbled up to my shoulders and got her feet in place on either side of my head, but it wasn't quite enough for her to reach the sill. "Hold still," she said, and started to climb on top of my head. She was a solid three feet of gnome, and was not as light as I had thought she'd be.

"Halt! Come down from there!" A loud voice commanded. Netty wobbled, and I managed to catch her as she tumbled down, landing on her feet behind me.

"And you are?" I heard her ask. I turned to see her staring up at a tall, pale, blond human. His broad chest strained the brocade tunic he wore, and he was pointing a large hand at Netty.

"I am one who does not abide thieves or assassins," he answered. His voice was smooth and loud, easily reaching a volume that was drawing the attention of the crowd in the market.

"That's not an answer. What thieves? What assassins?" Netty looked around in a parody of searching for something.

"You were attempting to break into this shop," the man said, losing none of the confidence in his voice.

"It's her shop," I said. "And you're not on the Watch, so what makes you think you can interfere either way?"

"I have vowed to right any wrongs that I come across," he said. He was starting to look confused. "Can you offer proof that-"

Netty began cursing at him in Gnomish. There's something special about the way Netty curses. She uses more than just foul words. She literally creates curses, banes and evil incantations, creative and devastating. It's mesmerizing, so long as it's not directed at you. She called on the fleas of a thousand sand rats to infest his armpits. The man began tearing at his armpits with his nails.

I tried to get between Netty and the man, but she skirted around my legs and shooed me away.

"This mountain of meat doesn't scare me," she said. Then she called down the forces of darkness and shadow to take his sight. The man went from clawing at his armpits to covering his eyes and moaning.

"I think he's got the point, Netty."

"He's still standing here, isn't he? Get lost, righter of wrongs. Move along, or I will shred your body and feet it to a ghoul."

As Netty uttered the last curse, another voice rose over hers, chanting a short phrase in perfect elvish. I caught the scent of vanilla and smoke. As the smoke wafted by, the large man was rubbing his eyes and blinking. I looked back towards the main street, and saw a man putting a candle back into the pouch on his belt.

"Are you all right, Thromm?" The new man asked. The large man nodded in response and backed away from Netty.

"Is this yours? You should keep him on a leash," Netty said. The new man took a few steps towards us with an odd expression on his face. I couldn't tell if he wanted to laugh or slink off without any more embarrassment.

"I'm very sorry," the new man said to Netty. He was an average looking human, no taller than me, with dark red-brown skin and thick black hair that fell around his collar in curls. His dark eyes were moving around constantly, stopping at each object or person and scanning it over like he was reading a book. "Thromm is very new here and doesn't understand how the city works. I am very sorry for any misunderstanding."

Thromm's face was turning deep red. "My apologies," he said, bowing. I would have thought he was being sarcastic, if his bow hadn't been perfect. "It appeared like you were breaking into the store."

"It's my store you ox," Netty grumbled.

"We were locked out," I said. "She is the owner. You could ask anyone on the street."

"Next time, just call the Watch," the new man said. He grabbed Thromm by the arm, and pulled him away. "We really are very sorry."

"Wait," I said. The man stopped, and Netty grumbled some, but didn't try any more curses. "Could you unlock the door for us?" The expression on his face became more pronounced. It was the look of someone weary of performing the same tricks every day. I had worn that expression myself the last few nights.

"I'm not a thief," he said, shaking his head.

"No, you're a spellcaster. Unlocking a door is pretty easy." At least, it should be easy for a spellcaster. If he was only a reader, like Harkor, he'd be stuck. They didn't print broadsides for lockpicking.

He grunted, then moved to the door. Rather than reach for anything in his pouch, he placed his hand flat against the door, and spoke a few more words in elvish, and closed his eyes, his face relaxing into an emotionless mask. Then a click sounded, and the door popped open. I was impressed. Not many spellcasters could work without ingredients.

"Thank you," Netty said, shoving through the door and disappearing inside.

"Thanks," I said. The spellcaster shrugged. I looked at his companion, still red-faced, and holding himself compactly as the crowd moved around us on the walkway. "Don't be too embarrassed. She has a quick temper, and it was an honest mistake."

I gave Netty a few minutes to calm herself and let her fuss around the counter while I sorted out the broadsides. Then I scanned the shelves, checking the levels of various powders and potions in the glass jars. Netty stopped muttering and was reading through the accounts when I finished.

"Look like the usual things today," I said and leaned on the high-level counter. Netty looked up at me from the lower level and tapped the book.

"All right, well, I'll let you do the honors. Too many bad omens for me to be making magic. What will you be making?"

"Health potions, seeking powder, some sleeping drafts." She scratched the list down in her book.

"You didn't happen to bring anything back for me from the border, did you? We're getting low on dew pods."

"Sorry, Netty, I didn't get a chance to gather anything useful." I squeezed back through the shelves, setting the jars ringing against each other, and popped out into the back workroom. It smelled of rotten eggs and burnt hair. Netty must have been putting together a special order.

I cleared off my workstation, and pulled out the basic ingredients for health potions, seeking powder, and sleeping draughts then got to work.

Working for Netty was probably my least illustrious gig, but it helped pay for clothes and supplies for the road. I also got a great discount on any potions or powders I needed. Working as a

Warden came with some distinctions, but the pay for border patrol was paltry, and we were expected to bring our own supplies. Spellcasters, and those skilled with a blade or bow got first pick of the Warden jobs. Artificers like me picked up the rest.

Health potions were easy enough to make. I mixed the three oils into a large pan, crushed lavender and rosemary together, and sprinkled it into the oil as I sang a song of rest and mending. The mixture glowed gold, and then turned a bright clear blue. I poured it into a few small bottles, already labeled, corked them and coated the corks with wax.

Seeking powder was simple as well. It was mostly talc, with a few crystals of quartz sprinkled in. I stirred the mixture carefully, not wanting to create clouds of the stuff, and made sure the crystals were evenly distributed throughout. I sang a song of seeking and finding, almost a child's song for hide and seek. The powder glowed gold again and then turned purple. I divided the powder up into lines and slid it into small parchment envelopes.

Sleeping draughts were a little trickier. Too strong and the drinker would have trouble waking, stuck in a dreamless slumber until a spellcaster could wake them. Too weak and the drinker only grew dizzy or drunken. They were also more strictly regulated, and the city kept tabs on how many we made and how many we sold. I nervously counted out exactly seven drops of poppy juice and two of foxglove into the honey water in my bowl and stirred. Then I sang a song of soft pillows and cozy beds. The potion glowed gold, and then mellowed to a golden-brown.

"I don't know why they worry you so much," Netty had said to me when I had first started working for her. "It's not like just anyone can use them. You still have to know how to work the right spell."

"I don't like them." She had wanted to be sure I actually knew what I was doing.

"You know an awful lot for a bard," she had said, as I finished making the draughts. "What happened, did you wash out of university?"

"No. I just had a very thorough apprenticeship."

"Who did you study with?" Netty had learned potion making from Amreel, who owned the largest shop in the elven capital.

"Delvine Aria," I said.

"And how did you manage that? You must have the voice of an angel."

"My father pulled some strings."

"So, your father is Tor Balladeer." She nodded as though she had suspected all along, though I hadn't told her my full name. "Well, you've got the job if you want it. Just be sure you let me know your Warden schedule in advance and be here on time every morning."

And I had been on time every morning for the past four years. I only worked border patrol for the Wardens, so my schedule was very regular. She hadn't even asked any questions when I told her I needed two weeks off every Midsummer. I suppose she assumed I was visiting back east. It wasn't the best pay, but it was regular work, and let me still work nights for Jinelle at the Wyvern's Den.

After making the potions, I cleaned up the workshop, swept and dusted in the front room, and helped Netty carry in any other deliveries we received through the day. Netty handled all the customers. In the evening I said goodbye and hurried home.

Against my better judgment, I took the same route back, hoping to pass by the Silver Bell and buy that pendant, even if it was more than I could afford. I looked over the trays, three times, but the pendant was nowhere in sight. Hala, the stall's owner, even pulled out the trays she had already locked away for the night, but it was gone.

Hala knew the exact piece I was talking about, proud of her new hire, and told me it had been sold that afternoon to an elf dressed in long red robes. I asked her twice if she was certain, but she said there was no forgetting that man. He had a deep ringing voice and gold rings on his fingers. I thanked Hala and started up the three flights of stairs to the top level.

There was no market up here, only broad walks, canals for transportation, and manicured gardens. It was beautiful, but I noticed none of it. Instead I strode along the walkways, ignoring the looks from the elegant pedestrians out for an evening stroll, and didn't stop until I reached the gate of Roya's palazzo.

It was a tall, narrow wooden gate, carved with images of cornucopias overflowing with fruit. I gripped the handle and rattled the gate as loudly as I could.

"Can I help you?" A young elf dressed in a red tunic and black hose emerged from the column on my left. I hadn't noticed a door there and, in my surprise, I turned all my ire on him.

"I need to talk to Roya," I demanded. "Tell him his cheap trick worked, and I'm here to talk to him."

"I'm sorry, do you have an appointment?"

"Is he here or not?" I leaned forward so my face was only inches from his. "He sent me a message, and I need to speak to him."

"Just a moment." He went back into the column and picked up a large shell. He mumbled something into the shell and then held it to his ear. When he noticed me watching him, he turned his back to me. He nodded his head, said something into the shell, and set it down. "Follow me, please," he said. He unlocked the gate, locked it behind us, and walked me into Roya's palazzo.

A long still pool split the marble walk to Roya's home. To the right was a small orchard, orange and fig trees just getting heavy with fruit. To the left was a formal garden with benches and shade trees. The doorman led me around the side of the building, rather than leading me to the massive doors that matched the front gate. A small set of steps led up to a recessed, plain door. Inside was cool and bright, and our footsteps echoed through the hall.

Roya's office opened off the hall, a large room with no windows, lit by a set of glowing orbs floating near the ceiling.

"I'm sorry that business has been so slow for you lately," I said. I pushed past the doorman and into the room, disappointed that my voice and footsteps were muted by the heavy carpet and walls lined with books. "But, really, if you wanted to hire a bard you could have just said so. I'd be glad to recommend some very talented friends."

Roya looked past me and dismissed the doorman, who shut the door behind us. He was seated behind a massive desk, draped in deep red robes and a round hat adorned with gold trim. His robes were actually dyed red too, not just under a spell to imitate the pricey color.

"I'm glad you could stop by, Glade. I've been meaning to have a word with you." Roya didn't speak so much as intone. It was like listening to big brass bells ring in the middle of the night. He calmly reached over to one of the stacks of paper on the desk and picked up the top sheet.

"Fine, you win. I'm here. And what a cheap trick too. How long have you had someone following me? I could complain to the Wardens. I don't care how many councilmen you know."

"Please, have a seat."

"It's a waste of time, Roya. You know it, I know it. There's no way you are going to get me to take up a quest for you. What good would I be anyway? I'm a rank four Warden, a bard. It would be a stain on your reputation." I was waving my arms, making some of the pages on his desk flutter.

"Please, have a seat," he repeated, gesturing to the chair behind me. I plunked myself down and folded my arms. "Thank you." He paused to consult the paper he was holding. "You've been a rank four Warden for two years. With your training and performance ratings you could have been at least at eight by now. And you were initiated at the temple in Rhiodeja."

"Any higher and I'd be required to take quests. And as I have been trying to explain, I prefer not to die on the job."

"I thought perhaps it had more to do with your less than stellar record at the border." He picked up another page. The rage in me died down, and was replaced by a dark sinking sensation, like being pulled into a cold pool.

"I don't know what you mean."

"I mean there are multiple reports of unfortunate accidents during your rotations at the border. For example, a captured Salvani, they didn't specify which type of wild man, mysteriously broke free of his bonds and escaped the Veiled Tower last year, while you were there." He picked up another set of pages. "Two Janas were caught stealing from the food stores at Black Tower and managed to get away when the flour exploded in the kitchen. And you were there. An Anguana was caught in the Lumina River, but never made it back to the River Tower, disappearing from the cart on the road, while you were there."

"I was there when they killed the ogre at the East Tower," I said quietly. "And I was there when they brought down the Spina de Mul." I shuddered at the memory of that one, a skeletal sorcerer had risen from some Wild grave and attacked the South Tower, killing six Wardens before we stopped it.

"Yes, I have noticed that things are different when people are dying. I am simply trying to understand your lack of advancement.

The reports of those two incidents show you to be a competent fighter. When you wish to be."

Roya picked up another page, this one a sheet of parchment, not the rag paper reports he'd been holding before. Then he opened a drawer, withdrew the sword and rose pendant, and set it on the desk between us.

"Is that supposed to make me feel better?" I asked. He studied the paper carefully.

Then he began to speak in a tongue I had only ever heard deep in the Wild at Midsummer, and that no one in Cyfar or any other civilized place should be able to speak. He spoke in the language of a tree nymph. He spoke the words clumsily, his deep ringing voice plowing through the light whispery words. The same burning sensation that had flooded into me the night before when I had helped the Aletta rose in me again. For a moment the fire on my skin burned through my illusion and I felt it dissolve. I clenched my muscles and forced my illusion song through my mind as quickly as I could, weaving the disguise back together, but I was not fast enough. Roya had seen it. He had been looking for it. He blinked slowly and dropped the paper.

"Oh, my," he said. Two long notes that hung in the air between us. I focused my eyes on him again, my mouth dry, trying to take even breaths. A thousand unpleasant things he could ask for flew through my mind, and I would have to do them. Or he could just turn me in. I looked him in the eyes and waited.

"What did I say?"

I blinked. "What?"

"What did I say? I found the words but there was no translation with them."

"I don't know that I can translate them, really." My thoughts were a noisy blur in my mind. "Basically, you were offering a trade."

"Hm. Interesting." He picked up the page again. "The text I took this from implied that these words would bind one of the Wild."

"All trades are binding among the Wild." My voice was weak and shaky, coming out as a mumble. I hoped that all Roya wanted was information, details about Wild creatures that most people didn't know, to improve the success of his quests. Though I doubted I would get off that easy.

"Ah, just so. Then, this pendant, in exchange for you listening to the quest proposal I have for you."

"It doesn't work that easily. I mean, I'm only half-Wild, and we are in a city, which makes the magic weaker."

"Must one be full-blooded to be compelled to obey Wild magic?" He fiddled with the pendant as he asked.

I squeezed my hands together, my eyes glued to the intricate pattern of the rug on the floor. In the back of my mind I heard the beginning notes of the Midsummer Song. "No, I am required to obey Wild commands or creatures stronger than I."

He nodded. "My offer still stands." He pointed to the pendant.

"In exchange for listening to your proposal?" Even without the compulsion of the trade pulling at me, and the longing I had for any clue about the Lady, even something this small, all Roya had to do was send one note to the Chief Warden or a councilman, and I'd be finished. "I'm listening."

"This quest calls for the utmost discretion. You must also agree not to discuss any of the details of this quest proposal, or the quest itself, unless it is with the parties involved in the quest."

"Very well."

"I have been retained by House Carvallo to hire Wardens to investigate the disappearance of their daughter, Meia, from their home in Casavera. She has not been seen or heard from in three weeks. They are seeking any answer to what has happened to her, even if it is only proof of her death. Rather than arrive as investigators, you will go to their house as entertainment for a party they are having."

I almost laughed out loud in relief. Roya didn't need some high ranking spellcaster or swordsman to delve into a dungeon or trek into the Wild. He needed a spy.

"Has the Casavera Watch not been able to find anything?"

"They did not enlist the help of the city guard. They specifically requested Wardens who were learned in Wild lore. And as I said, they are very concerned that news of this disappearance not reach the public."

"They think she was taken by the Wild?" It was an interesting case, and I took the chance to think about something other than how much my life belonged to this man now. "Did they leave the baby unattended at a picnic or something?"

"Meia is not a baby. She's a girl of sixteen."

I looked up at him. "You're saying a girl of marrying age was taken from a city, before Midsummer, by the Wild?"

Roya spread his hands, unable or unwilling to answer that question. As unlikely as it was, it was not unheard of for youths to go missing in the Wild, but only when they were foolish enough to venture in on their own. Getting taken from their own home in a walled city like Casavera would be nearly impossible.

I lowered my eyes again. This job was not as bad as I had feared. But the next one might be worse, and I was sure there would be a next one. I would be at Roya's beck and call. Would that be better than going back home? While I was pondering, Roya lifted the pendant from the desk and held it out to me.

"You listened. This is yours now." I held out my hand, and he dropped it into my palm.

"Who else have you hired?" I asked. I tucked the pendant into the pouch on my belt.

"I'm afraid I cannot tell you that unless you accept."

"Of course, I accept."

"Thank you. I have the contract for you to sign here. You will meet with your companions here in the morning. You are entitled to stay the night here if you prefer. That is part of the standard benefits."

"No, thank you." If my quick and curt response offended him, he didn't show it.

"The party you will be performing at is tomorrow afternoon. I will send a boat for you in the morning."

CHAPTER THREE

That night had to be the worst set I had ever played at the Wyvern's Den. The regulars didn't notice; they were always more interested in their food and drink than what I was playing. But Jinelle did. She stopped me before I headed to bed and asked if I was all right, though her tone and body language told me that I had better be all right the next time I played. I told her Roya had a job for me, and her expression changed. She wished me good luck and hurried back to the kitchen.

I worked more on my illusion the next morning, though I had not let it down overnight. It was only by continuously weaving the illusion that I was able to keep it whole, even while I was working other magic, so I often would weave it every morning while on a job, just to be safe.

As Roya had promised, a boat pulled up in front of the Den to collect me and my things. Another young person in the same livery as the doorman hopped out and helped pile my bag of sheet music and clothes into the bobbing boat. I carried my guitar on myself.

The trip up was longer by boat, but much prettier. I sipped my coffee, enjoyed the view, and thought over the job. He had hired others, and if Roya had truly earned his reputation, these others would include a skilled investigator, probably a spellcaster. I was merely providing a cover story so that spellcaster could gather the information. This would be just like doing any other gig, a performance and nothing more.

The canal ended in a series of locks that slowly raised the boat to the higher level, giving me a view of the market and the surrounding buildings that I rarely got from the stairs. Cyfar spread out in a neat grid, wide walks crisscrossed recessed canals, framing sections of colonnaded buildings or patches of gardens. It was not as intricate or ostentatious as the top level, but it was practical and ideally laid out to serve the most people in the most pleasing way.

The boat bumped into the top-level canal and pulled up before Roya's palazzo. This time I was led into the formal gardens, to a shaded grotto, where Roya was speaking to two familiar figures. Thromm and his spellcaster friend both looked surprised, and Thromm looked embarrassed, to see me walking towards them on the gravel path.

"Ah, here she is," Roya said. "Glade Balladeer. Glade, allow me to introduce Otsoa Stranero, and Thromm." Thromm made another of his picture-perfect bows. Otsoa held out his hand.

"Pleased to meet you, Glade." His handshake was firm, and his smile felt genuine. "I haven't met many bards who prefer guitar to lute. Is that a more common instrument in Guowtan?"

My eyes snapped to Roya. "How long were you talking about me before I arrived?" Roya put up his hands and shook his head. I looked behind me, but the boatman hadn't brought my bags or my guitar into the gardens.

"You can tell all that from a handshake?" I pulled my hand from his.

"And your accent," Otsoa said. "And sorry to be taking you out so soon. Just coming back from border patrol, you were probably looking forward to some time off."

"I don't really get time off," I mumbled. I looked down at my clothes, at my hands, and then looked up with a grin. "I forgot to take the sash off." I untied the strip of cloth from my belt that marked me as a Warden on duty. "That's very impressive." It was problematic. If he could tell all of that from spending two minutes with me, what would he find out during the job? I would have to be cautious. "And you are from Rheste, judging from your accent, and the beads in your hair."

I hadn't noticed them yesterday, but he had two braids tucked behind his ear, with several beads at the ends. Otsoa was an old human name, harsher in sound than the elvish names people seemed to prefer at the time. But Stranero was not a family name familiar to me. The beads in his hair represented the Ocelote family, but he could just have been wearing them for decoration. I had never been to Rheste, and I wasn't sure how many of the old traditions they held to.

I turned my attention to Thromm. He was wearing another fine tunic all-in-one piece, crisp white linen shirt, and trousers rather than hose. A broadsword was strapped to his side. "You aren't from Rheste," I said.

"No, I am not."

There was a long pause. I let it draw out, but Thromm didn't continue. He did exchange a look with Otsoa. Strange, but not any of my business.

"I suppose you're our fighter?" I hadn't seen anyone wielding a broadsword in a long time. The hilt was golden and inset with gems. I assumed it was a ceremonial blade of some kind, a symbol of his family like Otsoa's beads.

Thromm nodded. Again, there was a long pause, an exchanged glance.

"All right then, cover story." I clapped my hands once and we started walking back towards the boat. Roya followed behind us, his hands clasped behind his back.

"You'll be performing at a garden party in Casavera," Royasaid.

"I am to provide added security," Thromm said.

Roya added, "That was at the family's request as well. Apparently, they have someone of note attending the party."

I looked at Otsoa.

"I'm not a performer," he said.

"Oh, don't worry, you won't have to perform. If anyone asks, you're my porter."

We piled into the boat. Thromm settled in the front seat, and Roya's servant at the back. Otsoa and I had to share the center bench.

"We're not staying long, what is all of that?" Otsoa peered down at my many bags.

"Roya didn't give me any specifics about the performance," I said, raising my voice a bit to sound more childlike. "I had to bring options. Different sheet music in case they wanted high elven tunes. Different outfits in case tavern chic isn't their preference. What about you? Don't you have a few bags full of tomes you need to bring along?"

Otsoa grinned. "No." One of Roya's servants had brought out two bags, but they were nothing more than a typical pack.

"Really? Not even one spellbook? What, do you have them all memorized?" The boatman pushed us off from the walkway.

"Many of them, yes. But if there's one I don't remember, I improvise."

"You can't improvise spells." I frowned.

"You can, actually."

"They're very precise formulas," I said. I raised three fingers and counted off the requirements every student of magic, spellcaster or not, learned their first day. "A specific set of materials, a specific amount of time, and the right amount of will. You change any of those up and things get messy."

Otsoa shook his head. "It's like any other recipe. You just have to know what substitutes for what." Otsoa gestured to my guitar. "Do you always play the same song when you heal someone?"

"That's different," I said. "Artificer's don't have a recipe, we have a talent."

"Right, a talent that impressed the old gods into granting you power." The sarcasm in his voice stung.

"I don't know where it comes from," I said. My voice wavered, and I cleared my throat to make it more solid. "The old gods or our own hearts, it doesn't matter. We train hard to learn the right... Vibrations? Resonance?" I had never had to put these thoughts into words. Once I had passed my initiation the magic just flowed when I called it.

"Exactly. Each part of a spell has a resonance. Find something else that matches that resonance, and the spell still works."

"It's not the same at all. Spellcasting has rules."

"All magic has rules. All magic is the same. It's just a matter of figuring out how the rules apply."

"Is he always this stubborn?"

Thromm was looking over his shoulder at us. He didn't answer, but he smirked at Otsoa.

"What do you think?" I asked him.

"I think arcane magic is arcane magic." Thromm sounded bored. "It is all the same to me." We had come to the locks that would lower us down to the ground level, and Thromm took hold of the sides of the boat. "A lot of symbols and math and fancy words. The only kind I know that is different is that granted by gods."

"So, I suppose it comes down to where you believe your power comes from, Glade. Is it arcane, or divine?" He tilted his head at me, his hair fluttering around his ears as we were lowered down the steps of the canals.

"You know, I just met you, and I've only had one cup of coffee today. I think it's a bit early for philosophical debates."

"You're probably right. Is it too early to speculate about the job?" We reached the bottom canal with a thunk. Otsoa adjusted his tunic, a longer one than most younger men wore, almost reaching his knees. The smell of stale, dirty water accosted us, and Thromm pulled a handkerchief from his sleeve and covered his nose.

"Never too early for that," I said. "Let's wait until we're in the coach, though." The lower level was crawling with people, even at this time of the morning. The streets were narrow, cluttered with refuse and horse manure. The coach had drawn up as close to the canal as it could get, but we still had to push and pick our way through an alley to reach it. Thromm led the way, and the canal workers hurried to get out of his path.

"Why all the secrecy," Otsoa mused once we were seated in Roya's carriage. It was lined in red velvet and cushioned, and even with Thromm inside it was spacious. We jerked into motion, riding out through the columns that held up the city and into the surrounding farmland.

"People in Casavera can be touchy about a lot of things," I said. "Especially a house like Carvallo. And old high elvish house living on this side of the river is something of a disgrace."

"Is Casavera not a desirable place to live?" Thromm asked.

"It's a wonderful place to live," I replied. "But it's not Rhiodeja. Most of the wealthy elven houses still live there."

"So, what sort of thing would drive elvish nobles to move to this side of the river?"

I sat up straight and stared at Thromm. "Nobility?"

Otsoa tensed. Thromm raised an eyebrow. "Is that not what you meant by 'old elvish family'?"

"Where did you say you were from?" I asked.

Thromm grinned, and Otsoa glared at him, nearly hissing.

"I do not believe I mentioned it," Thromm said, looking back at Otsoa. I looked back and forth between them as they tried to stare each other down. As much as I wanted to know the story between these two, I couldn't start prying into their background. It would just give them an excuse to start prying into mine.

"Nobles, hm? You did tell him not to call them that, right?" I switched my attention to Otsoa.

Otsoa rubbed the ridge of his nose. "I tried. He hasn't quite grasped the idea."

"No, I understand the idea very well. I just happen to think it is a very foolish one. Not having kings and queens because the fairies have kings and queens is nonsense."

I winced at the word fairies. People do not speak of the Wild that casually, and they certainly didn't call them fairies anymore. At least, not since the wars. I couldn't have him talking like that at the party, we'd be thrown out before we could learn anything.

"Let me tell you a story," I said, settling into my seat. "Something they don't teach much, unless you dig into the old lore. Before the Breaking, there were only the Wild. All of them were under the rule of the Queens of Summer and Winter. They still are. When Ventor the Breaker came, he fought against the Wild with fire from the gods and led as many as would follow him out of the forests. Elves, dwarves and all the Free Races came to be. The Breaker offered freedom, and many took the offer.

"Once they were free, the elves tried to set up their own king and queen. They had a son, and the Wild stole him away. He went through many trials, proving himself to the Wild, and was saved by the Lady. When she brought him home, the king and queen were dead, and the city they had built had become a mound of thorn bushes." I leaned forward, and Thromm leaned forward to mirror me, engrossed in my tale. "We have mayors, and provosts, and doges, and councils. We do not have kings or queens." Thromm nodded, and then twisted his mouth.

"So, these great houses, do the sons inherit their wealth from their fathers?" I started to argue, but he spoke over me. "Then it is the same thing, the name does not matter. And why all the tiptoeing around it? Are you not hired to kill the Wild all the time?"

"When they break the treaty, sure. If they are found in our lands, we can kill them. Same applies if we are found in theirs. These are ancient rules, Thromm, and they've kept us from another war for ages. So, for now, why don't you just tiptoe."

"If you wish, I will guard my tongue more wisely," he said. It wasn't convincing, but it was the best I was going to get. I made a mental note to keep my attention on Thromm and be ready to silence him with a spell if I had to.

The Carvallo estate was not within the walls of Casavera, but around the south side of the town. The carriage skirted around the wall rather than muddle through the narrow streets. It jostled us over stony, rutted roads and through fields of still green barley. It was just around noon when we rolled down a straight path lined with trees trimmed to a point. The villa was a low building in a C shape around a central courtyard. We were driven to the gap in the building, and two servants ran out to tend the horses and open the wrought iron gate stretched across the opening.

We were greeted at the door by a stocky elf with a long, hooked nose. He appeared in the doorway with a welcoming smile until he saw who stepped out of the carriage.

"We do have a servant's entrance," he said in heavily accented elvish. Either he had grown up in Rhiodeja, or wanted to sound like he had.

"I'm sure you do," I retorted. "But that means we would have to traipse through the house on the way to the courtyard. Instead, we are already here." I pointed through the gate.

"I really must insist. It is just around the side there."

"We even arrived early so we wouldn't disturb any guests." I sighed and shifted my guitar on my shoulder, slumping some as though it were growing heavy. I put on an expression that I hoped looked tired but accepting. "But if we must, we'll go around."

"Very well. My name is Tellar, I am the chief steward here. If you have any questions you will put them to me. Lady Carvallo will be out shortly to give you instructions, but I don't want you pestering her with questions."

"Oh, of course, thank you, sir." The gates swung wide, and we entered the central courtyard which was already decorated for the party. Strings of flowers and bright strips of silk were stretched between the columns. Small tables draped with cloth surrounded the round fountain in the center of the courtyard.

Otsoa set down my bags and my music stand. Tellar pointed us to a small raised platform at the back of the courtyard in front of a set of double doors. I gave vague instructions in a crabby voice to Otsoa as he struggled with making sense of my music stand.

"Don't get too comfortable in this role," Otsoa said to me, dropping another leg of my stand into the grass. "I'm not taking orders from a bard this whole job."

"Embrace the part," I said as dramatically as possible. I watched him struggle a while longer before having mercy on him and putting the stand together myself. Servants buzzed around us getting things ready, setting out chairs on the grassy areas, sweeping the tiled walks, and adjusting decorations.

One of the doors on the right of the courtyard flew open, and a balding, breathless man hurried towards us. He was round, and his tufted beard had gone out of style several years ago. When he reached us, he had to pause to catch his breath.

"Thank you," he said in perfect elvish. "I am so glad you have come. I apologize for the conditions." He paused and looked over his shoulder. "There can be no discussion of your purpose here until after the party."

"Master Carvallo?" I answered in elvish as well and bowed as best I could. Thromm showed me up of course. Otsoa merely nodded in greeting. "Of course, as you wish. We are at your service."

He nodded, and smiled, but it was a weary smile. A woman appeared in the doorway he had come from and looked around the courtyard with a critical eye. She made a few comments to the servants to adjust this or that. She was tall and willowy, with flawless hazelnut skin, and was much younger than I had expected. I wouldn't think she was old enough to have a nearly grown daughter.

"This is my wife, Matra," Master Carvallo said as she glided over to us. She examined us with the same exacting look. I waited on her judgment. Depending on what was in style that summer, she could prefer the tavern bard to play quaint folk music. Or she could scold me for arriving in such tawdry attire and insist I play elven concert music.

"You are Glade Balladeer?" she asked. There was something sour about her voice that made the question sound more like an accusation.

"Yes, Mistress," I said. "Thank you for inviting me to play for you."

"Yes, well, I have heard that you can make even the staunchest and stuffiest of people enjoy a good party. That's what I'm hoping for from you today. Joyful, fun music." She looked me up and down again. "Though I had hoped you would be more appropriately dressed for the occasion."

Master Carvallo clicked his tongue, but I nodded.

"Of course. I didn't want to risk fouling my clothes on the way here. If you would allow me a room to change in, I will put on something more appropriate." The smile felt stiff on my face, but Matra accepted it.

"Good. Taller will see to that, as well as where your porter can wait while you are working." That was all the attention she paid to Otsoa and moved on to Thromm. "I would like you to stand by the gate. No need to hover around our guests. I really didn't think you would be necessary, but Veiro insisted." She took her husband's arm.

"Just a precaution, dear," he said, patting his wife's hand. "It's not every day we have such a controversial guest."

"If any of our guests thinks him controversial, they aren't the sort I want to be friends with." She sniffed a bit, then called Taller over. "See to whatever they need, we have to get ready." She floated off with her husband.

CHAPTER FOUR

Taller led us to a room just to the side of the double doors behind us.

"You may stay in this room during the festivities," he said to Otsoa. Then he left us there, surrounded by shelves of delicate glassware and cushioned seats. I dumped my bag out onto one of the chairs and started picking out my outfit.

"It's good you'll be watching the gate, you can keep track of people coming and going." Otsoa spoke to Thromm as I laid out a gown and camisa. I dug into the pockets of the bag searching for something for my hair, a cap or some ribbons.

"I will do my best, but I am not sure I know what to look for."

"You just need to notice if something is not like the others," Otsoa said. "Someone that doesn't belong."

I flipped the camisa over my head, untied my hose, and then started shrugging out of my tunic. I heard Thromm mumble something and then the shelves rattled.

"What are you doing?" he said. I glanced over my shoulder to see that he had turned his back to me.

"Changing. Don't worry, you won't see anything important." The camisa formed a large formless tent over me and was heavy enough weight linen that it wasn't see through.

Otsoa chuckled, but he too had diverted his attention to the fine glassware.

"Otsoa's right, we just need to know if you spot a guest acting unusual." I gathered my tavern garb up and shoved it into the bag and flung the green gown over my head, adjusting it around the voluminous camisa.

"Do you think I should take some time to look for other entrances? Somewhere something Wild may have snuck into?" Otsoa asked. He had turned around now that I was tying my sleeves on. He nudged Thromm who turned around, glancing first to be sure it was safe.

"Nothing Wild is sneaking in here," I said, quickly weaving a ribbon through the braid in my hair. "It's not going to come waltzing through the front door either. Either Meia went out into the woods south of here, or someone her family knows took her."

"Or she ran off on her own," Otsoa said. "Or with a lover."

"There are too many options," I sighed. "We need to narrow down the choices." Thromm was staring at me, not gaping with his mouth open, but his brows raised. "What?"

"You look... I mean, that was a rather quick change."

"I've had a lot of practice." I had forgotten to pack fancy shoes, but no one could see my boots beneath the gown. "It's kind of nice, for a change. I don't get to dress up often."

"I still think I should look over the place while everyone is distracted." Otsoa said. "No one will miss me for a few hours."

"Yes, but now you are the only one not dressed up," Thromm said.

"Heh, point for Thromm," I said, smirking at Otsoa.

He frowned and looked down at his clothes. They were practical, and in good condition, but plain. "I thought I looked fine."

"You want me to make you invisible?"

"Can you do that, and still play?"

"Yes," I said. "Just don't let anyone bump into you, stay out of direct sunlight, and don't cast any spells. That will disrupt it."

"Great." He held his arms out like I was going to measure him for a new tunic and waited.

"What do I do with him while you're sneaking around the house?" I nodded my head towards Thromm. Keeping an illusion on Otsoa meant I wouldn't be able to silence Thromm if he started to say anything inappropriate. It would have been difficult anyway since we would be on opposite sides of the courtyard.

"I will be acting as a guard. I doubt anyone will speak with me," Thromm said. "And if anyone does, I will speak only of the weather."

I started to smile, but I quickly straightened my mouth, and started humming, then lowered the volume slowly, until the sound was barely audible. As I did, Otsoa began to fade until he was a shadowy shape. Actual invisibility was impossible, so far as I knew. But becoming part of the shadows, blending in with what was around, that could be done. In the weak light that filtered in through the curtains into the room, Otsoa could just have been a trick of the light.

"Be careful opening doors, too," I said. "Make sure no one is watching."

"All right." Otsoa's voice was muted, like he was speaking through a wall. I motioned for him to wait, opened the door, and checked that the hallway was clear before motioning him out.

"Did they tell you anything about the special guest?" I asked Thromm as I shoved my bag under the chair.

"Only that he would be arriving late, and that he is on the city council." I headed for the door, but he moved to stand in the way. "I know that you have your doubts about me, Glade. But I want to assure you that I will not jeopardize you or Otsoa in any way."

There was a level of intensity to his words that made me want to believe him. But, so far, he seemed like any other spell reader I'd seen sign up in the last few years. They didn't know how much they didn't know, and that put everyone in danger.

The first hour of the party was torture. I did my best to keep an eye and ear on Thromm, but my focus was already split. It didn't take a lot of concentration to keep Otsoa invisible, but combined with having to play more complex music than my usual fare was as much as I could handle. Matra had given me vague instructions, but I knew the sort of people that would have been invited to a party like this, all the local politicians and merchants and landowners. They would be expecting joyful music, sure, but of a high caliber, nothing I could play without sheet music. I did the best I could, but I'm sure it came out mechanical and rough.

I glanced up now and then, between songs. I was sitting in the only place in the courtyard in full sun. Most of the guests were lounging on seats in the shade or filling their glasses at the ice sculpted wine fountain. It was all very sedate after the night before. Thromm kept to the main gate. He watched people coming and going, but looked nervous, his hands fidgeting as though eager to pull his sword. Towards the end of the first hour, he perked up, and began shooing guests away from the entrance.

Matra swept by and asked that I pause the music, then tapped on her glass with one of her rings to get the crowd's attention.

"Ladies and gentlemen, I am so honored to present to you our honored guest for today's festivities. Some of you may already know him for his brilliant lectures at the university in Cyfar, and his amazing contributions to the rebirth of magic across all of Drakir. And now, of course, he is visiting us as our newly elected councilman, Rayul Vitabon."

The crowd erupted into applause as a tall, gray-haired man appeared in the gate. He was dressed in a knee length, black tunic, and a simple black cap. There were two people with him. One was a dwarf with a book tucked under one arm and a similar, simple tunic. The other was a tall woman dressed in leather armor, carrying a saber.

Many people in the crowd came forward to shake Rayul's hand, and he patiently greeted each of them as he made his way into the courtyard. It took some time, but eventually he made his way to the small stage. I hurried away as the attention of the crowd shifted my way, not wanting to get caught on stage behind him. I didn't have time to grab my music stand, but I took my guitar with me, and managed to snag a seat in the back of one of the shaded areas. Most of the crowd was still standing so they could keep their eyes on the special guest.

Rayul held his hands up and the crowd fell silent. He stood smiling out at them, pausing to make eye contact with several people, and then began to speak in a commanding tone that radiated out from him like a gust of wind.

"Thank you, honored friends," he said. "I am so pleased to be able to join you today at the home of our distinguished hosts, the

Carvallos." He paused, and then started clapping, stirring the audience up to applaud the couple. Matra looked flustered, but Master Carvallo waved their attention away.

"I am also proud to have been elected to the council, thanks in no small part to all of your efforts on my behalf. You will expect a lot from me in the coming months, and I intend to deliver all that and more." The crowd cheered again. I kept half my attention on the speech, and the rest I spent trying to see if Otsoa had returned from his investigation.

"I know that you all want decisive and immediate action in response to the recent attacks on our town, and I assure you, plans are already in motion to do just that. Not only have we increased the number of Watch to patrol the town at night, we have several top spellcasters investigating the attacks themselves, to see if there is any pattern, and find if there is a cause."

I turned back to the crowd. Before I had time to think that over, the crowd started murmuring and whispering the same word over and over. Changelings. Rayul held his hands up again, and again the crowd obediently fell silent.

"I know the rumors but let us be reasonable here. I cannot endorse taking any action without proof. Once I have any evidence to bring before you, only then will we take action." The crowd burst into cheers again. Rayul's voice rose over the crowd, vibrant and triumphant. He must have been using some kind of magic to be heard over the crowd. "We will defeat these attacks, together. We will protect our town, and families. Reason and order will prevail."

Rayul descended the stage, mobbed by the crowd now barraging him with questions. I caught Matra glaring at me from her place across the courtyard, and hurried back to my place on the stage, striking up a song the *Beauties of Reason*. I didn't sing the words, but a few people nearby caught on to the song and nodded their approval.

It was another long, warm hour before I was able to take a break. I hurried back to our changing room and found Otsoa waiting in one of the seats, still a blob of shadows. I let go of the spell and he materialized completely and rubbed his arms.

"Is it always that cold to be invisible?" he asked.

"Something to do with the shadows," I answered.

"So, did you know anything about attacks happening here? Roya didn't mention them to me."

"Me neither," I said, setting my guitar on another chair. "And he doesn't seem the kind of person to leave out an important detail like that."

"So, either the attacks were incredibly recent, or they were keeping news of the attacks to themselves." Otsoa tapped his fingers on his leg. "Why wouldn't they ask Cyfar for help?"

"Who knows. Pride? I imagine they have a decent Watch, and they can hire Wardens independently too. It's not as though there's a shortage of funds here."

"But the Carvallos hired us out of Cyfar, and are assuming their daughter's disappearance isn't related?"

"We still have to talk to them. Maybe they have some clue that we don't know about." I hurried to change back to my travelling clothes.

"I hope so. I went through the whole house. You are right, there is no place something from the Wild could have gotten into. They have iron bars on all the windows, and a fence farther out behind the house." Otsoa looked away from me. "The most likely story still seems to be that she left on her own."

50

I played for another two hours, ignored by the crowd. So was Thromm, for the most part, though he caught a few side glances now and then from those in the crowd now lucky enough to be close to Rayul. I wouldn't have paid him much attention, except that Matra seemed more attached to him than the other guests. And it was more than just introducing him around to her friends. They spoke alone, away from the other guests, several times.

Once Rayul left, the party broke up quickly. As soon as the last guests wandered out of the courtyard past Thromm, Otsoa appeared and helped me gather up my music stand, chair, and carry them back to the room. Master Carvallo was there waiting for us.

"Thank you again for coming. I know this was not your typical work, and I really appreciate your patience." He spoke mostly to Otsoa. "I am sure you have many questions."

"First, if you could, describe the events leading up to your daughter's disappearance," Otsoa said. He leaned back against the table and focused his dark eyes on Carvallo.

"Three weeks ago, Meia was helping Matra prepare for the arrival of her cousin. He often comes to stay with us for the summer. While they were airing out his room, we received word that he was not going to be coming after all. Meia was very disappointed, and I'm afraid she had an argument with Matra, who then took to her room with a headache, and Meia retired to her room to play music."

Carvallo stopped as his voice caught. He cleared his throat and went on.

"She played and played for hours, the same song over and over. I didn't know what to do, she wouldn't come to the door or answer us, so we broke into her room. And she was gone." The last word came out choked.

51

"I'm so sorry," I said, giving him a chance to recover his voice. Otsoa frowned at me.

"Thank you," Carvallo said, after a few deep breaths. "That was the last any of us saw of her."

"Now, I'm going to have to ask you a few hard questions, and then we would like to see her room," Otsoa said. Carvallo nodded, and straightened himself up, locking his face into an emotionless mask. "Do you think it's possible that Meia fell prey to one of these recent attacks?"

"No," Carvallo said quickly. "Those have all been within the city walls. And so far as I know, no one has been taken. There has been some destruction, but the creature responsible is always killed."

"Creature?" I asked, earning another frown from Otsoa.

"Yes, the attacks have all been by Wild creatures."

"Did Meia have any suitors?" Otsoa said, taking control of the conversation back. He narrowed his eyes at me, but I ignored him.

"No, no suitors. She was still young." He said it defensively, and I could easily imagine Meia wishing she did have a suitor, and her father disapproving.

"Why was her cousin unable to come for the summer?"

"He's fallen ill, I'm afraid. He lives a good ways north, in Taunton, and his parents didn't want him to make that journey while he was ill."

Otsoa nodded. "Thank you. I know it pains you to speak about this, but we will need all the information we can to help you."

"Of course, anything you need. Here, let me show you to her room."

He led us through a long corridor to the back corner of the house and opened the door to his daughter's room. It was huge. A large feather bed dominated the room, draped in white. The blankets, the pillows, sheets, even the wood of the frame were pale and pristine. The back wall was divided into five tall windows framed by long ethereal curtains. Thick white carpets covered the floor. The room was blinding. Through the windows I caught a view of rolling hills, and a long stripe of dark woods beyond.

We moved around the room slowly looking over things, under things. Carvallo remained just outside the doorway. There was not much lying out. All of her clothes were neatly put away in a closet, her vanity was bare, her bed neatly made. In one corner, close to the windows, I found a small wooden flute on a chair. There was no written music anywhere in the room. I guessed it was just something that she played for enjoyment, and not something her parents had expected her to learn. There was probably a music room in the house somewhere with a harp or a forte.

I lifted the small flute. It was a simple instrument, amateurly made, and painted with bright simple patterns.

"That's what she was playing on that last day," Carvallo commented from the door. Otsoa came to look at it as well, and I held it out to him on my palms. He maneuvered so he was between me and Carvallo and showed me that he had a bit of hair in his hand. He kept his voice low.

"I have enough to try and trace her," he said. "But if you think we would learn more from that we can ask to take it with us." I nodded, and Otsoa took the flute in one hand, tucking the hair away in a pouch with the other.

"I think we should take a look at a picture of her too, if possible," I murmured. He nodded, then turned around to Carvallo.

"May we take this with us?" he asked, showing the flute to Carvallo.

The man nodded, a weary smile on his face. I looked out of the windows, through the delicate iron bars, at the stretch of woods behind the hills. There was something strange about those woods.

I moved closer to the windows to try to get an idea of how wide they were. There was a scent in the air like Hyacinth, but it was too late in the summer for those to be blooming. I had been to nearly every tower on the border of the ancient Rhiandon Forest, and none of them had felt like this place. There was something alluring there, something calling to me.

"I think we have all we need, but we would like to see a picture of Meia, if we could?" Otsoa asked. Carvallo nodded and motioned for us to follow him. He took us into the dining hall, a long narrow room dripping with colored crystal. There were portraits scattered along the walls in no sense of order, ranging in size from the palm of my hand to the full height of the walls. Carvallo motioned to one of the largest portraits.

"This is Meia."

We looked up at the portrait of a girl in a pale green gown that matched her huge eyes. Her hair was thin, long, and raven black. Her nose and the shape of her chin looked vaguely like her father's. She was posed carelessly on a bench somewhere outside of her home. Beside her was a young man who might have been related to her.

"Is that her cousin?" Otsoa asked. Carvallo nodded.

"I will have to ask you to go now, I'm afraid," he said, slumping where he stood. "I haven't told Matra that I've hired you. She insists she just... ran off. I need to know for certain."

CHAPTER FIVE

We walked around the back of the villa, where the carriage Roya had sent us was parked. It was late afternoon, and the air had finally cooled. Soft breezes drifted to us across the hills from the woods.

"I'm going to try and track her," Otsoa said to Thromm. "It's been a few weeks, so I'm not sure if it will work, but it's worth trying first." Otsoa handed the flute to me and started pulling items from the pouches on his belt; Meia's hair, a vial of purple powder, and a small piece of cloth. He packed the hair and some of the powder into the cloth and tied it into a ball. Then he held the ball between his hands and began reciting a seeking spell. The ball glowed red, then darkened to a dim purple and faded.

He tied the ball to the end of a string, and then let it dangle from his hand. The ball began to pull towards the woods. I sighed, and we started off for the woods, explaining things to Thromm as we went.

"It does not sit well with me that he did not tell his own wife about hiring us," Thromm said.

"But it's understandable," I said. "It's also why he's been keeping things so quiet."

"I wouldn't have guessed it," Otsoa commented. "Not until I saw the picture."

"Guessed what?" Thromm asked.

"Meia is not Matra's daughter. She has Wild blood in her." I tucked my hands under my arms. "The last thing he would want to do is admit that. Everyone will assume she went back to the Wild of her own accord."

"Which is still a possibility," Otsoa added. I nodded. I agreed, especially considering the feeling I was getting from the woods. If her real mother was nearby, she may have run off to join her. Though living out here, it would have been easier for her to meet up with her mother, and to feel connected to the Wild. I barely felt any of that connection in Cyfar. And I had never met my mother.

We followed Otsoa onto gentle hills dotted with old tree stumps and wildflowers. It was about half an hour before we reached the forest. It was old. Even the trees at the edge were bowed and gnarled, like old men's knees, and the floor was tangled with brush and thorns. It was mostly oak trees with birch and maple sprinkled in. The glow of Summer ran all through the leaves.

We stopped at the edge of the forest where a long log covered in dark bark had fallen years ago. Otsoa motioned for us to stay where we were, and started to sidle along the edge, trying to guess where the pull was greatest on his spell. It was starting to act strange, pulling in different directions, and when he held it out into the woods, it went back to hanging straight down.

Otsoa huffed and tucked it back into the pouch at his waist. Then he started to step into the woods.

"What are you doing?" Thromm asked, holding him back. Otsoa looked at me with an apologetic smile, then turned to Thromm.

"Is there a problem?" Otsoa asked.

"Do you think it would be wise for you to go in there?" Thromm's voice was strange and had lost the stateliness I was growing used to. "Alone?" he added, after a long pause.

"Yes, I think it would be very useful to go in there. Alone." Otsoa smirked, imitating Thromm's pause. "The spell has been thrown off by something. I'm just going to take a quick look around." Thromm backed off, and Otsoa stepped into the forest, walking so softly that not a leaf rustled.

I tried to find something to focus on, but my eyes kept going back into the trees. I could hear a song calling to me, something like the song that called at Midsummer, but different. I had never heard another song call to the Wild, but I knew there were others. Winter's was different, of course. Maybe each forest had a different one.

Otsoa emerged from the trees about twenty feet away, again without making a sound, and I jumped. Thromm sighed, and moved to meet him, leaning down to look into his face. Otsoa waved him away.

"There is no sign that anyone has been in these woods for a long time," Otsoa said.

"Are you sure?" You didn't find anything?" I tilted my head. "It's very..."

"Very what?"

"Enticing," I said. "You don't hear it?"

"There is magic here," Thromm said. "I feel it too."

"I don't feel anything," Otsoa said, shaking his head. "Too much intuition, not enough evidence."

The song grew in strength, and before I knew what I was doing, I stepped over the log.

There was a sudden drop in sound, a moment of complete silence, and then a burst of noise as I stepped through the trees and out into a clearing. I turned to smile at the others, but they were no longer there, only the wall of trees. The clearing was surrounded by green, moss covered trees with trunks thick as houses. I felt submerged in gentle sunlight, a sweet taste clung to my tongue, and the song burst into my mind clear and joyful.

After taking some time to drink in the feeling, I raised the flute to my lips and began to play along with the music, tapping my foot to the rhythm. I caught up to the galloping speed of the song and let it carry me with it. I took off dancing around the edge of the clearing, hopping tree roots and ducking under branches like they were the proper steps. One, two, one two three, jump.

As I danced, insects came to join me, spinning around my head and buzzing in time to the song. I was surprised there were no smaller Wild things. At other times when I was so caught up in song, they would join me, compelled by the music to dance to my tune. Several butterflies flitted around me, and the crickets filled in the background.

A cold, resounding snap brought everything to a halt. I tumbled to the ground, a fiery pain shooting up through my leg. The light was gone, the music silent. I lay, rocking back and forth, my right leg curled up to my chest, and stared up through distorted , dark tree limbs at a clouded sky. My face twisted, and I felt a shameful heat flush my cheeks, as hot tears filled my eyes. I had been taken in so easily.

I sat up slowly, and looked down at my leg. I had just missed getting caught in a bear trap. The metal contraption was grinning at me a few feet away from a patch of thick grass. It managed to scrape along my leg, and I was oozing blood through a tear in my hose.

"Glade? Can you hear us? Glade, where are you!" Thromm's voice barreled through the trees. I looked over the rest of me. There were places where my illusion was growing thin. I tossed the flute aside, closed my eyes tightly, and hummed scales in my mind to weave it tighter. I didn't have time to check my face, so I had to trust my work was good enough.

Thromm appeared through the trees, Otsoa right behind him. They hurried over to me.

"I'm fine," I croaked. Thromm crouched down as though to lift me, but I swatted him away. He took a look at the scrape on my leg, then offered me a gourd of water from his pack. I nodded my thanks and washed the blood away. "See, it's not much of a wound."

"Would you like me to-" Thromm began, moving his hands toward the injury.

"I got it," I said, cutting him short. "Thanks though." He stood up and gave Otsoa a glance, but they both stepped away from me. I frowned down at the cold feeling spreading through my leg and pulled a small packet out of a pouch at my belt. While I set my hand over the wound and sang a short healing song, I also rubbed a special salve into it. Same as any Wild thing, if something forged by fire pierced my skin, the wound was problematic, resistant to typical healing. My salve was mostly honey and beeswax with a few herbs mixed in. I spread it on my leg, rearranged my pant leg and hopped up.

"So, what now?" I said as cheerfully as I could. I tapped my leg on the ground a few times to shake the numbness away.

"That was a bear trap." Otsoa's voice was flat, his brow furrowed.

"This trap wasn't set for a bear," I said. I looked around us. The woods looked mundane now, the colors dim and muddy. It was not a Wild place at all.

"How did you get here so quickly?" Thromm asked. "It took us some time to get through those woods."

"I don't know," I admitted. "But it looks like someone is protecting this area from intruders." At least, I hoped they would believe that was the case. Whoever had devised that spell knew a very specific and effective way to lure and catch Wild people.

"But why?" What would you do all of this to hide?" Otsoa asked.

"That." Thromm pointed to the far side of the clearing. The crumbling remains of a wall was just visible between the trees.

"That's just some old stones," I muttered. But as I spoke, Thromm walked across the clearing, drew his sword and raised it towards the ruins. As he walked, he began unravelling the illusion spell that hung over the ruins like a mist. It pulled out and stretched apart like a spider's web. The house underneath was not in ruins. It still looked old but livable.

I hadn't stopped to consider what Thromm's role was in our group. I had assumed he was just a fighter from his build and his sword, the sword that was now glowing white in his hands. My worries about Otsoa discerning that something was different about me dissolved as I watched Thromm. If he could spot illusions and unweave them, I was sunk. The spell that had been cast over the mansion before us had taken power and skill, had fooled me completely and lured me into its trap. Thromm melted through it like it was spun sugar.

We followed Thromm. Each step he took revealed more of a moss-covered walkway that led to the doors of the mansion. It was a low house, wide and sprawling, like it had been added to many times without a plan. The door was open, and the frame stuck out at strange angles. I stopped on the path, frozen by the sight of that door frame. It looked as though a giant animal trap had been built into the door, but one that had already sprung. It looked broken, or rusted shut, clamped onto itself right where a person would be standing if they had opened the door.

Otsoa had stopped too, a sour expression on his face. "It doesn't smell right," he said, mostly to himself.

"What?" Thromm looked back at us, one eyebrow raised.

"It smells like death," Otsoa said.

Thromm nodded, and moved forward more carefully, prodding the door trap with his sword. It rang dully, and a few flakes of rust snapped off. He stepped over it and disappeared into the house. Otsoa went next, his nose wrinkled up. I held my breath and slipped in after them, turning sideways to keep from coming anywhere near the trap. I was so focused on the door I tripped over the head of an ax buried halfway into the floor. There were two of them in the entrance way, plunged there by two tall suits of armor, one on either side. I managed to turn the trip into a set of hops that got me into the main hall.

There were more traps here, an iron cage that had crashed down from the ceiling, and a set of chains that were wrapped around the remains of something. I could only see a mound of cloth there now as I passed on the far side of the hall. We left a trail in the grit on the floor and moved carefully around the sheet covered furnishings that smelled of must and rot. Thromm was leading us to a door on the back left of the hall, somewhat hidden by a partly collapsed set of stairs. It was the one thing in the house that looked new and whole.

"It is locked," he said to Otsoa, and stepped out of his way.

"It's not just locked." He raised his hand towards the door and a faint blue glow rippled around it. "I'll try to be quick."

"You don't have to rush. If whoever lived here was still here, I think they'd have shown themselves by now." I shivered, keeping Thromm between me and the door the best I could.

"None of the traps are set," Thromm pointed out. "That usually means the master is home."

Otsoa pulled a roll of leather from inside his tunic and unfurled it on the floor before the door. The leather bore the seal of the council of Cyfar and tucked into pockets along the inside was a set of delicate wands, each with a different size lens fitted into the end. Otsoa chose two, then waved at the door again, studying the ripples. He put one back and chose two others, fitting them together so the lenses overlapped. He straightened up, pointed the wand at the door, and uttered a series of heavy words. There was a quiet ringing, then a click, and the door creaked open.

Beyond was a small room, clear of dust. A low iron table fitted with restraints took up the left side. On the right, laid out neatly side by side, were three bodies wrapped in sheets.

I pushed past Thromm into the room and began to look under the sheets at the faces of the dead. Meia was not there, but the third one in the row was her cousin. They were all part Wild, even dead their nature made the burning feeling rise in me. They all seemed to have died around the same time, and from the same sort of injury. Their eyes were red. Not just irritated red, but red like the vessels in their eyes had burst. Some had bloody tear trails on their faces.

I heard Otsoa enter the room behind me, and start examining the table and the area around it. I closed the eyes of those under the sheets. There were shelves above the table, with a few stray papers on them. Otsoa was looking them over. Thromm stayed in the doorway, keeping an eye on the hall.

"Meia is not here," I said quietly.

"What happened?" Thromm asked, glancing down at the bodies.

"Their eyes were blighted," I said. "I'm not sure how."

"I've heard of spells that can do that, but they are difficult spells, and not usually controlled enough to just affect the eyes." Otsoa looked ill.

"Could someone use a wand to do that?" I guessed.

"And the restraints, to keep the victim still. Are all of them..." Otsoa started to ask, then stopped and looked at me.

"Yes. All of them are partly Wild."

"How do you know?" Thromm asked.

"Iron burns," I replied, circling my wrist with my other hand.

Otsoa started gathering the papers, and something fell from the shelf, tinkling across the iron table. He snatched it up, then held it out on his palm. It was a small, sharp piece of glass that looked like it had broken off something longer. It was dark red, almost black.

"We have enough to start with," Otsoa said. He let down his pack, and pulled out an oiled skin bag, and laid the papers and bit of glass inside it before packing it away again. "I think whoever did this planned to return. The magic that had this room locked was preserving the bodies."

Thromm nodded. "I would like to search outside as well." Otsoa headed for the door, and I followed. When I passed through the door there was a loud click that resonated through the hall. As the last echo died away, a cacophony of metal grating shook the walls around us.

"It's the traps," I heard Otsoa shout. "The traps are resetting."

"No no no no no," I said. My knees wobbled, and I grabbed hold of the door frame to keep from sliding to the floor.

"Stay calm." Thromm's voice hummed low in my ear as he gripped my arm. "We will get out safe." Then we ran.

The cage trap in the main hall was easy enough to avoid, but to dodge it we pushed along a wall lined with portraits that shot iron tipped arrows at me. Otsoa drew his wand and threw a gust of wind at them, but it was hurried, and some of the arrows tore at our clothes.

I don't know if Thromm noticed that the traps only triggered as I passed, but he did an amazing job of protecting us from them. As we skirted around the chains, they reached out for us, and Thromm batted them away with his sword. They kept crawling after us, scraping along the floor like rusted snakes. They were trying to force us away from the door and into a nave in the side of the hall. With a quick slash, Thromm knocked down a moth-eaten tapestry onto the chains, leaving them scrambling to find a way out.

Rather than run for the door, Otosa took us toward a large window that had fallen out of its frame. Otsoa jumped through it, and as I sprang after him, the curtain rods bent down to grab me.

I twisted enough that they didn't get a hold of me, but they did knock me back, straight into the charging form of Thromm. He caught me up as easily as he would a child, and plowed through the window, knocking the iron bars aside, and landing us safely outside. We didn't stop running until we reached the clearing.

Chapter Six

We rode back to Casavera, and I directed the coach towards the one request I had made when drawing up the contract with Roya. It was the same request I always made if I happened to have a job near Casavera. We were going to stay at the Fonte.

The gate of the city opened onto the main street, and we traveled north along the bumpy cobblestone way to the main piazza, a broad stone paved area lined with manicured trees and showy flowers, the kinds of flowers cultivated to the point of losing their scent. Little iron fences were erected around the trees and grassy sections, keeping people on their paving and the plants in their place. I hated it.

The Fonte wasn't on the main street, but down a side way too narrow for the coach to fit through. We climbed down from the coach, and the driver let us know he would stay in the city as well, should we need his services for the rest of the job. A narrow stone floored alley led us to a courtyard with a massive marble fountain in the center.

It was not a quaint building. It had been constructed by dwarves, and showcased some impressive stone carvings, mostly mountain scenes and intricate geometric patterns around the door. The other buildings around the courtyard were daintier, plainer. The Fonte looked like the tough older sister in the neighborhood.

I shoved open the heavy door and took a moment to let my eyes adjust to the dim light. There were neat round tables draped with white linen set with flickering candles. The walls were covered in carvings as well.

"Glade!" The familiar voice was like a warm blanket after a walk in the rain. A moment later I was being hugged by my best friend.

"Hello, Josie," I said, letting her embrace envelope me. No one gave hugs like her. They are warm, soft, welcoming, but strong and always from the heart.

"What are you doing here? You haven't aged a day." She pulled back and I looked her over. She hadn't changed much since we had studied together, maybe a gray hair or two, and a wrinkle around the eyes. She wore her hair in braids, tucked up behind her gently pointed ears. I was always jealous of how well she filled out the high waisted gowns that were in style, though she always complained about being short and stout because of her halfling heritage. I thought it added to her cuteness. It certainly softened the dwarvishness of her chin.

Before I could answer her, Thromm and Otsoa pushed through the door behind me. Josie looked up at them, and I watched the look on her face change from curiosity, to confusion, to embarrassment.

"I'm, um, on a job," I said.

"Oh, I see." She dried her hands on her apron. "So, do you need the back room?"

"We're just here for dinner," Otsoa said, stepping around me and bowing to Josie. She brightened up, happy that we wouldn't be disappearing into a secret conversation.

"Well let's not keep you waiting, then. Friends of Glade get the family discount." She was smiling widely, not the painted-on grin of someone who has to work with people every day, but a real smile.

"No, now, none of that," I said, starting to relax. "This is going on the company expense account."

"Hm, we have veal ravioli today, creamy mushroom stew... Want the Vaster wine too?"

"I have never tried Vaster wine," Otsoa said.

"Oh, I have to remedy that. You know, they say, once you go dwarf you never go back. I'll be right back with the wine. Please take your pick of the tables." She hurried into the back of the room, and Otsoa watched her go. When he finally turned back around to see what table we had chosen, I smiled at him brightly.

"Nice place, right?" I asked.

"She is an old friend of yours?" Thromm asked. He pulled back his chair enough to have a good view of the tavern's exits before sitting down.

"Yes, my best friend. We had the same instructor."

"She sings, too?" Otsoa said, glancing over his shoulder towards where Josie had disappeared.

"She has the most beautiful singing voice I have ever heard." She was the only person I've seen make Delvine cry.

"Do you perform together?" Thromm asked.

"Oh, it's been ages. I don't make it out this way often." The Fonte was more than I could afford most of the time. Despite the ritzy neighborhood, it was still cozy, and smelled of bread and spices. "And it takes a lot to get her to perform."

"Why is she working here, if she is such a fine bard?"

"This is her family's place. When her mom got ill, she felt she needed to come home and help out. I imagine she still performs here, now and then. I wouldn't be able to resist it if I owned a place like this."

"Do you think we could risk taking a look at our findings?" Otsoa glanced around the room. We were mostly alone in the dining area. There was an older couple a few tables away, and one server checking over saltshakers and candles.

"If you're concerned about Josie, she knows how to keep a secret. She has Wardens come through here all the time, and there's never been a problem."

Otsoa nodded, reached into his pack and pulled out our finds from the mansion. There were a few sheets of paper with strange sketches on them, and the piece of red glass. The papers were all just sketches, half done and scratched out as though the writer hadn't gotten them right. Most of them were attempts to draw regular geometric shapes, representations of them in three dimensions, but each was just a little off.

"What is that thing?" I asked, pointing to the glass.

"I think it's the tip of a wand," Otsoa said. He folded a clean sheet of paper into quarters and then unfolded it onto the table, setting the glass in it so it wouldn't roll away.

"You mean part of the lens?"

"No, I think the whole wand was glass." He set out a small bottle of powder and strips of paper. "I've seen people use them to try out new spells, a control of sorts, to see how the spell works without any modifications."

"What was it doing there?"

"It means someone was experimenting with magic, on people." A cold edge entered his voice as he spoke. He sprinkled some greenish powder onto the glass and whispered something to it. It flashed green. "Luckily, it is also good at remembering what magic has gone through it." He touched the papers to the glass. Streaks of color drew up the strips, ranging from dark purple to a brilliant green, and last a small line of inky black.

"Looks like there were three parts to the spell. The purple is for seeking, and the green is to target the Wild. The black, it's a kind of destructive magic, but not very strong. There's not a lot of artificers who could make something this precise, or spellcasters who could balance the spell this well. Do you think the town would let us see the registry?"

I grimaced. "Roya has a lot of pull, but that might be pushing it. Worth a try though."

Josie arrived, two servers behind her laden with all sorts of amazing food. Josie held up two bottles in the signature shape of a Vaster winery; short squat bottles with a volcano pictured on the label.

"White or red?" she asked.

"Red," Otsoa answered, scooping up the papers and the glass in one quick motion and tucking it into his pack. The servers started covering our table with trays. Josie set to uncorking the bottle.

"You're going to join us, right?" I asked Josie. She shrugged.

"I don't want to intrude. I'm sure you have business to discuss."

"No, I've had enough business for the night. We have to catch up!" I squeezed her arm. She looked around, noticing the dining room was still fairly quiet.

"All right, but if it gets busy..." She pulled a chair over and sat between Otsoa and me.

We couldn't talk about our current job, so I regaled Josie with tales of the border patrol and some of the people I've had to work with. Thromm had a large appetite, and both men drank their share of the sharp, smoky wine. It brought some color into Thromm's cheeks and loosened Otsoa's tongue.

"Do you remember the place we stayed at in Trent?" Otsoa tapped Thromm's arm, and Thromm let out a tortured sigh.

"Now, don't go comparing the Fonte to other inns. You'll make me jealous," Josie said. Otsoa laughed and shook his head.

"No need to worry about that. That place could have been an outhouse for this place." Otsoa tapped Josie's arm next. "And the proprietor was nowhere near as lovely."

"No need for flattery, you're not paying for your rooms," Josie laughed. She looked down, rearranging the plates so the cheeses were closer to me. She had also ordered me a bottle of mead.

"He is being very accurate," Thromm said, his nose wrinkled. "It smelled like one. And the room we shared barely held the both of us together."

"I told you it was going to be terrible. But you insisted we needed to stay somewhere-"

"It was cold," Thromm interrupted, sniffing. "And it was going to rain.

"Which made the smell even worse." Otsoa laughed again, louder. "The place didn't even have a name, or I'd warn you away from it."

"The blessings of not having to travel." Josie sighed. She was still smiling, but this one wasn't real. "I'm going to get you all some more rolls." She grabbed the half full basket from the middle of the table and hurried to the kitchen. Otsoa leaned towards me and lowered his voice.

"Did I say something wrong?"

I shrugged. "I have no idea."

"Perhaps she wishes she could join you on your adventures," Thromm said, swirling his wine glass.

"On border patrol? No one wants to go on border patrol." The thought dampened the cheer I had been feeling from the mead. Josie always spoke so proudly of the inn and her family. When she had left our classes, she had been more concerned about her mother than qualifying for Warden.

A large hairy arm intruded over our table and set down a full basket of bread. We all turned to see a broad dwarf with a thick cut beard and a gold hoop earring. Once the bread was on the table, he pulled a knife from his belt and stabbed it through.

"You guys need anything else?" he asked. His voice rumbled like a landslide. He was glaring at Otsoa, who gulped down whatever he had been chewing on and shook his head. Thromm sat forward and put both hands on the table.

"No, no, we're good," I said, holding my hands out, though I knew I could not have stopped Thromm or the dwarf from doing anything if they chose to start something.

"Josie's not going to be able to get back to you guys tonight. There's a problem in the kitchen." He looked at Thromm and clicked his teeth. "If you guys need anything just ask me." Then he walked away.

"Who was that?" Otsoa had been gripping the tablecloth. He let it go and started to pour himself some more wine. Most of it made it into the glass.

"That's Josie's uncle. Joff? Joth? Something like that," I said. "He came to get Josie at school when her mom fell ill. But I remember him being a lot nicer than that."

"Did we do something incorrect?" Thromm asked. Uncle Joff had gone behind the bar and was wiping the counter, but still watching us.

"Who knows. Josie tried explaining some of her family traditions to me when I went to visit them over the holidays. Never made any sense to me." Josie had told me her clan was old fashioned, and I should just be prepared for occasionally uncomfortable situations. They had been very nice to me, however, and forgiving if I did something 'taboo', knowing that I just didn't know any better.

"She's going to inherit the inn, right?" Otsoa asked, tapping his fingers on his wine glass. "And her mom is ill, so her dad is busy taking care of her?"

I nodded.

"So, the uncle is her patron. He's training her to run the business. I guess he wants to make sure she stays focused."

"Yeah, well, he didn't have to be so creepy about it," I said.

"Yes, that was a bit much. But I don't give up easy." Otsoa yanked the knife out of the breadbasket, saluted Joff with it, and used it to eat with for the rest of the evening.

We saw Josie now and then through the rest of the dinner, but the dining room got busy, and she did seem to have something she needed to stay on top of in the kitchen. I stayed up late, waiting until Thromm and Otsoa headed up to their rooms, and then headed over to the bar.

Joff nodded to me and waited to see what I wanted.

"Is she still busy?" I asked. The bar was empty, and only two tables had customers. He narrowed his eyes at me, but put the glass down that he was drying, and headed into the kitchen. Josie came out a moment later.

"Hey, everything all right? Did your companions enjoy the dinner?"

"They would have enjoyed it more without the death threat." I nodded towards the kitchen. "What's with your Uncle Joff?"

"Oh, he's harmless. Sorry, I hope he wasn't too terrible." She leaned over the counter and started playing with some stray water drops that had pooled there. "This is a nice inn, but it's still a tavern. Now and then we get some rough characters in here. You know how Wardens can get when they're just returned home. Anyway, he just likes to be sure they all know he's here protecting the place."

"Are you doing all right?" I took hold of her hand.

"I'm fine. And it's really good to see you, even if you are working. Maybe you can stay a little after your job is done, and we can go to a concert or something, like old times."

"I'd love that." I sighed. "Um, so your uncle isn't worried about these attacks I've been hearing about?"

"Everybody is," she said. "It's been so random, no one knows what to do about it. So far, it's just been some small Wild animals getting into people's yards or hen houses. There was one Mazzi, but it showed up almost in the center square, and the Watch took care of it pretty quickly." She squeezed my hand. "I'm sure to you that doesn't sound like a big deal, watching the border all the time like you do. But having it happen in town is really troubling."

"It is troubling." There wasn't much more I could say without going into what we had found that day. If someone that close to town was actively trapping Wild creatures, the Wild would feel justified fighting back.

"Have you stopped by to see Glenn yet?" she asked.

I pulled my hand away and pushed away from the counter. "Nope. I don't like to bother him when I'm working. I should get to bed. Another long day tomorrow."

That night the dreams started. It was early, just the end of May, but the Wild song must have opened my mind to it. In the dream I was still in the bedroom in the Fonte, a small cozy room with a patchwork quilt made of fabric in all different shades of green. The moon was close to full, waning now, but still giving enough light to make the room feel cold. I was lying on my back, unable to move anything besides my head, and my heart was racing out of control.

Back in Cyfar when the dreams started, it was only small folk, Wild bees or butterflies, Alettas, maybe a Mazzi or two. Back home in Guowtan it had been Dryads from Fogwood, moss covered old men or leaf clad women peering through the window at me. Here it was nymphs. Flower nymphs always looked like children, as most flowers die and grow back every year. Sometimes there are a few who are older, like peonies or yarrow, those that pass through the snows. There was a mixture of them, five of them, dancing a circle at the foot of my bed, giggling and singing a little rhyme over and over.

A chill of fear ran through me, like when a mouse runs across the floor or you find a roach among your dishes. It was not as strong as what the larger, stronger ones made me feel. I knew they were something different, something not like me. I didn't even need to see their eyes to feel it. The one time I had been unfortunate enough to look a dryad in the eyes something rang through my ears, but I couldn't look away. She had been in a good mood, and those eyes promised the granting of wishes, and pleasures I could not imagine. In a bad mood, they could bite off my nose for spite and wear it as a necklace.

The flower nymphs were not really there, it was only a dream. But it meant that Midsummer was calling, and I would have to go to them soon.

So, I lay paralyzed, trying to calm my heart and watched them dance. I listened carefully to the song—it was one I had not heard before, all heather and meadow and a hint of something sharper like mint. They all wore ethereal short gowns in bright colors. Their hair was the color of summer grass and it bobbed around them as they danced. Their skin glowed a dull green in the moonlight.

Slowly a space opened in their circle, and they began to beckon to me with each pass, calling by my old name, Clara, as they whirled around. They knew that I was Wild, despite the illusion I was wearing. The Wild ones always knew. They beckoned to me, motioning for me to join the dance, but I still couldn't move. It wasn't time yet.

CHAPTER SEVEN

"You don't have to come with me this morning," Otsoa greeted me as I moved into the shared living space in the suite Josie had arranged for us. "I'll take care of the boring part."

"Paperwork," Thromm groaned. He was finishing a plate of bacon. I didn't think there had been anything else on the plate besides bacon. There was a plate of honey oat cakes and a cup of coffee waiting for me.

"You're going to the registry alone? I don't think they'll do much for someone licensed in Rheste." I sat down at the small table and blew on my coffee.

"I'm licensed in Cyfar," Otsoa said. He peered at me over his own mug. I paused, taking a drink myself to cover my surprise. Most spellcasters were registered as soon as they started training, and it was clear Otsoa had been doing this for some time. Maybe he had his registration transferred. Which would imply he didn't intend to ever go back home either.

"I still think I should come with you," I said, setting the mug down. "You could research in the registry, and I can dig around the library. See if I can dig up information on the crafting of wands, and what the purpose of the spell would be."

"Do I have to join you?" Thromm asked.

"What are you going to do while we're gone?" I asked him.

"Perhaps I will do some of my own reading," he said. There were a few books in the suite, volumes of poetry, a few legends and some histories. I looked at Otsoa. He shrugged.

"I don't think he can get into too much trouble sitting around here reading," he said. "And we won't be there all day."

"Just don't pester Josie all morning, all right?" I told Thromm. He nodded and got up to start perusing the bookshelves. I finished my breakfast then Otsoa and I headed out for the registry.

The Registry of Spellcasters and Artificers was kept in the Hall of Records in the main plaza of any town of a decent size in Drakir. In Casavera the main plaza was bounded by the Hall of Records, the council building, the cathedral to Ventor, and something that looked like it had been a temple to the old gods in ages past all worn marble and empty naves where statues had been. Wooden market stalls were lined up around the edges forming their main marketplace.

As we crossed the plaza, a few street cleaners came through sweeping up after horses and the detritus left by revelers. In Cyfar, all of that work was only done in the dark before sunrise and the workers all vanished back to the bottom level. Only what was beautiful, what was ideal, was to be seen. One of the sweepers was a Changeling. She had a hat pulled down over her shaggy hair, trying to hide her glowing eyes, but I could sense it. She and a waif of a human were pushing big brooms along the walks. I caught

Otsoa watching them as well as we climbed the wide stairs to the Hall of Records.

It was cool and quiet inside. The main doors opened on a rotunda capped with a fresco of Ventor giving gifts to the world; fire, writing, freedom. Several halls led off the rotunda. I waved to Otsoa who went to the right to request the records of spellcasters and artificers able to create the magic we had found. I went left to investigate the library.

I was met at the entrance by a dwarf in long dark robes, with a master's tassel on his hat. He folded his hands in front of him and looked up at me expectantly. I wanted to make an impression, so I licked my lips, and tried to remember what I could of Ancient Drakiri. I asked him if he would be kind enough to show me to the old magic books. He corrected my choice of words, calling them scrolls, not books, and then switched to speaking the modern tongue.

"Very nice. So few people take the time to study the old words," he said. "You have your license, of course?"

I nodded and pulled out my registration card, as well as one of the pages we had found in the mansion. "If you would be so kind, could you point me towards the making of glass wands, and spells that involve using these?" I showed him the page with the geometric drawings. He laughed.

"That old nonsense." He waved the paper away. "I can show you, but it was all foolishness. Like chasing the philosopher's stone."

"Is there a translator available today as well?"

"For a girl who knows the old words, I translate myself," he said. "This way." He led me through narrow stacks of books to a dusty back room lined with cubby-holes instead of shelves. Piles of tagged scrolls filled each cubby.

"This is a nice collection," I said. It was about the quarter size of what we had in Cyfar, and it looked like more of it had been cataloged and translated already.

"We are fortunate to have many wealthy patrons in this town." As he walked through the room, he pulled a few scrolls out and set them on the table. "Some who are also bored, I think." He stopped at one of the cubby-holes. It was empty. "It seems that someone else has been looking into these follies as well. Some eccentric rich man who likes ancient philosophy. I am sorry I cannot offer those scrolls to you."

"Thank you, whatever you can offer will be more than welcome." He stayed with me a while and translated everything we could find about using glass wands and targeting spells, until Otsoa came calling for me through the stacks.

There were very few spellcasters registered that met the criteria we were looking for. As we looked over the list outside the Hall of Records, we discussed the candidates.

"You do know this could be a rogue," I said.

"Sure. But they had to learn from someone. Even if it isn't one of these people, it may be someone they taught." He fanned out the copied cards. "So, take your pick. Chief of the Watch, retired artificer, and a gardener."

"A gardener?" I peered at the cards. "And that's not just a retired artificer. That's a veteran of the wars."

"Really? He'd have to be what, five hundred years old?"

"Something like that. I thought they were all living at the Bright Gardens in Rhiodeja. This one lives here?"

"Apparently he still lives in the barracks," Otsoa said, pointing to the address. "Doesn't sound like much of a retirement."

"I say we visit him first and get it out of the way." I headed down the stairs, towards the north side of town and the barracks. They would most likely be behind the cathedral.

"A veteran of the wars doesn't seem to be a likely candidate for killing Changelings to you?" he asked. He tucked the cards away in his pouch.

"If a veteran of the wars wanted to kill Changelings, they wouldn't be sneaking around in hidden mansions and using wands," I said. "They could set them ablaze in the town square and no one would blink."

The cathedral glinted and sparkled in the morning light. It was shaped from long strips of metal that spiraled upward to a point. Orange and red stained-glass panels stretched between the metal arms, making it resemble a brazier or the top of a torch. During services they would light the central fire pit and the whole building would glow.

"Did you find out anything in the library?" Otsoa asked. Past the cathedral were a few low stone buildings, stables mostly, and carriage houses.

"Some about making wands. But nothing about the strange drawings. I have a feeling there are two people working on this."

"Right, one to make the wand, and one for the spell. It's not likely someone would have the skill to do both."

I nodded. It was refreshing working with a real spellcaster. The newer Wardens couldn't deduce their way out of a sheepfold. That reminded me of how easily he had figured out what I did for a living, and how easily Thromm had detected the illusion at the mansion.

"Have you known Thromm long?" I asked. "Or did you just meet him on this job?"

"Oh, I've known him a few years now. I know he's a little odd, but I've never seen anyone better with a sword."

"A little odd?" I shook my head. We rounded a corner and found the wide, double storied barracks building. "Did he grow up in a cave?"

"Well, you know how some of the far east towns are. We don't get much news from out here. We don't see a lot of elves, or anyone other than humans and the occasional Dwarven trader. Just country bumpkins, ignorant and blissful." He ended with a flourish, and I couldn't help grinning at him.

"I know Rheste. It's nearly as big as Cyfar, though yes, it could use a few more dwarves. Can't get a decent cup of coffee anywhere."

"Maybe, but we do have the best toasted cheese in Drakir."

"Oh flames, I haven't had toasted cheese in years." I closed my eyes for a moment to remember the creamy goodness.

"Don't get home much?" he asked.

"No." I needed to change the subject. We were nearly at the barracks door anyway. "So, what rank spellcaster are you?"

"Just made nine," he answered, a touch of pride in his voice.

"Great. You can do most of the talking then. I'm still only a four." The symbol on the door was the sign of the Wardens, a single tower with a circle around it. But on the stone around the door the motto of the church of Ventor was still readable. 'By your light we shall see.' We knocked on the door and waited.

During the wars, when almost all knowledge of magic had been hunted out of Drakir or taken offshore by the dwarves, the only ones able to fight the Wild had been the paladins of Ventor. They had marched, clad in metal, and cut swaths through stretches of the forest, burning everything in their path. When the wars ended, they trained soldiers for a while, but nothing stirred on the borders, nothing that warranted armored soldiers. And as the dwarves returned, so did the knowledge of arcane magic, and the Wardens were created, trained to keep an eye on the border. Wardens like me, who took occasional gigs on the border and had to make their own living arrangements or find side jobs to get by. Career Wardens, who took special jobs, lived in the barracks.

The woman that answered the door was sun-beaten into looking older than she was. She looked us over quickly and raised her eyebrows when she noticed Otsoa's wand.

"Yeah?" she asked in a low voice.

"We were hoping to get a chance to talk to Andiel," Otsoa said.

"He's in the back, training. You'll have to wait for a break." She pushed the door open so we could come through.

"Thank you," he said. We pushed through a long hall, lined with doors that opened into rooms full of bunk beds and sweaty armor. The back opened onto a sandy floored practice square. Six people were paired off and sparring, some with swords, some with spells.

An old elf, tall, muscular, wearing his hair long in the former fashion, with skin almost as dark as a walnut tree, was circling them. Now and then he would stop someone, make a few comments, and tell them to start again. They were using real swords, and real spells, not the wooden staves I had used when I was trained to be a Warden. He noticed us after a few minutes and told the trainees to take a break. Most went straight to the water gourds on a nearby bench. One, a lithe young woman, noticed me and laughed, saying something to her sparring partner. The only word I heard was 'bard'.

"Can I help you?" Andiel said, walking over to us.

"Yes, thank you." Otsoa bowed slightly. "My name is Otsoa, and this is Glade. We have a few questions for you about some spell evidence we found."

Andiel bowed back. "Of course. What have you found?" His voice was rich, aged into full bodied perfection over the centuries. He didn't walk stiffly, though he didn't stand up perfectly straight, and his eyes were growing gray. Otsoa pulled out the small papers with the colored stripes and handed them to Andiel. He pulled a monocle out and looked closely at them. The trainees were now talking together and laughing, the lithe woman having pointed me out to the others.

"That's what we call bringing a bow to a ballista fight." He handed the pages back.

"I'm not sure I know what you mean," Otsoa said.

"It's incredibly precise, but there's not enough power behind it to kill anything Wild. Not even a mouse. It might annoy it though, aggravate it." The side of his mouth ticked up. "Where did you say you found this?"

"Unfortunately, we can't say," Otsoa said. Andiel nodded. "Do you know anyone who could create a spell like this?"

"None still living," he said. His mouth straightened out.

"What about glass wands? Do you know anyone in the area who makes high quality ones?" Otsoa asked.

Andiel was looking at me now, as though expecting me to add something to the conversation. I looked back at him but kept quiet.

"Possibly. I'm not sure if they are still living, but Vidria used to make the best wands."

"Thank you, Master Andiel. We won't take up any more of your time." Otsoa turned to go, but Andiel put his hand out and set it on my arm.

"No trouble at all. Actually, if I could borrow your companion for a moment. Glade, you said?"

"Yes." I tried not to sound worried.

"We don't get many bards anymore. I was wondering if you could provide us with a demonstration?" He motioned for the trainees to get back into position, and for a moment I feared he was going to toss me into the ring with them. As they paired off, he pointed to the lithe woman and her sparring partner, a smaller woman with two short swords. He commanded them to fight, and they began slowly circling, the lithe woman taking teasing jabs at two swords.

Andiel leaned close to me and whispered. "Buff the two-sword one."

I smiled, nodded, and began to sing. It was a simple song, and I sang it quietly. I don't think the other trainees noticed it. But the woman with two swords did. She started circling and bouncing, blocking the lithe woman's blows with more energy. Then in a quick flurry, she drove forward against her. The lithe woman faltered, and tripped, landing on her butt in the sand, with two swords at her throat.

"Never discount a bard in your party." Andiel announced to the trainees. "And keep them on your good side. Their song can make you stronger and swifter, heal you after a battle, or send you running away in cold fear. Thank you, Glade." He bowed to me again, and then clapped his hands and started barking at the trainees.

"Your turn to do the talking," Otsoa said. We were standing at the bottom of the steps to the Hall of Justice, staring up at the tall columns and the blue banners covered in white stars hanging between them.

"You're not wanted, are you?" I was not eager to talk to the Watch either. Watch duty was a cushy job, far from the dangers of the Wild, only fit as retirement for former Wardens. Though the

Watch would tell you Wardens were all thrill seekers with death wishes, and if any of us made it to retirement we were either too broken down or insane to enjoy it.

"Not in this town," Otsoa answered. "It's just you know this area better than I do. They may even know who you are."

"That may not be the best thing. All right, let's get this over with." I strode into the hall like I was supposed to be there and headed straight for the front counter. I had expected there to be a line, but the waiting area was almost empty. One of the Watch was behind the counter, reading something, and two others were talking and laughing near the door to the rest of the building, all wearing tunics bearing their symbol, a ring of stars.

I waited at the counter until he glanced up at me. He didn't speak, just looked back down at the book he was reading.

"Excuse me," I said, my voice poised between professional and urgent.

He looked up at me, closing his book but keeping his fingers on the page he was reading.

"I would like to speak to your captain. Official business." As I spoke, I showed him the pass Roya had given us, with his seal on it. The guard reacted to that, raising his eyebrows and letting go of his book. He snapped at one of the Watch talking by the door.

"Go see if the captain's free, would you?" The watchman nodded and headed through the door. The one at the counter went back to his book.

The captain poked her head through the door of the waiting area. She was a stocky woman, medium height, with a mop of dark curly hair.

"Can I help you?" she asked.

"I hope so. I'm Glade Balladeer. I'm in town on a specific job." I showed her my card as well. "But if you don't mind, I'd rather not discuss it out here."

"Sure, come with me." I followed her through the door into a long hallway. There were several doors, each with a small plaque hung on it. The hallway ended in a barred gate manned by two more members of the Watch, the entrance to the local jail. Her office was small, but very neat. In the center of the shelf behind her desk was a golden ring of stars badge next to a small portrait of an older man. She had his eyes.

"Thank you for seeing me so quickly," I said. The seat she offered was hard and wobbled when I sat down.

"I prefer to keep trouble to a minimum, and if there's something Roya is investigating nearby, it's best to give all the help we can. Is this related to the recent attacks?"

"Yes," I said, jumping on the excuse to ask questions. "We're looking into what's behind the recent attacks. We want to do everything we can to keep the town safe. I'm afraid I can't tell you much more than that."

She didn't look pleased, but she held her hands palm up. "We have the same goals. What can I do for you?"

I pulled out the small strips of paper Otsoa had used to examine the wand and set them on her desk. She picked them up and peered at them.

"We were looking into the possibility that someone was provoking these attacks." I pointed to the papers. "We found evidence of a glass wand containing this spell near some of the attack sites. We were thinking someone could be goading the Wild attackers. Do you know anyone able to create such a precise spell?"

"I might be able to make something like that, but it would take me a long while. Something like three months, at least. And that's three months of working on it all day every day. I wouldn't have that kind of time. Have you talked with any professors in Cyfar? Seems like the kind of thing they would have the time and patience for." She handed the papers back.

"No, not yet." I was really hoping we wouldn't have to go so far afield to find the culprit. Something was telling me the person was still here, waiting to provoke another attack. My mouth twisted. The gardener must be a retired professor. I couldn't think of any other reason he would be so high ranking. "Is there anything else you can think of that we should look into? I'm sure you have been working as hard as you can, but you have other concerns in town and only so many Watchers to go around."

She nodded, and some of the hardness melted from her face. "Yes, no rest for the Watch. And the attacks only made it worse. Most of the town is on edge, so tempers flare and things heat up between neighbors. This was such a peaceful town when dad and I moved out here. We'll get things back in order soon enough." She glanced back at the portrait behind her, her eyes hardening into a determined glare. "If you find someone has been using these wands to provoke the Wild, don't hesitate to let us know. We'll provide any back up you need. But so far, the theory is the attacks are centered around those in town sheltering Changelings. So, if I were you, I'd look into the Church of the Light. Do you know where that is?"

I squeezed my lips together and nodded. I knew it very well. *Oh, Glenn, what are you up to now?* "I will do that," I said. "Thank you for your help."

"It's good to know there are others helping in this case." She shook my hand as I stood to go.

"We'll do our best," I said.

"Not good news?" Otsoa asked me as we headed back into the streets.

"Don't you ever turn that off?" I asked him, half-smiling. The other half of me cringed every time he guessed something correct about me.

"Turn what off?"

"The whole 'I can deduce everything by just looking at you for three seconds' thing." I was walking quickly, trying to hide the anxiety I felt after the conversation with the Watch, but it hadn't hidden anything from him.

"You can't turn off your soul," he answered. I stopped short and stared at him. He only shrugged. "You know, if you want, you could just head back and check on Thromm. Let me talk to the last one. I'll be back before you know it."

"He's not just a gardener, is he?" I asked. Otsoa blinked. "You're not the only one with deductive skills. He was a professor before, right?"

"All his card says is gardener," he said, digging into his pouch to find the cards. He wouldn't look me in the eye. I didn't need to be a master investigator to know he was lying.

"He was your professor. Wasn't he?" He stopped digging through his pouches, but still didn't look up. "I didn't know there was a university in Rheste."

"There isn't." He looked back up at me, daring me to keep asking questions.

"So, you studied in Cyfar?"

"No."

I folded my arms and waited. Maybe I couldn't deduce everything, but I could be as stubborn as a pack mule. Otsoa recognized my attitude and shook his head, making the beads in his hair click together.

"They had professors that would come to visit Rheste," he said. "And take in students, like apprentices. They would stay a few years and train them and then head back to their comfortable homes, secure in the knowledge that they had given something of themselves to the less fortunate. Even if Rheste is as big as Cyfar, we're not nearly as wealthy. We're too close to the Wastes, too stuck on the old gods, too backwards for anything more than charity work."

It all came out of him in a rush, and I felt something twinge inside. It was pretty much how people felt about my hometown. After learning to change my appearance, the next thing I had done was lose my accent. Otsoa hadn't changed himself at all. Was Roya holding something over him too?

"Yes, sounds about right. Though back in Guowtan we didn't even get charity."

He looked away again. There was something more to this than shame at being from a poor town. But there was something more to my shame, too. I couldn't begrudge him his secrets.

"This isn't going to go well. I didn't want to drag you into it," he said. "Things didn't end well between him and me."

"I'll go back, if that's what you want." Then I smiled as mischievously as I could. "Or I can go with you and sing your praises. Make him regret ending things."

At first his eyes widened, but then a smile spread over his face. It wasn't a happy one, though. There was something dark in his eyes, regret or sorrow. But he nodded and led the way to the gardener's house.

His house was in a quiet part of Casavera. The houses were all tucked behind adobe walls with wrought iron gates. At the gardener's house we could see the tops of fruit trees peeking over the walls and hear the soft song of birds rustling through the branches.

Otsoa stood at the gate, formed a funnel around his mouth with his hands, and shouted, "Hello the house!" The door opened, and a stooped elf with short black hair peeked out of the door. When he saw us, he hurried out to the gate. He wasn't stooped with age, just from leaning over desks, and walked toward us with long stomping strides. He yanked open the fence and motioned us inside, then looked up and down the street before shutting it again.

"What are you doing here?" he asked Otsoa. His voice rasped like a bad viola bow. He had a scar across his cheek, or rather three parallel scars, from his ear to his chin. "Does anyone know you're here?"

"Probably one clerk at the Hall of Records, but I doubt they care," I said.

"And who are you?" he asked, frowning. I could tell just from that frown that he had been a teacher. It conveyed disapproval and the threat of punishment all at the same time.

"I'm Glade Balladeer," I said, thrusting my hand out. "We've been hired by Roya Sontuoso, and we have a few questions for you."

He looked over Otsoa again, taking note of the wand at his belt. Otsoa stood completely still under the inspection.

"So, you're licensed now?" the professor asked. Otsoa nodded. "Do they know-"

"Roya knows," Otsoa interrupted. The professor still hesitated, looking like he might run back to his front door at any moment. "It's all right, now. It's under control. I've gotten... assistance." The professor's eyes narrowed. He crept closer to Otsoa and peered into his face. Whatever he saw there must have satisfied him.

"What are your questions?"

I glanced around, mostly towards the street. It was a quiet neighborhood, but not so quiet that there was no one at all passing by.

"Couldn't we go inside?" I asked. The professor rolled his eyes, waved his hand through the air, and all sounds from the birds and wind in the trees stopped.

"There, no need to worry about eavesdroppers," he said. "What are your questions."

Otsoa took out one of the little papers and held it out to him on his palm. "Did you do this?"

The professor looked at them briefly. "What if I did?" I clenched my jaw, and my fists, and locked my legs in place. He hadn't even blinked.

"For who?" Otsoa asked. His voice was tight, like he was choking back other words.

"One of the Hunters," he said.

"One of the what?" I stepped towards him before I could stop myself, getting close to his face. "They've licensed Hunters in Casavera? Since when?"

"Since the attacks started," the professor continued. He didn't flinch or back away, just kept a steady gaze on me. "And I support them wholeheartedly. So why shouldn't I help them? I haven't been as fortunate as you in finding work again." The last he said to Otsoa.

"You know that this would be of no use to a Hunter," Otsoa said, matching his teacher's calm voice. "This wouldn't kill a Wild rat. What is it for?"

"I wouldn't know. I created the spell that fit their specifications. Perhaps they just wanted to stun the creatures so they could get them out of town."

Which would have made sense. If we hadn't found the bodies. If they hadn't licensed Hunters. Wardens could have been used to chase Wild creatures away from the town. Hunters were allowed to go out into the Wild in pursuit of a specific Wild creature that continued to cause trouble.

"Or blind them," Otsoa said, looking down at the papers. I turned to glare at him and shook my head the tiniest bit.

"Where can we find these Hunters?" I asked. We were done here. I just needed to know where we were headed next.

"They have a guild hall, same as Wardens," he answered. Otsoa and I turned to go, but he grabbed my arm to stop me, and traced the scar on his face with his other hand. "You keep an eye on that one. I don't care what Roya thinks."

I'm not sure if Otsoa heard him, he just pushed through the gate and kept walking. I pulled my arm away from the professor, wanting to spit into his face how stupid it was to have Hunters again, let alone give them murderous spells to work with. Instead, I brushed off my arm, as though wiping off his residue, and walked out.

CHAPTER EIGHT

When we returned to the Fonte, Thromm wasn't in our rooms. There were a few books left open on the table, and an empty glass. We headed downstairs, scanning the midday crowd for him, knowing he would stand out. Josie appeared from the kitchen and waved to me.

"He's downstairs. He was nice enough to help us load in today's deliveries." Josie started moving bottles aside on the shelves behind the bar. "He'll be up in a minute. Did you guys have a good morning?"

"I guess you could call it that," I mumbled. Otsoa took a seat at the bar, but I stayed standing, tapping my hands on the countertop. Thromm came through the kitchen door carrying a crate of bottles and set them down gingerly on the bar.

"What else would you like brought up," Thromm asked. His fine brocade tunic was covered in dust, and he had a smudge of grease or dirt on his face.

"Nope, that's everything." She started setting out bottles. "Have a seat, they'll be bringing out lunch for you guys in a moment."

Thromm came around the bar and sat beside Otsoa. I kept drumming on the counter, not ready to just sit and eat.

"I'm going to take a walk," I said. Josie stopped to look at me, and I smiled back, but she wasn't convinced.

"You don't want to eat first?" she asked. Her hair was still in braids, and she pulled it all back and rolled it into a bun.

"I just need a walk. I won't be long." I looked sideways at Thromm. "Make sure they save me some, all right?"

"If they don't, I'll stab them with a fork," Josie promised. I hurried out of the Fonte and into the afternoon sun. What I wanted to do was run out of the city, or hide in a locked room, let my disguise down and sing. The warm sweet delight of the dance at the ruined mansion caressed the back of my mind, and I wanted it again, the wild abandon of that moment. Instead I settled for walking fast circles around the stone courtyard, humming scales under my breath to keep myself under control. Eventually I found the sunniest spot in the courtyard and stopped there, closing my eyes and turning my face up towards the sun. I'm sure the others milling around me thought I was crazy, but I didn't care. I wanted the warmth to sting on my cheeks.

I heard a splash from the fountain, and the sound of wet squishy footsteps. I opened my eyes, but the sun dazzled me, and I had to blink before I could see well. By then whoever had been in the fountain was disappearing between two of the houses, just a shape in the shadows. I couldn't help smiling. I remembered summer days swimming in the fountains back home, one of my few happy memories. It was a little odd that someone would do that in such a ritzy part of town. Maybe a kid had done it on a dare. I was ready to head back inside.

The fountain began to bubble over, and exploded outward raining water and rubble down on me and the rest of the courtyard. In its place a massive minotaur appeared, soaking wet. It was taking deep grunty breaths and looking around in a daze.

"Oh, Holy Flames," I whispered. The minotaur made a loud snort and stumbled towards the swimmer. It took a few steps and lost its balance, slamming a massive fist into the closest wall. Stones fell from the wall and the house shook. I heard screams from inside. The minotaur steadied itself and continued tromping forward, and I stared open mouthed as it passed me.

The doors to the Fonte flew open and Thromm barreled out, throwing himself between the minotaur's fists and the next wall. He took the blow of the fist, staggering back but somehow remaining on his feet. The minotaur growled something about finding the little thief, but Thromm couldn't understand him.

"Back, fiend, back where you came from!" Thromm shouted. He was using his sword like a prod, trying to maneuver the creature away from the buildings and towards the ruined fountain. The minotaur repeated itself, asking about the little thief, getting louder in the futile hope that Thromm would answer.

Otsoa ran out next, and I skirted around the piles of wet gravel to meet him halfway across the courtyard. Thromm might be able to take a hit from a minotaur fist, but I knew I couldn't. It still looked confused and was growing angry. It lifted a large chunk of the fountain and tossed it at Otsoa and me. We ducked, and it went rolling along behind us and into the corner of another shop. Otsoa dropped to his knees and started pulling things out of pouches for a spell.

People were running past us, climbing out of the holes in the walls or pouring out of doors to get away. The minotaur took another step back to avoid Thromm's sword. Thromm wasn't just prodding now but taking full swings that clanged against the minotaur's hide. As soon as the minotaur stepped onto what had been the center of the fountain, it let out a roar, and rushed forward.

Thromm dove out of the way, rolling through soaked rubble and landing against a set of barrels. The minotaur kicked rubble and mud on top of him and let out a throaty roar as a warning for Thromm to stay down. The fleeing people caught its attention next and it started darting its head around and making grabs at whoever was nearby. Otsoa was still busy combining things and whispering a chant as he poured powders together.

I moved away from Otsoa, waving my hands and whistling. "Hey big boy, look over here!" The minotaur stopped, his hand poised above a lady who had been trying to inch by along the wall. "That's right, this way! Come catch the sparkly bard."

I started singing, weaving a glowing illusion between my raised hands, and the minotaur turned and headed for me with slow, swaying steps, his eyes dazzled by the display. The minotaur was slow, wincing as it moved from Thromm's slashing. As it came closer, I slowly started changing the song, and turned the glowing lights between my hands to cooler, calming colors. It came within a step of us and slowed, it's one leg still up in the air, wavering as though it had forgotten where it was going. Its foot stomped down, two feet in front of me, and its eyes began to droop. I waved my hand behind me at Otsoa to tell him to pick up the pace.

There was a poof, and the distinct smell of sulfur, and three black arrows swept over my head and struck the minotaur in the chest. Rather than piercing its hide, they exploded into oozing masses that began eating into its skin. The minotaur howled and fell to its knees, trying to rub the ooze from its chest. I raised the volume on my song, pouring every ounce of weariness I could into the music. It groaned and collapsed sideways into the mud of the courtyard.

"Sorry," Otsoa said. He stood up, brushing his hands on his tunic. "I usually have more things prepared. This was unexpected."

A barrel rolled aside, and Thromm stood as well, joining us by the slumbering hulk. He looked it over and nodded.

"Ah, good, you have eaten through its defenses." He raised his sword.

"No, wait!" I shouted. Thromm sunk his sword down into its chest. The minotaur moaned loudly, its eyes fluttering wildly, and then relaxed with a long sigh.

"Is there a problem?" Thromm pulled his sword out again, covered with green blood, and began to clean it in the water spraying from the ruined fountain.

"No," I said, closing my eyes. I don't know how it had gotten here, but I don't think it had known either. It seemed to be chasing the person who had been in the fountain—had they come out of the fountain too?—and had not intended to hurt anyone. I just wished I had a chance to ask it. "No, nothing. Thank you, Thromm."

He nodded and started checking around the courtyard for anyone who was hurt or caught under the rubble. I looked down at the bleeding minotaur and grunted an apology in its language. There were many things in the Wild that would kill or hurt without provocation. Minotaurs were generally harmless unless provoked. I took a careful look at its eyes, just in case I saw any evidence of the spell we had encountered at the mansion, but there was nothing odd about them. I sighed, and followed Thromm's example, looking around for anyone I could still help.

97

Thankfully, no one had been caught under any rubble. There were a few folks trapped in their homes, and some cuts and bruises, but no major injuries or deaths. Thromm turned out to have another surprise skill, he knew how to heal. We set ourselves up inside the Fonte dining room, which now had a massive hole in the wall, and anyone needing fixing up came in through the hole, received what help we could give, and sat down at a table behind us, where Josie was setting out soup and drinks.

I watched Thromm work with the wounded, his large bulk surprisingly gentle with the patients. His smooth voice and warm smile helped. It was odd for a fighter to know any kind of magic, let alone the type he knew, and I wondered if he had been trained by the church. He didn't talk much like a cleric, though he obviously had no tolerance for the Wild like a cleric.

Otsoa did his best to clear the courtyard of water and stone, using his wand to manipulate the elements. He tried patching some of the walls back together, but most of the stone had been reduced to gravel, so he settled for making a few neat piles of it, using it to turn the flow of water away from the buildings and into the street drains.

Part way through the clean up, I heard Otsoa's voice, loud and annoyed, arguing with someone. I poked my head out of the hole in the wall, and came face to face with a short, pale woman with short cropped white hair.

"Can I help you?" I asked, stepping out into the courtyard, even though it brought me only inches away from her. I didn't like the way she was looking at me. Her head was tilted sideways a little too far. She looked like she was examining something she'd found under a log.

"No, honey, pretty sure we're here to help you." There was something wrong about her voice. Too low? Too airy? I couldn't define it, but it made me shiver.

"Well, we're all fine here, thanks." I continued walking forward, seeing Otsoa facing off with someone behind her, but she blocked my way and I bumped into her. She was solid for someone so small.

"Are you sure? I think maybe you hit your head during the commotion." A faint blur started in my mind, just behind my eyes, as she spoke. I only had to feel the beginning of it to recognize a mind fogging spell and throw it off. She would have to be a high-ranking Artificer to be able to start such a spell just by speaking, instead of relying on music to focus the resonance. She wasn't focusing very hard, however, or I wouldn't have been able to throw it off so easily. I narrowed my eyes and pushed my face towards hers so we were nose to nose.

"Stay out of my head. I said we're all fine."

"Navala, stop playing with the hirelings and come help me with this." I looked past Navala and saw a tall, muscled woman, her bare arms scarred from her hands to her shoulders, standing over the body of the minotaur. I couldn't tell if she was referring to the minotaur or to Otsoa, who was standing beside her. The women were wearing a uniform of sorts, a long green vest with a seal on the left side over their hearts. I looked back at Navala and down at her vest. The seal looked like a dragon's claw clutching a sword.

"Hey, my eyes are up here." She snapped her fingers at me and pointed to her eyes.

"You're not my type," I muttered, pushing past her and heading towards Otsoa.

"No, but I know who is," she replied. Her voice was a low hiss. Thoughts of someone I hadn't pictured for years rose up in my mind. Instead of just fuzziness it felt as though she had punched me in the gut. I hadn't expected it to hurt so much, I mean, it had been years. Before I could stop myself, I called up the burning sensation I got whenever a Wild thing was near, and funneled all of it into my mind, blotting out the face in my memory. Navala squeaked and covered her eyes, though none of the light was visible. It was only in our shared mind.

"I told you to stay out of my head."

Thromm stepped out of the hole next, and Navala stepped away, giving him ample space to get by. We headed for Otsoa, who was staring at the scarred woman. She didn't acknowledge my arrival. The scars on her arms were not in rows. I knew some Wardens tracked how many Wild they had killed by marking their skin with thin cuts. But her scars were random, and all from the same time, older scars that looked like long stripes of raised flesh. She was a well-built woman, tall and striking, her hair pulled back into a thick braid, her pointed ears pierced many times and bristling with gold rings.

There were others with them in the same vests. They were hovering around Otsoa, keeping a nervous watch on him. I thought that was amusing, but to be fair, defending against a sword was much easier than the myriad of things a spellcaster could come up with.

"Stand aside, and let us collect our due," the woman said. I realized then that a shimmering bubble of water had formed around the minotaur, and was slowly solidifying.

"It was my kill," Thromm said firmly. "I will loot it first, if you please." Thromm was right about that, for once. As the party that had brought down the enemy, we had first rights to the body.

"You are on our lands. We have first rights to any Wild rewards here," she answered, looking past me to Thromm. He hesitated and looked to me.

"I'm sorry, who are you?" I asked. She finally looked down at me and gave a brief smile, as though upset at having to explain things to a child.

"You're obviously new here, so I'll let this slide this time. I'm Tara Ryo, head of the Hunter's Guild, and Casavera is our territory. So, unless you'd like to take this matter to court, you'll step aside."

"By all means, let's go to court. I'm sure they'd love to hear about your little mind witch's tricks, and how she uses them on Wardens." I tried to look intimidating, but she had nearly six inches advantage over me.

A clear, strong voice struck my mind, and all the anger and tension in me melted away. I could see the same change come over Tara's face as well. The song felt like an ocean breeze, lifting out every negative emotion and sweeping it away. Josie was singing. She had the attention of everyone in the courtyard, even Otsoa, who nearly lost control of the bubble. With another quick snap of his wand, he solidified the bubble around the minotaur. Tara frowned, but it didn't last long.

"We have people to attend to," I said. My voice was light as a cloud. "If you still wish to dispute this later, I'm sure it can wait until after we've seen to these people's needs."

Tara nodded slowly, made a motion towards the others, and led them out of the courtyard. We headed back into the Fonte and the sweet song.

Many of the refugees had gathered in the dining room, huddled together and whispering. Josie's song had a calming effect on them as well, stilling their jitters. I went upstairs to dry off and returned with my guitar and began to play along with Josie's song. It was the quietest, most peaceful tune I had ever heard. The song was about a brook that runs by Alte far in the north, and the little white flowers that grow only around that brook. As I played, I concentrated on the feeling of lying by that river and breathing in the scent of those flowers and sent it out into the room in soft waves.

She let me choose the next song, so I played a sunrise. I filled my music with the quiet slow creep of light and the feeling of waking slowly someplace safe and warm, and the triumphant feeling as the sun finally forms over the horizon bright and blazing. By the end of that song people had begun talking and eating, still slow and weary but no longer in a daze.

"Oh, Fires above, Glade, I miss hearing you play." Josie put her arm around my shoulders and squeezed. "Sorry it had to be like this." She set down a tray half full of little breakfast pies, as she called them, and sat down beside me. "I saved you some nut ones," she said, pushing a few across the tray.

"Have I told you in the last five minutes how much I love you?" Most of the pies she made involved sausage and eggs, but for me she saved her honeyed-nut and cheese pies. "So, a Hunter's Guild?"

"I know, it's a bit extreme."

"A bit? And you see what kind of people it attracts." I pulled one of the pies apart and started picking out the nuts.

"Well, there have been so many attacks. Though this was certainly the most destructive." She ran a hand over her hair as she looked up at the gap in the wall.

"And let me guess, it was a campaign promise from your new councilman?" I pushed the cheese back into the pie shells and ate them next. "Always have to do something flashy to get into office."

"At least he's doing something about it. Everyone else has just been pointing fingers blaming anyone who takes in Changelings, blaming new Wardens for not training as hard, blaming the planets for rising in the wrong houses." She flipped her hand in the air. "But no one wanted to do anything."

There was a knock at the door, a strange courtesy considering there was a hole in the wall. She answered the door to find two clerics, one carrying blankets, the other a basket of food. The hems of their dark orange robes were wet from the soggy courtyard.

"Hello, we were just coming around to see if everything was all right. We're working to get someone here to repair your wall as soon as possible. Do you need anything? Was anyone hurt?" The younger one held up the blankets.

"Thank you, that's very kind," Josie said. "But we're fine here. And thank you about the wall, that would be wonderful." As they left, I heard shouting from the courtyard, the raised voices of the Hunter's Guild against new voices, one of which I recognized.

I sneaked over to the wall and peeked out. There were several clerics and even an Auger, a leader in the Church of Ventor, trying to get the Hunters to leave the minotaur's body alone. Glenn was one of them. The clerics wanted to be rid of the minotaur's body as soon as possible, and the Hunters wanted to cut it up for parts. Glenn was staying quiet, but the Auger was standing up to Tara, his powerful voice ringing over the stones.

Another group was arriving as well. They looked official, like city Watch, but in finer clothes. Among them, being guarded by them, was Councilman Rayul. The argument stopped as the Watch spread through the crowd.

"What seems to be the problem here?" One of the guards asked. They pulled Tara and the Auger apart. Tara shrugged them off. The Auger stepped back quietly. Two other Watchers took up positions around the minotaur's body.

"This guild is trying to claim jurisdiction here." The Auger had turned to Rayul and was still using his booming behind the pulpit voice.

"We are fully licensed by Casavera," Tara said, also facing Rayul.

"You are licensed to loot Wild kills in the field. There is no looting allowed within the city limits." The Auger pointed to himself. "We are tasked with removing Wild creatures from the city wherever they are found."

"Then perhaps you should have kept it from getting into the city to begin with," Navala said. She was winding her way through the crowd of clerics. Several shied away from her as she passed. Glenn ignored her completely, his eyes glued to the councilman.

"Yes, the blame falls on us, not on the guilds for keeping pens of Wild animals within the city."

"Or the church for sheltering Changelings." Tara sighed as though she had spouted this argument before.

"You are right, of course, Auger Linel," Rayul said. Everyone stopped moving when he spoke. "The Watch will escort the guild back to their hall, so that you and others may fulfill your duty. I will ensure that they stay within their limits." He nodded to the Watch, who started pairing off with the Hunters. Tara stared at the Auger for a moment more, then she nodded to her guild and they moved away.

"Thank you, councilman." The Auger nodded and the clerics went to work, first dispelling whatever Otsoa had encased the minotaur in, then using some kind of magic that dissolved the body. I moved back into the dining room, looking for Thromm.

"If you want to loot anything from that creature, you should go claim it now. Once they get done with it, you'll be lucky to get bones." Thromm nodded and headed out into the courtyard. Otsoa was seated nearby, a mug in his hand. "You're not going out there with him?"

Otsoa shook his head. "I don't think he'll need more of an introduction than the fact that he killed that thing." He watched me for a moment. "You're going after them, aren't you?"

"We know they're involved. And they have Wild animals penned up somewhere? Maybe the spell started as a way to control them?"

"You shouldn't go after them alone. They know what we look like now."

"I'll be invisible. It'll be fine."

"I'm going with you."

"I can't keep us both invisible. Not for long anyway." I had already used a good deal of energy calming the neighbors.

"You can't just go stalking a legal guild. They'll have you arrested." He finished his mug and set it down on the table.

"Maybe we can find someone to watch them for us." I sighed. "Let me at least find out which guild hall is theirs and look over the place. I won't do anything on my own without discussing the options with you both."

"Your word on that? No action without talking with us first?"

I nodded, and he held out his hand. I took it to shake on the agreement. His hands were rougher than I expected for a spellcaster. He probably had several other jobs before he was licensed in Cyfar. I ducked out of the front door and faded into shadow.

CHAPTER NINE

I rushed through the streets as much as I dared, knowing that if I bumped into anyone the invisibility would end and I'd have a lot of explaining to do. The skills of spellcasters and artificers were highly prized for Wardens, but using those skills in town was suspicious. But then, there weren't usually Wild creatures showing up in town either.

Edging around the main plaza, I hurried down Guild street, distinguished by the bright banners hanging on poles sticking out of the faces of the buildings. Each banner bore the symbol of their guild. I scanned the banners and spotted the dragon claw clutching a sword on a green flag part way down the street.

Each guild hall looked much the same, two story white buildings criss-crossed with dark wooden beams. Most had large display windows in the front filled with the wares of the members.

The windows in front of the Hunter's Guild were boarded over. The buildings were built close together with tight alleys between them. Rather than risk running into someone by going around the block I squeezed into the alley and shuffled through to the back.

I peeked out when I reached the other side. The guild my backside was pressed against had several large pots and empty barrels lined up in the yard. The Hunter's Guild yard was fenced in with high slats of wood. No one was around that I could see, but something was scuffling or snorting inside the fence. I crept out of the alley, running my hand along the fence to see if any of the boards were loose. When I reached the corner, fortune finally gave me something, and there were a few slats missing.

A snort erupted and I jumped back. Looking down, I saw a snout pressed against them. I carefully inched back to the fence and peered through the gap. There were several pigs inside the fence, not regular pigs, but not Wild pigs either, or they would have eaten through the slats by now. They were only a little Wild, larger than regular pigs, with some spiky bristles along their backs. The others were crowding around the gap now, their noses pointed right at me. I took another quick look around the pen and realized there had to be another one. This one only took up half the width of the building.

I rounded the corner, looking for similar breaks in the other half of the fence. As soon as I stepped into the back alley, the animals in the far pen began barking and howling madly. I kicked into a run, my heart skipping to a wild rush. The howls chased me as I tore around the corner and towards the alley on the other side of the Hunter's Guild Hall. My foot caught on something hard and I went flying face first into the dirt, jolting me out of my invisibility. I had tripped over the cellar doors probably twisting my ankle in the process. The hounds inside the fence, Wild hounds at least in part, were clawing and barking at the fence beside me and howling like they had scented their prize.

I climbed to my feet, testing my ankle, and was immediately dizzy. I tried to steady myself against the fence. Looking at the doors my vision split. Multiple doorways opened up and stretched out in different directions. I squeezed my eyes shut, took a deep breath and the images faded. I heard the door at the back of the hall open up, and someone came out into the yard fussing at the dogs to be quiet. I ran again, shoving myself into the space between the buildings.

It was a tighter fit than the other side had been. I gritted my teeth and tried to pull my sleeves down over my hands. I couldn't leave a trace of blood behind, not when they had hounds like that at their command. I checked again quickly before popping out and strolling down the street like I had been walking there all along. I made it past the Hunter's Guild when a bout of shouting rose up behind the hall. My heart was still racing. I needed to get somewhere that would cover my smell. Keeping my pace even and slow, I looked around at the nearby guild flags. The very next one was a golden color bearing a mug topped with foam. Perfect.

I stepped into the Brewer's Guild just as the entrance to the Hunter's Guild flew open. I closed the door and waited, listening as several people ran out and past the door. I took a long breath and tried to slow my heartbeat. Two halflings were seated on the counter at the far end, one looking through a ledger, and the other half asleep.

"Good afternoon," the reading one said, looking up over a pair of spectacles.

"Good afternoon. Is your mead maker in?" I asked.

"I like a lady who knows what she wants. Hey, wake up." He elbowed the sleeper who stirred and sat up, bleary eyed. He was much younger than the reader, probably an apprentice. "Go find Morris and let him know a Warden is here looking to trade."

The boy hopped down behind the counter and disappeared into the back of the hall. The reader set aside the ledger and motioned me to come closer.

"Like a taste of anything? Meads on the left there, ale on the right, wines along this wall." He waved toward each place as he spoke.

"Gladly," I said. I turned away from him and browsed the shelves while I caught my breath. There was a surprising selection of mead flavors, not just fruit but flower and spices, some that they must have traded with dwarves for. I chose a bottle marked cinque, a popular blend of spices, and poured some into one of the small tasting cups on the table.

I took a whiff and smiled. Anise, cardamom, ginger, cinnamon and a touch of cloves calmed my nerves. And it tasted fantastic. I stopped to look at the maker's mark so I could watch for it next time I was in the market. The boy appeared again, hopping up onto the counter and resuming his leisurely posture. A few moments later a round human appeared, wiping his hands on a worn apron, his smile hidden under a shaggy beard.

"That's one of my specialties," he said in a lilting halfling-like accent.

"I can see why," I said. I raised the little cup to him. "It's delicious."

"I hear you may have something to trade?" All of the guilds knew to welcome Wardens looking to trade. We picked up some interesting things while out working, and while any being from the Wild was considered dangerous, items from the Wild like silk or skins were highly prized for their innate magical powers. I leaned towards him and lowered my voice.

"What do you think a few gallons of Snow Dew honey would be worth to you?"

Morris narrowed his eyes. "Depends. Do I get to be sure it's the real thing?"

I smirked and reached into a thin pouch I kept tucked under the corner of my tunic. I had a few small vials of Wild honey there that I mostly used for healing salves for myself. I passed it over to him and he popped the cork out and sniffed at it. Then he put some on the end of his little finger and tasted it. His bushy eyebrows went up.

"And you can get gallons of this? How?"

"I have my ways." He offered the vial back. "Oh, no, please keep it."

His brow furrowed, and he looked over his shoulder at the reading halfling. He didn't look up from his book, busy scratching figures into it with a long feather quill.

"It's all right Morris, I like her," he said. Morris pocketed the vial.

"How much do you think you can get?"

I tilted my head, calculating. It was early in the summer, and I hadn't gathered very much yet. Assuming no one had found my usual spots so far, it could be a fair amount. "I can get you five for sure. Probably more if the weather is good."

He wiped his hands again on his apron. "And what would you want in payment?" He motioned to the bottle I had tasted. "We do have a good amount of cinque left."

"As tempting as that is," I said, "I have more of a favor to ask. Could you keep an eye on the Hunter's Guild? You wouldn't have to do anything. Just watch. And keep me informed?" I held my breath and waited. It was all well and good to offer something as good as liquid gold to brew, but if they liked the Hunters they could turn on me and warn them, or the city, about what I was up to.

Again, Morris turned to the halfling who was still making calculations in his book. The small man finished a line, then looked up at Morris and waved him back into the hall, pointing to the now dozing halfling as well. Morris moved back around the counter, picked up the sleeping boy, and headed out of sight in the back.

"My name's Anurin," the halfling said, standing up on the counter. He had dark wooly hair and an impressive nose.

"Glade," I said, moving over to the counter.

"I don't imagine you'd like to tell me why you want someone keeping an eye on the Hunters, eh?"

"I'm sorry. I'm not allowed to speak of it."

Anurin nodded slowly and looked me over. Then he sat down on the edge of the counter and swung his legs back and forth. I wasn't charmed though I might have been if I hadn't been so flustered. Halfings are disarmingly cute, and even though this one was older and obviously a savvy businessman, sitting on the edge of the counter and swinging his legs made me want to tousle his hair.

"I have to say, what you're offering, its enough to make me suspicious." He paused, and I took a shaky breath. "But you gave us more than enough in exchange to make it all right. I'll send a report around this evening to start. Where are you staying?"

"Fonte. If we aren't in, you can leave the report with Josie."

His face lit up at the mention of her name. "Do you know that darling?"

"I do. We were in school together."

"Hm. I may come around myself," he said, straightening his collar. "Never pass up a reason to go by there."

"Thank you. I greatly appreciate it."

"As do we. There aren't many left around who know where to find Wild honey."

"I'll be sure to bring you the best."

The Fonte looked more like itself when we returned. The wall was almost completed, the fountain's rubble had been cleared away and the flow of water stopped. Josie and Otsoa were sitting at the bar together. Josie was telling an old dwarf tale about the Wild creatures that live in the mountains, and Otsoa looked enthralled.

Thromm was sitting at a nearby table, eating something. I motioned for him to stay quiet, and tiptoed up behind Otsoa. Josie was getting to a suspenseful portion of her tale where three campers were caught in an early snowstorm while strange growling and howling surrounded them in the snow. Just as she described the beast jumping at the campers out of the cloud of white, I let out a fierce growl and pounced onto the counter behind Otsoa. He jumped and made a strange yowling noise, throwing himself between Josie and me, before realizing it was me. I slid down the other side of the bar, laughing too hard to catch myself, and ended up sitting on the floor.

"What did you do that for?" he asked.

"I couldn't resist," I said. I stood up and leaned over the bar, still giggling. "You were so lost in her eyes." Lucky for me I was still laughing too hard for the last few words to be understood very well, or Josie would have slapped me.

"She weaves a good tale," he said. He was pouting. "If you could pull yourself together long enough to fill me in, I'm hoping you found out something useful."

I took a few deep breaths and looked at Josie. She was trying hard not to laugh, but her cheeks were pink and her eyes merry.

"Where's Uncle Joff?" I asked her. She shrugged.

"He headed out after the lunch rush. He likes to check if any caravans arrived during the day." She looked around the dining room and I could see her making mental calculations. "He'll probably be back soon." She glanced at Otsoa. I slipped onto the stool beside him, facing the table Thromm was at.

"Let me know if you need anything," Josie said before moving to the end of the bar to give us some privacy.

"The accusations are true. The Hunters have part-Wild pigs, and Erl Hounds penned up behind their guild hall."

"Erl Hounds?" Otsoa hissed.

"Well, like I said, only partly."

"Still, that can't be very safe. And they don't think the Erl might come looking for them?" I shook my head, but fought the urge to clarify the situation. Minotaurs wouldn't work with or for the Erl, Lord of the Hunt. They tended to buck any allegiance though they would have to obey commands like the rest of us. I should have gotten more information on the other attacks from the Watch, but I didn't want to attract suspicion. If we were already investigating, we would have those details.

"I have the brewers watching them. But I couldn't give them details about what to look for. And whatever they are doing with those wands is probably going on in the basement."

"Whatever the cause, it would appear that they have their reasons for fighting back," Thromm commented.

"Sure, I mean, a few random Wild attacks are perfect reasons for torturing people to death," I said. Otsoa clicked his teeth at me.

"I did not say I thought they were good reasons." Thromm raised his head. "But if in their minds it is Changelings, people or animal, that are driving the Wild to attack, they may be pushed far enough to create something this terrible."

"I think we need to refocus," Otsoa said.

"I think we need to report to Roya," I countered. "This is beyond the Warden's reach."

"We were hired to find Meia. I know you want to help the others too, but we have to stay on target. Once we've done that we'll report back and see what can be done for the rest."

I frowned. Yes, we had been hired to find one girl. But I couldn't make them understand how deeply this was burning into me. What they did understand was returning to Roya without reaching our goal meant we wouldn't get paid. I would have felt the same way on any other job.

"Fine, then, what should we do next? For all we know Meia's in their basement already." Thromm somehow managed to get paler at that statement.

"True. That's why we're having them watched. If the brewers see her around there we'll know." Otsoa's logic couldn't possibly more annoying.

"I doubt they'll be parading her around. No one has noticed Changelings going missing yet. Her own parents didn't suspect this sort of thing was going on."

"All the more reason to think she isn't being held in town. Who knows how many hiding places in farms or other old homes they have around this area?" Otsoa kept his tone level and calm. I sounded like I was raving in comparison, though I was doing my best to keep my voice hushed.

"Could you at least do your job and try to track her in town?" That finally got a reaction from him. He pressed his lips together and narrowed his eyes at me.

"Of course. It'll take a while though, this many people in the way. But by all means, allow me to spend the rest of the day trying to track her." He stood up, taking the small seeking stone he had made before out of his pocket. "Coming?" he asked Thromm. Thromm looked from Otsoa to me. I kept my best I-don't-care-what-you-do face on. Thromm shrugged and stood as well. I watched them weave their way out of the inn, and then slumped against the bar.

"Going that well, huh?" Josie asked. She settled across the bar from me.

"Do I look that depressed? I thought I was doing a great job of hiding it." I didn't even raise my head, rolling it back a bit so I could look up at her.

"You all do," she sighed. "It's enough to make me think you're not happy staying here. I mean, we have such great ventilation, exciting floor shows." She waved her hand at the partly finished wall.

"Well, as much as I love this place, I do have to say I think the neighborhood is really going down hill." I propped my head up with my elbow on the counter. "I don't know how the others feel though. Maybe you and Otsoa can get together later and discuss the accommodations." I wiggled my eyebrows at her. But she frowned and turned away, pretending to straighten the bottles on the shelves.

"Don't start, Glade. It's not funny."

"I'm not trying to be funny." I sat up straight and frowned. She kept her back to me. "Come on, he's smart, and talented, and I think he likes you."

"He's just being nice," she said. She shook her head and turned to look at me. Her eyes were large and a little wet. "Your friends are always nice to me. And then the job will be over and I'll never see him again. So, let's not pretend, all right?"

"I'm not pretending," I mumbled. "I mean, not even the threats of your scary uncle have warned him away."

"You think Uncle Joff is scary?" She smirked. "You haven't met Aunt Joan."

"I think Thromm thinks your Uncle Joff is scary. Aunt Joan must be a monster." I patted her hand. "How are things with your mom?"

"It's all right, for now." She squeezed my hand. "Dad took her back to the Suderburgs for a while. We thought the dryer weather would be better for her. The last letter was pretty encouraging. I'm actually fortunate Uncle Joff was willing to come show me the business. He's very successful back home. I'm learning a lot about how to run things here."

"As long as he doesn't threaten all your customers with knives."

"I think the Wild attacks have him on edge. And I do need to stay focused on the business. This place is my responsibility now. It takes a lot of dedication."

"I know. And current damage aside, the place looks great. And you seem pretty busy."

"Thanks. I know you've traveled to some amazing places, so if you think it's doing all right, I 'll consider it a great compliment. Just no more teasing about Otsoa, please? It just makes it harder when you leave."

I nodded and gave her a small hug over the counter. I had never been able to convince her to court with anyone, not even back in school. She had it fixed in her mind that none of it was real. If I ever found out what fool had hurt her enough to make her believe that, I'd use his guts for guitar strings.

"Well, it's not as if you aren't turning heads around here," I said. "Just today I was talking with a fairly well to do halfling-"

"Anurin?" Josie flopped her head backwards. "Is he going to be coming here?"

"Yes, he might be by later. What?" Josie glared at me. "He seemed nice enough."

"You haven't had him shoved at you at every social engagement you go to. He's fine, you know, if your goal is to cement a great business deal. They are the finest brewers this side of the Lumina."

"That sounds like torture." I could imagine Josie running things at the inn, keeping track of inventories, making sure her guests were happy. I could not picture her navigating ritzy parties and avoiding sticky social situations. She hadn't even attended our own graduation celebration.

"Yes, it's all part of the glamorous life of an *hovding*." She used the dwarvish word that I've always heard translated as business person. Another thing I didn't understand about dwarven culture, they talked about business people like the rest of us talked about landowners.

"And you're all right with this?"

"It's worth it to make sure things keep running smoothly." She smiled and looked around the dining room, raising her chin. "Not as exciting as Warden work, I know. You'd probably rather be stuck playing lute for the symphony in Rhiodeja. But it's worth it, really."

I nodded, knowing that one day she might actually believe that. She could have gone so far as a Warden, or an artificer. Her songs could calm any fear, or excite any crowd.

"And a wealthy *hovding* like you can't afford to have a little fun on the side now and then?"

"Fine, if I get a chance to, maybe I will see if anything is there." She pulled away from me. "I've been getting braver since you've been away. It's just scary, you know? Well, I mean, you don't know. You've never been afraid of anyone."

I had to look away at that. As much as I loved Josie, as long as we had been friends, I had never told her my secret.

CHAPTER TEN

Otsoa returned with Thromm before dark, hot and tired. He didn't look our way at all but went straight to his room to clean up. Thromm at least waved first.

Anurin was true to his word and came by to the Fonte that evening. He was dressed in a full suit this time, his hair combed back and slick. Josie saw him coming and tried to rush through the orders she was giving to the servers for the night.

"Good evening, beautiful," Anurin said. He hopped up onto a stool with almost no effort so he was sitting across from Josie. "How are you tonight?"

"Fine, thanks. Your usual?" Josie asked him. She smiled as warmly for him as she would for any other customer.

"You know it, darling." She started mixing something complicated and colorful. When she was finished, she slid a glass layered with colored liquids that I swore was sparkling on top. Anurin was smiling so widely his dimples were deep divots in his face.

Joff appeared at the bar then, I'm not sure from where, and tapped Josie on the shoulder. I expected him to treat Anurin to a similar display as we had previously with the bread and knives. Instead he whispered a question into Josie's ear. She nodded and answered back with a flavor of pie.

"Oh, no, I couldn't, really," Anurin said. "I won't be here for long."

"Please, it's on the house," Joff answered. He headed into the kitchen himself to get it, brought it out with a flourish and a fork, and then headed out into the dining room with a long glare at Otsoa.

Josie waited until he was out of sight and then curtsied to Anurin. "Excuse me, I have to check in on the kitchen." She darted away. Anurin shook his head.

"That girl breaks my heart every time I see her." He spun around on the stool she he was looking at me. I was watching from a nearby table, sipping on my mead to hide my smirk. "So, here's the news," Anurin continued. "The white-haired woman, I think she's fairly high up in their guild, she arrived this afternoon. And the she arrived again, just an hour ago."

"What?" I asked. I thought I had drunk too much mead. "She arrived again?"

"She went in this afternoon. I wasn't the only one to see her. Then a few others came out. And then nothing happened until she went in again this evening. I promise you by all the flames she had not come out from the front or the back of that building at any time in between."

"That is strange," Otsoa agreed. "And we're sure they only have the two entrances?"

"As far as I know. I mean, it was formerly just the weaver's guild, so there shouldn't be anything else in there." Anurin took a large bite of pie and washed it down with his colorful drink. I looked at Otsoa, but he shrugged.

"She could have made herself invisible," I suggested. Anurin shook his head.

"We were watching for that." He grinned. "We had a bit of an accident with a certain shipment of ale. Spilled it all along the walk for half of the street. One even leaked all along the back alley. If she left that building, she wasn't walking. We'd have seen the footprints."

"I think we need to get in there and take a look around ourselves," I said.

Thromm slapped his hands on the table. "I agree. I think we should plan to confront this problem head on. What do I need to prepare?"

"Hold on, let's not get too excited." I looked around the busy dining room. There was a lot of noise, but this wasn't the Wyvern's Den, and we couldn't sit around planning to break into a private building, even if it was to rescue someone. Thromm sighed, but relaxed and lowered his voice.

"You took a look at the place. Did you see a weak spot to enter?"

"There is a storm cellar, with a large door. But I think it is protected by magic. Something very disorienting." I tried to explain the split vision I experienced over the door. Again, Otsoa looked puzzled.

"Sounds like a clever spell," he said. "Keep the intruder too disoriented to try to get in. But it's sure to be better than whatever they have guarding the front."

"What about the hounds?" I asked. "They're a surer alarm than any spell would be." The only way I could keep them quiet would make more noise.

"I think I know a few tricks. I'll make sure I have a few things prepared." Otsoa pulled a small book from his belt, opened to a blank page, and started making notes.

Anurin finished his pie and drink, then hopped down from the stool. "I'm going to head out now. I didn't hear any of this. I'd like to get back before our neighbor's lights go out. Should be in another hour or so." He nodded to us, looked around for Josie, but she was nowhere in sight, and left.

We headed out early in the morning, several hours before sunrise. Josie waited up with us until we left, telling us all to be careful. Before going out the door I made the three of us stand in the doorway to the inn, and I sang a quick vanishing song.

Invisibility is so easy at night, it felt like cheating. We had to stick close to the walls of buildings, and rush across any streets to avoid the moonlight. But the only people out this time of night were the Watch, and we managed to avoid them easily enough.

Otsoa pressed through the narrow alleyway first, his hands filled with a powder he had prepared for the animals. I heard the hounds stir in their pens, a few growls and scratching, but then everything fell silent. Thromm would not fit through the alley, so I took the long way around with him. We met Otsoa at the cellar doors.

"Will they still be like that in the morning?" I asked. I peeked through the slats to see the hounds all snoring in a pile in the middle of the pen.

"It only lasts an hour," Otsoa answered. His invisibility had already gone, the spell he had cast cancelling out mine.. He was leaning over the cellar doors, peering through the lens on his wand.

I tried to keep away from it, wondering if it triggered the way the mansion had triggered, around Wild creatures. Otsoa didn't seem disoriented by the doors at all.

He opened a pouch at his belt, took out a few things to look at them in the moonlight, and selected a reddish-brown powder, sprinkling it over the doors. Rather than settling on the doors it landed on something unseen, just above the doors, in the shape of a giant X. The powder glowed red where it landed. Otsoa whispered something over the shape, and the light began to fade. Then he took a long iron key from a different pouch, inserted it into the air over the doors and turned it. There was no click, but the spectral shape dissolved in a flash of red light.

Otsoa held up a hand to keep us from approaching just yet. He tried the handle of the doors, and they gave easily, opening to a dark space below. We let him head in first, the better to check for any further magical alarms. Thromm kept a wary eye out, and I listened hard, but so far no one else was anywhere near the alley or stirring in the guild halls.

We waited an uncomfortably long time. Thromm grew impatient and whispered to me that he would go down next, in case something had happened to Otsoa. I told him I would give them another few minutes before I followed them down myself. I heard the stairs creak as Thromm went into the basement. After another few minutes of rubbing my arms to keep warm, I crept to the edge and peered down. I couldn't see anything. Then the strange double vision of multiple doors with paths stretching away in many directions pulled at me. I shook my head focusing on the one door, the one path down, and rushed down the stairs.

After three steps I found that instead of packed dirt or stone I was walking on soft grassy earth. The wet smell of a forest at night filled my nose. I looked up and saw stars through the tops of trees. Otsoa and Thromm were standing a few feet in front of me crouched behind trees and looking further into the forest. Whatever we had just walked through must have canceled the invisibility.

"What was that?" I whispered, coming up beside Otsoa. He shook his head.

"I have no idea. I was seeking for magic as I came down the stairs and I didn't feel anything."

I frowned. I had felt it, the many doorways, and now that we were in a forest on a summer night, I still felt the lingering cold on my arms. It must have been some kind of Wild magic that had created these things, and Winter Wild at that, something that was rare this close to Midsummer which would account for the cold feeling lingering around me. It was the only reason I could think of why Otsoa wouldn't have known it was there.

I set my hand on the tree, and warmth flooded into me. We were in Rhiandon, the oldest and largest forest of the Wild. I couldn't imagine they would take lightly to any magic creating pathways into their home. Otsoa and Thromm didn't seem curious about our strange form of transportation. Instead both were focused on something in the clearing beyond the trees.

There was a tall fence of wood pikes, similar to the pens we had just left behind. I couldn't see it very clearly from this distance, but I could feel that it was bound by iron bands. There was a campfire glowing inside the fenced space, and there were low voices murmuring. The Hunters were camped in the middle of Rhiandon, and not just a camp to go hunting from, but a permanent structure to spend days and nights in.

"Can you tell where we are?" Otsoa asked me.

"Can't you?" My whisper was harsh. I had to swallow back some of my fear and anger. "We should go back. Now."

"Can we?" He looked behind us. "Just step back through it? Is it even still there?"

I looked as well. The same double vision floated before me. I could feel the path back to Casavera, but there were others that felt longer, leaning more northwards.

"You can't see it?" I asked, careful to word it so it didn't sound like I could. He shook his head. I looked at Thromm, and he shook his head as well, though he barely glanced back. He was completely focused on the camp in front of us. "I have to imagine they have a simple way back. They aren't hiking through the whole wood everyday to get back to the guild."

Otsoa nodded at that. "What is it Thromm?"

"There is something very evil in there," he said. He tightened his hand around his sword. "They have captured something evil, and it is angry."

I'm sure it was, whatever it was. This far into Rhiandon they could have caught all kinds of terrible things. I wasn't sensing anything like that, but then, I might not through the iron banded wall.

"All right, time to do your job and get in there," Otsoa said. He turned away from the camp and leaned back against the tree.

"What? Why me?"

"You're the best at staying hidden and silent. There's no way one of us will be able to sneak in there as well as you. Just see if Meia is in there. We can make a plan to get her out once we're sure."

Sure, because of course it was that easy. The invisible bard would sneak in through the massive iron-bound fence, through what was sure to be a field of iron traps, and spot the missing girl with no problem at all. At least, I hadn't seen anyone patrolling outside the fence. Maybe they were relying on the same sort of thing they had at the ruins, and rather than guards they had set traps everywhere. I shivered.

"Fine, sure, I'll go."

"I would rather go in with you," Thromm said. I couldn't help smiling at him. He would, too, charge in there with me intent on destroying whatever wicked thing they had locked up in there and slice through anyone who dared get in our way. And probably get Meia killed.

"It's all right. Thank you. Just watch for a signal in case I need help." I took a deep breath, made myself nothing more than a shadow, and headed toward the camp.

There is nothing worse for one of the Wild than to be near forged metal. It burns our skin, sickens us after long exposure, and any wounds created by it, especially iron, would not heal without using Wild magic on it. As I crept towards the fence I had to take slow calming breaths to keep from gagging. I got as close as I dared, trying to get a glimpse inside, but the staves here were built snugly together. Any crack and the people inside would have been devoured by Wild things the moment night fell. But there would have to be a gate somewhere.

I found it on the far side. Rather than forming a complete circle, part of the fence had been built to overlap the other side for several feet. A guard was posted in the space between. There was no way to slip past him, there wasn't enough space. I stood just around the edge of the fence, running through my options.

I felt the Wild magic around me, tasted its sweetness cloying at my tongue with each breath. If I stopped to gather enough of it together, I could charm the guard to sleep, or into a daze, or into my arms. There was something else there too, a deep muskiness that made me feel energized, as though I could run through the forest forever or jump the fence in one bound. Gathering that magic

I could rip the guard's throat out before he even saw me coming. I shook the feelings away, and instead thought through one of the harder songs I knew on guitar, picturing each fingering position, until the pull faded. Using Wild magic now would attract the attention of anything lurking around the woods, and as much as I didn't want the Hunters to guess I was there, I wanted attention from the Wild even less.

So, I settled for an old bardic trick, and cast a clanging sound out in the woods nearby using only my voice. At first the guard just peeked around the outer lip of the fence, peering into the dark woods for the source of the sound. I cast the sound again. The guard took a few steps beyond the edge of the gate, and I slipped past him and around the inside edge. I waited there, holding my breath, until I heard the guard huff and resettle back into their position in the gap. I let my breath out slowly and took a look at what I had stepped into.

The area was bare dirt, about twenty yards across, and five people were sitting near the fire at the center, chatting and passing a bottle. Spread around them, reaching towards the wall like the spokes of a wheel, were lines of cages. Most of the cages had something in them, Wild animals huddled in the center of the cage, or smaller Wild folk listlessly staring up at the sky. Most of them were harmless.

The one they should not have caught, the one that had Thromm uneasy, was across the fire from me. It was not cowering at the center of its cell like the others. In fact, it would stop now and then and press against the bars to stare at its captors, puffs of steam exploding from its beak as the iron bit into it. The people around the fire would jump when it snorted, but would not look in its direction. The basilisk would slink its long tongue out between the bars, and then turn back to pacing, bobbing on its two clawed feet.

126

It was not large for a basilisk, probably only a young one. It was only the size of a pony, and its wings hadn't grown in yet.

The other cage that caught my attention contained a young woman. She was standing completely still in the middle of the cage, staring up at the sky with wide green eyes. She too was in a cage closer to the fire, dressed only in a nightgown. Her cage was three spokes from where I was. Even if I managed to sneak over and get her out of the cage without burning my hands, I had no idea how I'd get her over the wall.

I didn't know how I was getting back over the wall.

I watched the figures around the fire. The white-haired Navala was there, but not Tara. I didn't recognize the others, though a tall figure in long robes caught my eye. The others were all slumped around the fire, but the robed one was seated tall and alert, and seemed to be working on something by the firelight.

I took stock of the cages near me: Alettas, Mazzi, a few Wild pigs and a badger. To my left I saw an Erl Hound. It was staring at me, its eyes glowing in the light from the fire. I nearly bolted then, but something glinted on its muzzle. They had bound its mouth shut with metal, and it was too weak to even growl at me.

But that basilisk, that had promise. If I could avoid having to sneak out again, plot some crazy plan with the men, and then probably have to sneak back in, I would. I followed the wall around towards the creature's cage, trying to get a glimpse of whatever locks they were using as I passed. They looked like simple padlocks, nothing fancy. I counted the steps between spokes as I moved, trying to guess how long it would take to get from the basilisk's cage to Meia's. Two spokes over, fifteen steps, and then forty back to the gap in the fence.

Creeping down the line of cages that ended with the basilisk, the other creatures peered out at me with large, sunken eyes. Invisible or not, they could tell I was there, and those eyes pleaded with me as I passed. I ignored them. I couldn't get them all out. Once I sprung one there would be mayhem, and I only had one chance to grab Meia and run.

Finally, I was there. A step away from the lock on the basilisk's cage, keeping an eye on the group around the fire. One bonus was that they knew better than to risk looking a basilisk in the eye, so they rarely looked this direction. The basilisk's scales glimmered in the firelight. It smelled like sulfur and sour bile. It snorted at me as I drew near, but kept pacing, unimpressed.

While I looked at the lock, the robed figure stood up from the fire and headed for Meia's cage. A hood obscured their face in the dim lighting, but I could see they were tall, and moved with grace. They unlocked her cage and reached inside for her. Meia shrank back, but stopped short of touching the cage itself. They grabbed her by the arm and dragged her out to meet Navala by the fire. The others around the fire fell silent and shifted in their seats.

Navala wrapped her arms around Meia from behind so the girl couldn't move her arms. She whispered something in the girl's ear, and Meia became completely still, her only motion her quick breaths. The robed figure stood in front of her, brandishing a long thin wand that glinted in the firelight.

"Rahkel!" he cried out. His voice rang through the air with practiced ease. I knew that voice and the casual command it carried. It was Rayul. "Rahkel, please! I beg you again to come and witness my triumph! I can bring you back, Rahkel, and I will prove it to you! For years you have been lost to me in this savage forest, bent to the whim of these deviant creatures, but no more. Look, I am about to free your daughter."

The creatures in the cages went still, even the basilisk. I was frozen as well. A Wild one, a powerful old Wild one was near, and it was not happy. I might have been able to fight it off, to try and reach Meia and get her away from whatever Rayul was about to do.

But it was able to control all of us through a wall of iron, and fighting back would only anger it further. So, I submitted.

"Watch what I have learned to do, to save you!" Rayul put one hand on Meia's cheek, positioned the wand at the corner of one of her bright green eyes, and pushed it upward in a swift jab. The girl jumped and let out a weak cry. He slid the wand from the socket and repeated the motion on the other eye. When he was done Navala sat the girl down and gave her a towel to hold against her eyes.

I had expected a gush of blood and screaming, but there was nothing like that. When Meia pulled the towel away from her face, she still had both of her eyes. He must have slid the wand between her eye and the bone — and then what? Shot a spell into her brain?

"Look, I have freed your daughter. I can free you too!" Rayul shouted. I realized he was calling out to the Wild one. I doubted it was Rahkel. Meia's mother, whatever she was, would not have been this strong. I did notice, however, that Meia could move now.

A roar erupted from the basilisk, from all the creatures around me, from the thing outside the fence, all at once. I nearly lost my balance as the force that had been holding me released. I caught the cage, my hand burning, but I ignored it, pointed to the lock on the basilisk cage and ordered it open, my voice drowned out by the roaring.

I was visible now, but no one noticed me. The basilisk shoved the door of its cage open, raised its feathered head and shrieked into the night.

The Hunters scattered, not in a panic, but in a clearly pre-planned way, rushing to weapons and cover and defensive positions. I took my chance during the commotion to run to Meia, keeping a line of cages between me and Rayul who was already rushing the basilisk.

Meia stood completely still, staring at the fire, unaffected by the shouting and screaming around us. I tried to pull her towards the gate, but she didn't move. It was like trying to drag a corpse.

"Come on, we don't have a lot of time," I said, tugging her again. She moved her feet, but she didn't turn her head to look at me, or where we were going. The creatures in the cages we passed braved the iron to stretch their arms or noses out towards us. "I'm sorry," I whispered to them. "Not today." One of the smaller people spat at me as I passed, and it sizzled on the ground.

When we reached the gate, Thromm was fighting his way in, making quick work of the guard with his sword. He smiled to see I was running towards him with Meia, and then he looked past me at the chaos of the camp. I could hear the basilisk still calling into the night with shrieking howls' snapping its beak as the Hunters tried to corner it.

"We have to go, now," I said, grabbing his arm to try and turn him around and push him back out of the gate. "That thing is calling his momma."

Thromm stumbled out of the gate and I rushed past him and a surprised Otsoa towards the thing we had stepped through to get here. The way was still there, still open. I tripped up the steps as we stepped through, but soon we were all rushing out into the alley and into the night.

CHAPTER ELEVEN

We were back in our rooms at the Fonte before the sun rose. Josie threw a blanket over the thin form of Meia, and tried to get her to drink some broth. The girl's hands were like ice and her feet were blue. She didn't react to anything Josie did. She would only do something if you told her to: Tell her to drink and she took a sip, or tell her to wrap herself up and she pulled the blanket around her. But soon she would forget what she was doing and resume staring off into nothing.

"What's wrong with her?" Josie asked, looking at me.

I was staring at Meia, feeling numb and cold myself. "I don't know," I muttered. Josie narrowed her eyes at me, but threw a blanket over my shoulders as well, and sat down beside me on the couch. She wrapped her arm around mine and squeezed my hand.

"Was she already like this when you found her?" Otsoa asked.

I couldn't answer. The image of Rayul shoving a wand into her eyes kept replaying in my mind. I didn't want to talk about it. They tried asking Meia what had happened and if she was all right, but she didn't answer. Otsoa tilted her head up and took a closer look at her eyes. They were still bruised and red, and a few bloody tears had crusted on her lids. He pointed it out to Thromm and turned on me with a ferocious look.

"What did this? It's the same as on the bodies we found." He didn't even care that Josie was still in the room. She gasped and looked at me as well. I didn't care if she heard it all at this point, so I just squeezed her arm tighter.

"Not the same," I said. My voice was low and dry, as if I had a bad cold. I was speaking around an enormous lump in my throat, but I couldn't cry. I just kept staring at Meia, her head still tilted up though Otsoa was no longer holding her chin. "It didn't kill her." He hadn't been trying to kill her. Perhaps he hadn't been trying to kill any of them. He claimed he was setting her free.

I jumped up from the couch and stood over Meia. For a moment I felt the sun warmth burn through me, and I might have let my illusion slip, just enough to let my eyes flare green. Whatever happened to my appearance, everyone flinched away from me.

"What?" Otsoa asked at the same time Josie asked, "Are you all right?"

"I'm fine. I need my guitar, and I need to be alone with her." There was only one thought shouting through my brain, an impossible thought, but one so terrifying and thrilling that I had to test it out. Rayul had fired a spell into Meia's mind designed to destroy something Wild. Rayul had claimed he was setting her free.

"Sit back down, Glade, it's all right," Josie said, trying to pull me back onto the couch.

"Do you know something you think will heal her?" Thromm asked. He was standing in a corner of the room, trying to keep his bulky frame out of the way as we were ministering to Meia.

"We don't even know what's wrong with her, yet," Otsoa said. "What are you doing?" He glared at me over Meia's head.

"I just need you all to get out of the room. I need a few minutes alone with her. I need to see something." I was trying not to scream at them, but my voice was growing frantic. I gulped down air and looked around the room at them. "I don't know if it will heal her. I just need to test an idea. And I can't do it with you in the room."

"All right, we'll give you a few minutes," Josie said. She looked at Otsoa and motioned with her hand for him to get moving. He kept his eyes focused on me, and I could see him trying to work out what I was going to test. Thromm tugged at his arm.

"Come along. I believe she will tell us more once she has tested her idea." Thromm turned and walked out. Otsoa followed, keeping his gaze on me the whole way. Josie hurried out after them, and I ducked into my bedroom to grab my guitar.

I dragged a chair over so I could sit face to face with Meia. I tilted her head down, so she could look at me. I didn't even bother tuning, I just started strumming the first tune that came to mind, the song I had played on Meia's own flute in the clearing by the ruins.

Wild magic doesn't fare well in cities, mostly because there is little Wild around to draw it from. No untouched trees or untamed beasts that are still connected to the web of life that can give power to someone who knows how to wield it. So, when smaller Wild folk are caught in a city, they have little to no defenses against the studied magic of a spellcaster or the forged weapon of a fighter.

But a strong Wild one, the Queen of Summer herself, for example, or a dryad from one of the Great Trees, has enough Wild magic within themselves that they can call at will. One of them could, if they chose, level a city in minutes. They had, during the Wars, taken many cities down by calling the roots of trees or flooding nearby streams, all using their own Wild power.

I had never met my mother, the Golden One. She had never spoken to me, or bothered with me since the day I was born. But I was still her daughter, and I still possessed a golden light that threatened to burn through me every day. It was not a lot, not so much as a Queen or my mother could call on, but it was enough to call on Wild magic even in the middle of a city. I had done it before.

On top of that, I had practiced long and hard how to project feelings and strength into others. An artificer's magic could reach into even the coldest of hearts and make them feel, just by letting them experience a work of art. Thanks to my father, I had inherited a great musical talent, and I had honed it through years of training.

I poured all of that into Meia then using her own Wild song, backed by the strength of my golden light and the skill of my guitar and the emotion in my voice. I pictured myself dancing wildly in that clearing, imagined Meia dancing there with me, crowning ourselves with flowers and laughing in delight as we were surrounded by butterflies. It was all I could do to keep from dancing around her in the room, but I wanted to stay in her sight.

Nothing. Meia didn't even blink. I played for a few minutes, changing the feelings from happy to sad or angry, changing the pace of the song, but her face never reacted. I finally simply stopped, my guitar slipping off my lap and thudding against the floor.

"That was very nice," Meia said, her voice flat. I blinked and the tears in my eyes welled over and fell down my cheeks. I didn't have the energy to sob. I dragged myself to the door, opened it, and then collapsed onto the couch, burying my face in my arms.

Josie was by my side in an instant, hugging me. I heard someone pick up my guitar and set it aside, and someone else closed the door. Otsoa started to ask something, but he stopped suddenly as though someone had hushed him. Josie pulled me up so I was crying against her shoulder. She patted my hair and whispered to me.

"What happened, darling?" she asked. I gasped and tried to answer.

"I couldn't stop him. I wanted to so badly and I couldn't stop him." I don't think anyone other than Josie understood my answer.

"You did what you could, Glade. You brought her home. This is not your fault."

"But I didn't stop him." I pushed away from her and pointed to Meia. "And look what he's done. I just played her own song, a song so strong it embedded itself in her flute, with every bit of magic I could muster, and she felt nothing. Nothing." I was shouting, but Josie looked calmly up into my face, her eyes wide and sad. "I should have stopped him. I should have come back out and signaled for help. I should-"

"There is no sense talking about shoulds," Thromm said. He set his large hand on my shoulder. "You did your best. If we had tried to take her by force, he may simply have killed her. All that matters now is what did happen."

"Yes, tell us what happened," Otsoa said. "We may be able to find a way to reverse it."

It took a few moments to collect myself, and steady my breath, and then explained the procedure as simply as I could. Josie groaned, and Otsoa's mouth fell open as I described it. I left out the part about Rahkel and the Wild one arriving.

"Flames, Glade," Josie said when I finished, and held my arm again.

"We should take her home," Otsoa said. "If we can get her parents to help us, we can expose what's going on, and get aid in trying to repair what they've done."

135

"Could it be possible," Thromm asked, "that this is why the Wild has been attacking the town? To try to claim back their children?" His hand was still on my shoulder.

"No," I said. "They have never felt a need to come after them before, and they can call them out when they wish. There's no need to attack the town to get them."

"Could they call her now?" Thromm's hand grew heavier.

"No." I lowered my head. "No, she will never hear them call again." Thromm released my shoulder and I felt like something released from around my throat. "But I'm telling you, that wouldn't bother them. They're probably more upset that there's a camp full of Hunters in their woods. They've captured all kinds of creatures in there. And I think they're breeding them." I thought of the hound they had muzzled in the camp, and the half-breed animals in the pens behind the guild.

"Whatever is doing it, they've stirred up the Wild, and it needs to stop." Otsoa took Meia's hand and got her to stand up. "Let's get you home."

We had Josie order us a coach to take us back to the Carvallo villa. Though the Hunters had probably spent the rest of the morning getting away from, or recapturing, the basilisk, by now they would be looking for Meia. I hoped they believed it had been the Wild one that had caused the commotion and that they hadn't seen me, but there was no way to be sure.

We sent word ahead and tried to explain the state Meia was in, but I didn't have the words. I simply stated that she had been through a traumatic ordeal, and that she would be greatly changed. Josie helped me get Meia dressed and arrange a veil over her head and around her face. It was like dressing a doll. I guided her out of the inn and into the coach, arranging her in the seat beside me. Otsoa and Thromm climbed in and we headed out of town.

Even in a coach we were waved around to the back side of the house. The coach stopped at the gate to the kitchen garden, neat rows of herbs and vegetables around the outbuilding that housed the kitchen. I could see Meia's windows beyond, white curtains waving in the wind.

Matra came to the gate first. Her face was pale and tight. She stopped at the gate and stared at the coach. I glanced at Meia to see if she reacted to seeing her mother. She was staring at a spot on the side of the coach, just over my head. She had barely moved the whole trip. Thromm shoved the door open and stepped out first, so he could help Meia down.

Carvallo strode out of the house and down the dirt, pushed past Matra and hurried to the coach. His face was dark red, and his voice came out in a raw rasp.

"Where is she? Let me see her." He shoved past Thromm, not an easy feat, and started climbing into the coach. Thromm stopped him and pulled him back out.

"Give her some room," Thromm said. He reached in and helped Meia down from the couch, and as soon as she was free of the coach Carvallo took her into his arms and hugged her tight. She didn't react, just stood still and let him hold her.

"Meia, darling, I'm so glad you're home. Are you all right?" He turned to us when she didn't answer. "What happened? What's wrong with her?"

"We are not certain," Thromm said. His voice was soft, and humble. I stayed in the coach, hoping he wouldn't demand more explanation. "We found her in the Hunter's camp. She has been affected by a strange magic that they have used before." While Thromm talked, Carvallo tried all manner of things to get Meia to react, including pinching her arm. That made her jump, but that was all.

Matra sighed. "Just bring her inside. She probably needs to rest. She's been through such an ordeal. You'll see, she'll be much better in the morning."

"Don't," Carvallo snapped. "I'm done with your excuses. You did this. You should at least own up to the consequences."

"They are not excuses." Matra's voice was bored. "You can see how much calmer she is."

"Stop it," Carvallo commanded. Matra turned her head away quickly, suddenly more interested in the vegetables at her feet than us. Carvallo turned back to his daughter and brushed his hand over her hair and down the side of her face. He closed his eyes and whispered, "Is there any way to heal her?"

"We are not certain," Thromm answered. "Perhaps if we could investigate further. With your connections and the help of the Watch—"

"No," Matra interrupted. Her glare was on us again in an instant. "You are not parading this around town."

"It might be the only chance she has," Otsoa said, peeking out from the coach. "Even if we could take her to a cleric. We need to make it known that this is going on."

Matra laughed a short slap of a laugh. "And what cleric would want to heal that? You can't tell me you didn't want her to be free." Matra stepped through the gate and started stalking towards her husband. "This way she won't raise such a ruckus with her music, or draw so many looks in town. This way she won't disappear every summer for what might be the last time. She will stay home, and do as we ask. It's better this way."

"Better?" Carvallo turned to look at Meia again. "You call this better?" He sounded deflated; his voice lifeless. He looked up at Thromm with blank eyes. "Thank you for bringing her home. I will send a message to Roya that you have completed your contract. Let me know if you need me to cover any of your costs here in town. It may be a day before he can get back to you." Carvallo took Meia's hand.

"Sir, you do not mean to make a complaint against the Hunters?" Thromm asked.

"We made it quite clear we didn't want any outside interference. And as you hear," Carvallo glared up at Matra, who leaned away from him. "This was pre-arranged. I expect you to keep that promise, even after the contract has ended. Or I will lodge a complaint with Roya."

I stared across the coach at Otsoa, who had to travel hundreds of miles west to get licensed for this job. And I thought of how much Roya knew about me and how many hundreds of miles I would have to move if he revealed it. I didn't know if Thromm was hiding anything, but I doubted he wanted any trouble either.

"Understood, sir," Thromm said. Carvallo nodded curtly, turned back to his home, dragging Meia behind him. She stumbled a few times, but he didn't slow or stop. He also never looked back at Matra. Matra gave us a triumphant glance, and then swept back up the path as well.

I fumed the entire way back to the Fonte. No one spoke. I didn't know what either of them intended to do, but I meant to head back to Cyfar and let Roya know what was going on. He might not care either, but at least I could talk to him about it without breaking the agreement. I hoped I would feel a little less in a rage by the time we got back and had to face people again, but I couldn't let it go. It was obvious Carvallo was furious at how his daughter was treated, but not enough to do anything about it. Not enough to face the shame of having a daughter with a Wild one.

As we pulled up to the inn, things looked busy. Josie hurried us inside and insisted we eat something, but once she saw the look on my face, she brought us bread and meat and light summer ale, and left us alone. I went straight to bed without a bite and collapsed into a dead sleep.

There were Wild animals in my dreams this time. Instead of the bedroom at the Fonte, I was lying in bed beneath the Summer Tree of Rhiandon. Its trunk was twice as wide as my bed, and the branches spread out in all directions for yards, so it felt like the roof of a house. Every Midsummer all the Wild creatures, those of us born to Summer, are called to this tree. None of us can resist that call, not even those with only slight amounts of Wild blood. Matra had been right, most chose to remain in the Wild eventually.

For those few of the longest days, we lose ourselves. I never remember what goes on there. I just know that afterward, I wake up on the edge of the forest tired, starving, and filthy. I don't stop to figure out what I'm filthy with either. I simply wash it all away, sleep for two days straight, and then eat like a bear coming out of hibernation.

Having animals dance around and call to me was unusual. Most Wild animals were the lowest of us, not able to command another of the Wild folk. There were exceptions of course, like basilisks, or unicorns or gryphons. The tales say dragons were the greatest of the Wild creatures, but they had died long before the Wars. Frozen to my bed, I had to lay still and watch as the creatures beckoned for me to join them, wolves and bear cubs and badgers, some on their hind legs and waving to me with their paws.

"I can't go just yet," I told them, my voice weak and strange like my tongue was asleep. "I have to make this right first. I have to make them pay for what they are doing to you. To us."

I heard a deep hiss, and a dark shape moved just outside of my vision, emerging from under my bed. My muscles strained against the paralysis of the dream, but it did no good. The dark shape bobbed just out sight, until it rushed out into the circle, scattering the others. It was a basilisk, a small one. It joined the circle, and the others continued on, keeping a safe distance from the creature's beak.

"You know what they're doing, don't you? That's why you're fighting back. But don't worry. I will get them to stop. You don't need to attack them." The basilisk hissed again and turned toward my bed. It bobbed forward, its two scaly legs clawing at the floor, its stubby wings spreading outward. Its beak snapped at me, tearing up the quilt at the foot of my bed. I wanted to pull my legs up and away from it, but they wouldn't move.

"I promise," I said, my voice rising as it chomped away. "I will stop them. I just need a little more time." The basilisk took one more hard bite, feathers from my blanket flying everywhere, and then in one heavy leap it was standing on the foot of my bed, screaming upward at the ceiling. I tried to scream too, but no noise came from my throat.

I awoke to the sound of banging on my door, my throat raw. I stopped screaming and pulled the covers over my head to take stock of myself. There were times after a dream like that when I would lose my illusion. I looked over my skin and pulled some of my hair around to inspect it. Everything seemed all right.

"I'm coming in, Glade," Josie said. I heard the key in the door, then it opened and shut. I felt her sit down on the bed, and she set her hand on my stomach. "Glade, are you all right?"

"Yes," I said through the blanket. I closed my eyes and concentrated on everything I was feeling. I tried to push away every warm, burning feeling, pictured my illusion covering me perfectly. Then I slowly slid the blankets away from my face. Josie was looking down at me with a concerned smile.

"Yes, Josie, I'm sorry. Just a bad dream."

"It's been a rough job. You're all really shaken up," she said. I nodded, and tried to sit up, and got dizzy, so I laid down again. "But it's over now, isn't it?"

"We did what we were hired to do." I tucked the blankets under my chin and squinted up at her.

"Not a great ending?" she asked, patting me lightly.

"No. Not a great ending. Not an ending at all."

"You always did prefer to write your own endings."

I smiled finally and took a deep, shaky breath. "Yes, yes I do."

"Come on, I'll get you some dinner before you head home."

"Dinner? Did I sleep that long?"

"Just about. I think you needed it. Do you want some coffee too?"

"I love you, Josie."

"I know. Aren't I the best?" She hopped off the bed.

Chapter Twelve

Otsoa had run out on some errand or other by the time I made my way downstairs, but Thromm was at a table in the corner downing a pint. Josie sent me a glass of mead before disappearing into the kitchen.

"Has it been quiet?" I asked him.

"So far. It does not seem like anyone is looking for you."

"Small blessings," I said. "It was dark, and there was a lot of commotion, so I'm hoping they didn't even know I was there."

"I think that is a safe assumption." Thromm had changed clothes and was in one of the few relaxed outfits I'd ever seen him in, just a shirt and trousers. He'd also let his hair down. I was always jealous of how sleek a man's hair could be. His lay in soft golden waves to his shoulders.

"I know you aren't happy about this..." I waved my hand to imply the whole situation we found ourselves in.

"No, I am not." His hand went to where his sword would be, if he were wearing it, instead hooking around his belt.

"What about Otsoa?"

"I believe he is out seeking evidence from another angle." He frowned and took another long gulp.

"You don't seem too happy about that."

"It is not always best when he goes out alone. He is not always in control of himself."

"Hmf. Who is?" I said. "I'm sure he'll be fine."

"You have not seen him in a fight," Thromm said, shaking his head in a slightly exaggerated way.

"How long have you been sitting here drinking?" I asked him.

"A little too long, I think," he admitted. "They serve very good ale here."

"They do indeed." I chuckled at him, and he smiled back with a lazy grin. Josie appeared at the bar and waved the mead bottle at me. I shook my head. If Thromm was going to be tipsy tonight I should remain sober. Then she waved to the cask of ale at the end of the bar and pointed to Thromm. I shook my head again. He'd had enough for tonight.

It was busy in the Fonte, but not overcrowded, a peaceful dinner crowd. I started to get the urge to be picking at my guitar and rose to go get it. The door of the Fonte opened, and I caught a few strains of a song out in the courtyard, a street performer I thought from the quality of the voice. It made me smile, and I started humming along.

Then I stopped still. I knew that song very well. It was a song I thought only I had ever sung at least in recent times. It was the song of the Lost Prince. The door shut and the song cut off abruptly. I headed for the door so fast I knocked my chair over. Thromm was close behind me.

"Where are you going?" he asked, grabbing the door handle before I could open it.

"That song, I've never known anyone else who knows that song. I wanted to meet the singer." I looked up at him. "Does that meet with your approval?"

"I am coming with you."

"That's not necessary. I'm just going out into the courtyard to meet a singer."

"Well look what just happened in the courtyard." His hand remained firm on the handle. "Either I come with you or you do not go."

I threw my hands up. "Fine, but if you pass out, I'm not dragging you back inside." He let go of the handle and I flew out of the inn. The singer had already moved on. I turned slowly and managed to catch a few stray notes coming from between two of the buildings. I hurried along the cobblestones, Thromm trailing behind me, and we came out onto a neighboring street. The singer was down at the far corner, just disappearing around another house.

"Oh sparks," I muttered, and took off after him. It was easy enough for Thromm to keep up, his legs were so much longer than mine. We chased after the singer for a few blocks, until I finally lost him in a narrow street in a section of town I didn't recognize. Several of the houses here were unoccupied. One was barely more than a pile of stone, having collapsed in at some point. Someone had made a lean-to against it, and a nest-like bed of blankets stuck out from under the splintered wood. I was suddenly very grateful that Thromm had come with me.

"What have we here?" A slippery voice asked. There were two men emerging from one of the buildings. Thromm was between them and me in an instant.

"Aw, come now, John, ain't no way to show off your goods," a second man said. His voice was whistle-like and high.

"Come on, Thromm, let's get going." I turned to head back out of the street and walked into the arms of another man. He was not much taller than me, but he was broad and his hands were huge. He put both hands on my shoulders and peered into my face. A strong smell of liquor exuded from him.

"Especially when they're such lovely goods," the broad man said. "I bet you can look like anything we choose, can't you, beautiful?" He grinned and looked me over completely. "She's got true skill, fellas."

I couldn't look at him. I looked at the ground, at the mud-spattered toes of his boots, and stayed completely still. An entirely different sort of burning when through me, one that felt like bile was rushing through my veins.

"Take your hands off of her," Thromm said, turning to the broad man. He released me immediately and backed away a step.

"Sure, John, sure, hands off the goods till we've talked price." He raised his big hands in a gesture of surrender.

"Right, so how much you asking?" The whistling voice demanded. I turned so I could see all three men, or tried to. I could only manage to keep two in sight at a time. Looking up at Thromm I shook my head a tiny fraction and tried to point him up the street with just my eyes.

"I am not asking anything," he said. "I am telling you that we are leaving now." He scooped his arm around behind me and started shepherding me away from the men.

"Here now, I didn't waste a good sighting spell for nothing. You ain't heard our offer yet." The big handed man grabbed Thromm by the arm. So that was what had set them off. He had cast a spell to let him see illusions. I must be lit up like a bonfire in his eyes.

Thromm glared at him, and then looked disdainfully down at his hand which looked normal sized on Thromm's massive arm. The big handed man didn't flinch.

"We've got you outnumbered, if you don't want to make a fair deal," he said. Then he made to swing at Thromm's jaw.

In two swift motions, Thromm caught the man's fist and pulled him forward, using his own momentum to send him crashing into the lean to. He continued into a spin and punched the whistling man so hard he flew into the slippery one, and they both went down in a tangle of arms and legs. While they struggled to get back up, Thromm picked up the big handed man by his collar and held him against the stones of the ruined house.

That was when the Watch found us.

They dragged us to the Hall of Justice, which should have been my first suspicion that this was more than just breaking up a brawl. We were shoved into separate cells, Thromm into one by himself, our opponents into their own, and I was thrown in with the women. I found a corner that was unoccupied and as far away from the other occupants as possible, wrapped my arms around myself and tried to ignore them all. The Watch would be through to question us eventually, but it might take them until morning before they bothered, so I settled in for a long night.

A few of the other women were sporting illusions as well, though mostly only over their faces. One woman who had claimed sole ownership of the one bench in the cell was covered head to toe with one and it held up pretty well through the night. The others all faded after an hour or so, but hers remained as clear as mine. I wouldn't have guessed it was an illusion except that she looked too perfect, her dark skin smooth as ebony, her hair piled around her head in glossy curls, her amber eyes almost glowing in the dingy room. I watched her out of the corner of my eye and how she held herself above the others.

"You're not from around here, are you?" she asked. Her voice was silky as her hair. She didn't turn to look at me, she was examining her nails, and rearranged her skirts to be certain they didn't touch the floor. Her gown was deep red with flowers and pearls embroidered around the edges. She easily outshone me in my traveling clothes.

I shook my head, not eager to start a conversation with her.

"I didn't think you looked familiar. Or your John either." She glanced across the hallway at Thromm who was pacing in his cell like a tiger. "You don't intend to stay much longer, I hope?"

I looked up at her then. Her voice had a strange inflection to it that made it seem more like a strong suggestion rather than just a question. She was boring into me with her bright amber eyes.

"I suppose that depends on the boss," I said. I drew my words out lazily, overdoing my old back east accent.

"Maybe you should convince your boss it would be better for business if you guys headed out of town." I didn't like the way she emphasized 'your boss'.

"I don't know, we've gotten such a warm welcome." Some of the other women were watching us, mostly watching me, and raising their brows like I had just challenged their queen to a fight.

"It'll only get warmer from now on," she said. One of the Watch came down the hall and started to unlock the door, motioning for her to come forward. She stood up, straightened her perfect gown, and headed for the door. "I think you should take off, while you can." I followed her with my eyes as the Watch escorted her out.

Not the most subtle message, or messenger, and I was trying to guess who had sent her. I hadn't though Rayul knew that we were here and investigating him, but I didn't think this was the sort of thing Carvallo would come up with.

Once she was gone, several of the women made a move for the bench. The one with the best glare won out and took their place on the bench. One of the others, her face scarred and gaunt, eased closer to me. She hissed at me to get my attention.

"Hey, got any tips for a simple working girl?" I looked down at her and took a shaky breath. This was not the time to be having flashbacks of home.

"Get a better job." She shot me a sour frown and moved back to the others. She whispered something to them, and they laughed.

"Thromm and Glade." A bored voice called out from the end of the hall. I shuffled forward. Thromm stopped at the front of his cell and grasped the bars. "Who wants to answer a few questions?"

"I have a few questions of my own," Thromm said. "I would like to know what right you have to hold me here with no formal charges. Your officers did not even attempt to question us at the scene, or we would have explained everything."

"All right, looks like it's you then," the guard said, moving to unlock my cell. He motioned me out and led me to a small office far down the hall from the captain's. A woman was waiting there, sitting at a desk with Thromm's and my Warden's licenses and our cards from Roya on her desk. She dismissed the guard and gestured for me to take a seat.

"Are you going to drop the illusion?" She said, tilting her head to look at me. She had her hair pulled back tightly, and she had small dark eyes that reminded me of Otsoa's.

"Are you going to explain to my employer why I had to break the terms of my agreement?" I looked down at Roya's card. I hoped the strength of his name would be enough for her to stop

149

questioning me about the illusion. Though if they took the time to send a messenger to Roya about the whole thing, I doubted he would be thrilled that his team had been arrested.

"Fine. Did your terms include luring those men out to get their faces pounded in?"

"No, ma'am." I shook my head. "We had been walking through town and gotten lost. Those men attacked us, and Thromm defended himself."

She nodded. "I'm sorry to have kept you for so long. We know those guys, but we don't know you. I was going to wait until we could verify things with Roya in the morning, but it seems you've already crossed paths with our captain this morning." She gathered up the papers. "We'd appreciate it too if you gave us a heads up about keeping illusions up if you're on job. Keep us out of your hair."

"Of course, ma'am. I'm sorry for the trouble." I kept my voice quiet and my eyes on hers.

"Do you think you'll be able to calm your companion down? We don't want him causing a ruckus on the way out."

"I'll explain things to him. He'll be fine."

"Good. I'll let you back in with a guard so you can explain things to him. Then you can head home."

"Thanks so much. Again, so sorry for the trouble." She handed me our papers, and I was let back into the cell block as they were releasing Thromm.

"I demand to know—"

"Thromm, please, I'll explain everything, all right? Let's get out of here." I waved for him to follow me. He brushed past the guard who stumbled a bit out of the way and followed me out, stomping loudly. But he kept his mouth shut as we left and waited a whole block before starting the questions.

150

"Can you explain what happened to us? We were thrown into jail for defending ourselves against obvious ruffians? And you are not the only woman in this town to bear an illusion." He waved his hands around as he shouted. I tried to shush him.

"First, could you find a better word than ruffians? And yes, that's exactly what they did. That's their job. If there is a disturbance in the city streets, they take care of it. So please, just calm down. Maybe where you're from you can get away with breaking someone's nose whenever you like, but that's not how it works here." I was walking as fast as I could, trying to get Thromm away from the plaza and crowds of people.

"And why were they saying such things about you? He is fortunate his nose was the only thing I broke." He curled his hands into fists.

"As flattered as I am it's an easy assumption," I muttered.

"An easy assumption to lump you in with those... those..."

"Prostitutes. What, you can't even say it? Yes, they lumped me in with all the other women who go about wearing illusions." I shrugged and brought my voice back under control again. "It happens sometimes."

"But Glade," he stopped and stared down at me, a deep furrow on his brow. "You are not..."

"Not anymore. You think I learned this from a singing master? Most of those women were just using the cheap spells you can get on the street. But you saw the beauty in there. I learned how to disguise myself, and then I left. And I never went back." I couldn't tell if Thromm was turning red from anger or from embarrassment. "Could you always tell I had an illusion on?"

"Yes. But as I said, many do. Many women wear them on their face, at least."

"Right, just cosmetics. A lot of women do that." We were speaking quietly again as we approached the Fonte. "But when it's more than that, most people assume." I stopped before we got to the door and looked up at him sideways. "Can you see through illusions?"

"No." He stopped as well, turning to me and leaning down so he could look me in the face. "No, I cannot. Nor would I dispel one unless it was to protect someone from harm."

I swallowed hard and nodded. "Thank you."

He held the door for me, and I hurried inside.

"Where've you guys been?" Otsoa asked. He was seated at the bar, a plate heaped with bare rib bones in front of him. He was in the middle of a piece of pie. "Josie saved dinner for you. Come on, it's splurge night."

"Splurge night?" Thromm sat down beside him. "That sounds perfect." Josie appeared with another plate of ribs and set them in front of Thromm.

"Splurge night." I frowned.

"Yes. Official letter came from Roya already. Job well done and all that." He gestured to the ribs. "Eat up, tonight's the last one on his tab." Josie winked at me and disappeared back into the kitchen.

"He's sending the coach for us in the morning?" I asked. Otsoa nodded. I would have a chance to tell Roya what was really going on, and much sooner than I thought. I tried to fend off the feeling that he wouldn't want to listen, and instead focused on what Josie was bringing out from the kitchen. She had made several of my favorite dishes, salad with fresh cheese and basil, flatbread covered with mushrooms and herbed oil, and a small loaf of honey cake.

"You are a goddess," I said, catching her hand on the counter. "Thank you."

"My pleasure." She shot a look across the room, and I noticed her Uncle Joff was watching. "Eat up. Though, I know no one would mind if you happened to play a few songs before you left." She headed out into the dining room to check on her guests. The Fonte was full for the dinner rush. If I was going to have to be in public tonight, I may as well be armed with my music. After eating as much as I dared before a performance, I hurried up and retrieved my guitar.

"Are you sure you are up to performing?" Thromm asked as I sat tuning.

"This is what makes me feel better," I said, plucking at the strings. I wouldn't have to play anything flashy, though this was an upper crust crowd. It would just be background music, simple and pleasant. It calmed my nerves as I began to play, and slowly the noise of the Fonte and the terror of the past few days faded into the back of my mind.

A loud bang and loud slurred voices jolted me out of my calm. Several elves had piled onto the stools beside me. They weren't arguing—they all seemed to have the same opinion—but they were stating them over and over as though daring someone to disagree. I tried not to listen and focused on remembering some of my favorite songs. As soon as I began playing, one of the elves turned to me and waved his half full glass.

"Oh, none of that old rot. Play something new." The woman beside him, emerald pins glinting in her hair, nodded in agreement.

Not wanting to offend Josie's customers I obliged and played the newest elven song I had learned. They went back to their emphatic conversation.

"The Wild is so much more out of hand than it has ever been," the emerald studded lady said. "And Hunters are all well and good, but it isn't enough."

"Not nearly enough." A thick, hunched elf agreed. He kept tapping his glass on the counter after each sentence. "We need the cities to stand united against this threat. Pass unified laws, send out unified, uh, units." He paused, worried that he had not sounded as strong as he hoped.

"Unification, yes, that's definitely the key. It's the one thing that has kept us free of the Wild. We banded together and invented new ways to combat them. We need to do that again. We need to invent new and better ways to protect ourselves from Wild incursions, from without and within."

The other two grew quiet, as though he had said something taboo. They looked around to be sure no one was listening, though I'm sure most of the guests just wished they would be quiet.

"I have heard of these problems," the hunched elf said. "It would seem there are towns even readying to give these half-breeds full citizenship."

The woman gasped at the word half-breed, and then gasped again when the man finished. "How could anyone choose such a thing? I mean, don't get me wrong, I feel sorry for those unfortunates, they had no choice in the matter. But they should be kept in their place. It could be dangerous letting them have full run of a town. What if they began to pollute the civilized races? We fought so long to rise above such things."

I hadn't noticed when, but I had switched to a much faster song. My fingers flew over the guitar and I finished with a loud flashy chord that made the strings twinge. A few customers clapped for me, but I barely noticed. I began a new song, quietly and slowly. *Rise above such things*, I repeated in my mind. *Rise above?* When I know there is a full-civilized-blooded elf in this city murdering us, and our parents don't even care? Oh, but no, these were the Free Races, broken out from the control of the Wild Queens, so of course they were better than lowly, pathetic me.

The song I played grew louder. I cleared away all thoughts and focused only on the glowing light rising inside me, channeling all of it through my song. All I could think of was teaching these elves just how successfully they had risen above the Wild. So far as I could tell they were all three pure-blooded elves, supposedly, completely out of the control of the Wild. And true, perhaps they couldn't be commanded, not the way I could. But they could still taste it, still feel it, still be carried away on the torrent of it I was about to unleash.

When my song reached full volume, rising over the sound of the crowd, the three elves paused and looked at me. For a moment they just stared, their eyes wide in surprise, and the whole crowd fell silent. I saw it come over their eyes. It's hard to describe what happens when a person hears the Wild song. It doesn't only happen the first time, but every time. For a Wild person it calls us, commands us to do the callers bidding. For the Free folk, a light comes into their eyes, a look of delight like a child watching fireworks, or a dog spotting his master. Pure, unadulterated delight. Then a grin spreads across their face, as though they have heard this song before and they are beginning to remember how it goes. These three felt it pulse through them, and they hopped out of their seats and began to dance.

Their drunkenness helped. It took longer for others in the Fonte to join them, but soon enough, all of us were whirling around the room, dancing in complex circles and laughing like schoolgirls. Otsoa managed to find Josie in the chaos and pulled her close as they danced. Dishes and glasses clattered and shattered around the room as we stomped and jumped. The heat rose within me until I could feel it pouring out of my eyes, and then I lost hold of memory.

I woke up under a table, cradling my guitar and being cradled by one of the drunken elves. All three of them were under the table with me, asleep. I slipped out of the pile, dug my tunic out of the mess on the floor, and climbed out from under the table. The place was a mess. Glasses were spilled and shattered across the floor, chairs tipped over, food everywhere.

No one else was around that I knew. Not Josie or Thromm or Otsoa. I tiptoed across to the washroom and closed the door behind me and examined myself in the mirror over the basin. My skin looked like it should, for the most part, but my hair was a fuzzy mess, and my eyes were glowing green. I managed to get most of it under control, at least, my eyes stopped glowing. My hair turned dark again, but it was still puffy and difficult. I wove it into a thick braid but wisps of it stuck out around my face.

Once I had myself covered again, I went looking for Josie. The elves in the dining room were still sleeping and would be for a while longer. When they finally woke up, they wouldn't remember what had happened any more than I did. Hopefully they would chalk it up to drinking far too much and would be too embarrassed to mention it to anyone. But Josie, even if she didn't remember what happened, would know it was my fault.

I tapped on Josie's bedroom door, rehearsing through my speech in my head as I waited. I would help clean up, offer to pay for damages, whatever she wanted. Though I knew she wouldn't take any money from me. She would ban me from playing at the Fonte ever again. I didn't hear anyone stirring in her room, so I knocked again, a little louder.

"Just a moment," I heard from within the room. It was Otsoa's voice. I heard him moving around inside the room, quietly rummaging through things. I remembered how they had looked dancing together the night before, holding each other close and ignoring everyone else in the room. At least that was something to smile about, but I would make even more of a mess of things if I walked in on what should have been a pleasant, sleepy morning for them. I hurried towards my room, hoping to hide out there until Josie woke and came looking for me. Any excuse to delay that discussion.

Thromm wasn't in our rooms either, though I wasn't too surprised. I could imagine a number of people from the night before wanting to lure him away to their rooms. Another bit of luck for me, I'd have the rooms to myself until I could get back under control. Back in Cyfar I had an abandoned house I would run to when I did something this stupid to wait for things to blow over. But Cyfar was a bigger city, and a noisy, messy party didn't get too much attention. As I locked the door to my room in the Fonte, I knew it wouldn't be as easy to cover up here, especially not in such a wealthy part of town, but I could spin it right. I just needed to make sure I talked to Josie first and convinced her I was just under too much stress and had done all this using normal, legal, artificer magic.

I was just burying myself under the blankets on my bed when someone started pounding on the front door. My heart dropped into my stomach. There was shouting from the street now too, and though I couldn't make out the words, I understood them well enough. It was the Watch, and they wanted to get in. I dropped any control I had on my illusion and instead concentrated on making myself invisible. Throwing open the window I looked around the alley. They hadn't surrounded the inn, at least not yet. I climbed out and crept down to the end to peer around the corner.

"Open up, this is the Watch." There were two watchers banging on the door. One of their coaches was pulling into the courtyard behind them. "We got a report about last night. Is everyone all right?"

The people that emptied out of the coach were not Watch, but Hunters. One reached back into the coach and pulled a dog out on a leash. As soon as the creature reached the pavement it planted its feet and howled, pulling on its leash in my direction.

My blood caught fire and I took off running down the alley and out behind the houses to the street, heading away from the main plaza. The howls followed me as the Hunters gave chase. Coming out onto the street the morning sunshine hit my face and I stopped, trying to orient myself while it felt like everything was spinning around me. I took off left, trying to keep to the shadows by instinct, even though that hound, an Erl-descended hound, would be able to smell my trail.

How had they known to bring Hunters? If anyone had managed to report last night it should have just sounded like a ruckus party, but someone must have made accusations of Wild involvement. I made another left again, rushing between two houses, and then running up another alley, circling back to head north through the town. I would have given anything for this stupid backwards town to have a canal, I could have thrown them off the scent in the water. But here everything was stone and dirt and neat manicured lawns.

Another howl rang out, at the end of the block I was crossing through. They were trying to get out ahead of me and cut off my path. I stopped, crouching in the shrubs beside a house, and held my breath. If they continued to rush ahead, I could try and make a break behind them and find another route to the one place I thought I might be safe in this town. I heard another howl and then more shouts, moving away from me. Whoever or whatever they had run into was drawing them away.

I tripped coming out of the bushes and bolted up the street trying to reach another bit of shadow under a tree on the corner. I only had one more block to go.

"Back this way!" I heard behind me, and the dog bayed again. I forgot about keeping to the shadows and ran with all I had left, trying to get to the church on the next block before the hound could get to me. It was close enough now that I could smell it, a mixture of wet fur and fallen leaves. I jumped the wooden gate that ran around the small churchyard and ran up the dirt path to a green door and threw myself at it. It was locked. My illusion fell away and the burning feeling in me went out.

"Glenn! Glenn, please it's me! Let me in!" I pounded on the door. The hound reached the gate and yelped, stopping short of hitting the gate. The Hunter holding the leash was Navala. She slowly opened the gate, but the hound still wouldn't cross. There was only so much you could breed out of an Erl Hound, and even they wouldn't approach a house of Ventor. They could feel it too, the aura that dampened any connection to the Wild. It could be painful if you weren't prepared for it, and Wild animals couldn't abide it at all.

Navala handed off the leash to the other Hunter and sauntered up the path toward me, her head tilted to one side.

"How did you get in here, little weed?" she asked, her voice sing-songy. "You should know better than to go traipsing through our town. Or weren't our warnings enough for you?" When she was halfway up the path the door opened, and I nearly tripped inside. Glenn was standing in the doorway looking down at me. He stepped aside to let me in and glared up at Navala.

"What do you want here?" he asked. Glenn had a clear voice, like a trumpet call. It was out of place in his thin, graceful frame. Navala stopped on the path.

"We are pursuing a criminal," she answered, pointing at me. I had sunk to my knees on the step, completely exposed as Wild, my skin amber and glistening, my hair straw colored escaping the

159

hasty braid. There would be no denying I was Wild now, but at least they wouldn't be able to tell I was Glade.

"I know the Hunters respect very little," Glenn said, stepping past me and out onto the path. "But you will respect the sanctuary of this place. Get off my grounds."

Navala scowled. "You would protect one of them? After all they have been doing to our town?" She grimaced down at me like I were no better than a bug she wanted to crush.

"I would protect anyone who asked for sanctuary here. One does not enter the house of Ventor lightly." Glenn raised his hand palm out toward Navala. "Go away, and leave this one to me."

Navala shrugged. "I'll leave. But there will be others looking for this one. I hope it likes stone walls and flames." She bent over so she was eye level with me. "Don't worry, weed, we'll be back soon." Then she turned and hurried back to the hound and pulled them away.

Glenn turned around and helped me up. I leaned on him as we entered the kitchen. He locked the door behind us.

"I'm so sorry. Is there anyone else here?"

"No, it's just me." He set me into a chair. I stayed slumped against him, tears flooding out of me.

"I'm so sorry Glenn. I did it again."

CHAPTER THIRTEEN

I first met Glenn when I was twelve. It was on a trip to Cyfar. The woman who raised me was an herbalist, and a good one. Now and then, she would come west to purchase certain supplies that were hard to find back home in our tiny country town.

She had learned after her first trip that leaving me home was not an option. So, I had to come along, draped in an oversized cloak and glued to her side. I don't remember exactly why we visited the church that day, or why that one in particular. I guess Mom wasn't used to giant church buildings filled with worshippers, so she had opted for a much smaller one away from the main plazas in Cyfar.

She had made me go to every service with her at home, enduring the glares from everyone else. I prepared to be glared at again as we entered. It was different here, though. No one knew who we were. They didn't know that the little cloaked figure was anything other than a cold child hanging on to the skirts of her mother.

When Glenn had come and sat beside me before the service, I tensed up, expecting to be asked to leave. He was just a pupil then, about fifteen. He looked even scrawnier at the time, a tall gangly youth, whose pointed ears were still too large for his head.

He didn't speak. Instead he reached into the collar of his robe and pulled out a small wooden medallion with the image of a lute painted onto it. It was worn, the gold background paint had been rubbed off in spots, and it was glowing.

I almost laughed out loud, but instead I reached into the folds of my cloak and pulled out the identical medallion I wore, which was also glowing. Mom had elbowed me to stay quiet before she noticed what we were looking at. Then she sighed and waved us away. We both hurried out of the sanctuary to a nave off to the side. It was stacked with extra chairs and dusty books.

We asked each other a lot of questions, but not the ones you would expect. We didn't talk about our father. We both knew from the medallions he had left each of his children, that our father was Tor Balladeer, the famous bard of the bower, who could woo anyone anywhere and sing to melt a heart of stone. And woo he had. Glenn was the third of my half-siblings that I'd found. He'd only met one before me.

Instead, he wanted to know about me. Who I was, what I did, and wanted to share his life with me. He was a foundling, an infant left on the church steps. So, the church had raised him. He was an honest, devout kid.

He was so disarming, so friendly that he managed to get me to take my hood down, convinced no one would see us where we were sitting behind a long pew. He was the first boy to tell me I was beautiful. He scolded me for the scars on my ears from when I'd tried to remove the exaggerated points with mom's sewing sheers.

Though he did admit trying to make his pointier to fit in with the elves that ran the church by tying strings around the tips.

He felt bad for me. And when I moved to Cyfar he was the first person I had contacted. There had been incidents before, and I wanted him to know that things might happen if I lost control. And he had offered me sanctuary. So, that's where I often went when I was in trouble.

I didn't remember falling asleep. I awoke in a small stone room on a stiff bed tucked under a gray blanket. I was disoriented, trying to guess where I was and what time it might be, but there were no windows, just a small lamp on the table nearby. The burning inside was gone, and when I tried to call it up nothing answered. I gripped the blanket and stifled a sob when I realized I was back in Glenn's church, and I had ruined things again.

"Are you all right?" A thin airy voice asked. I noticed someone in the room with me. They had been sitting nearby but stood and stepped closer. They had a boyish frame, but their eyes were wide and framed with dark curled lashes.

"Yes," I said, and tried to sit up. The room began to tilt around me, so I laid back down. "Almost."

"Take your time. I brought some bread, and some water, and some nectar... I'm sorry I wasn't sure exactly what would be best. What would you prefer? I can fetch anything you need." As the person came closer the light caught their eyes, glinting blue and brilliant. She didn't walk so much as float over the stones of the floor.

"Sylph?" I asked. It was rare for Changelings to be born of air nymphs. Trying to get a sylph to pay attention to anything for more than a few minutes was a challenge. She nodded as she set a tray of food on the table by the bed, and I caught a scent of salt air.

"My name is Ura," she said.

"Clara," I said, introducing myself by my old name. Even if Glenn had told her who I was, I wanted her to know that name. I knew very few other Changelings, and the few times I had met one I was acting as 'Glade the Warden', so they hadn't been warm friendly meetings. "What kind of nectar?" I generally preferred honey, but nectar was nearly as good if it was fresh.

"Hyacinth, and some lily. It was all I could get on short notice." She pointed to one of the cups on the tray. "You're sure that's all right? I can find something else if you want."

"This is wonderful, thank you." The cup smelled overly sweet, but the bread smelled sharp and warm. I sat up, trying to get a closer look at Ura as I tore off a chunk of bread and shoved it into my mouth. The voice sounded young, but again that was common among even aged sylphs. But it also sounded motherly and warm. I took a long drink from the cup and sighed as the dizziness began to ebb away.

"Are you dryad?"

"Napaea," I said. "From a glade in Fogwood."

"Ah. I'm from Finger Cove," she said, naming a small bay north of Cyfar.

"How did you get here?" I spoke around bits of bread. It was full of herbs and clashed with the watered-down nectar she had served me. "It doesn't bother you being so far from home?"

"Not really. I went to Cyfar looking for work, but it was too crowded. They mostly only hire naiads anyway, you know, to work in the canals. You're even farther from home. What brought you here?"

"Same thing, looking for work." I set the cup back down. "I help tend gardens." Ura's face fell a bit as I lied.

"Glenn said, I mean, well, Glenn told me what you are to him. I haven't told anyone else, of course." I looked up sharply and she flitted away from me a few steps. My eyes flared and she looked away, whispering something in sylph that sounded like an apology and a supplication.

"Of course not," I said. I swung my legs off the bed, ignoring the cold. "Who would you tell?"

"There are others that stay here. No other Changelings, right now, but other clerics come and go. Glenn is so hospitable." Her eyes kept flicking towards me, but she didn't turn her head, like the sight of my eyes was painful. There was a different burning in me now, brought to life by the sight of her deferring to me. We were cut off from the Wild here, divorced from it by the aura of Ventor, but we were both still what we were, and still carried our own amount of Wildness inside us. Mine was stronger than hers, and it frightened her.

"Did he tell you what else I can do?"

"Only that you're his sister, and an excellent musician." She turned her face to mine, forcing herself to look into my eyes. "He didn't say you were Archon."

The fire in me dimmed and I blinked at her. "What?"

"You're obviously very strong," she continued, growing bolder as my eyes faded. "Much stronger than I, stronger than any Changeling I've met. You must be more than just a nymph."

"Hardly. If I'd been Archon, they wouldn't have abandoned me the moment I was born." The last bit of Wild light in me snuffed out, and I sagged back against the wall.

"I'm so sorry, I didn't mean to—"

"It's fine." I flattened my shirt over my lap. "So, how long have you lived here?"

"Two years," she said. I looked up at her and blinked.

"Are you kidding? Two years? You mean you've been in and out for two years."

"No, I've stayed here for the full two years." She lifted her chin. "We just celebrated the anniversary a month ago."

I squeezed my eyes shut. I hadn't been able to make it two weeks before the desire to feel the Wild burning within me drove me back out into the world. And she had managed to stay here for two years.

"I don't have nearly as much Wild blood as you," she said, setting her hand on the bed.

"True." It wasn't much comfort. If I had tried harder to stay, maybe I wouldn't have sent my friends into a Wild frenzy the night before. "Not that much of an excuse though. Glenn has tried to help me so many times."

"Maybe this time it'll take." She smiled and I felt a warm breeze fend off the chill in the room. "Are you feeling up to a visit? Arno, she's the other cleric that lives here at the moment, she was hoping to speak to you."

I nodded, and Ura wafted across the room and out the door.

Arno was a heavy, fair-skinned elf with plain brown hair and a superior smile. She and Ura came into the room together, Ura carrying another chair, this one with a cushion, that she set near the bed. Ura didn't sit until Arno did.

"Hello, Clara," Arno said. Her voice was slow, and she drew out her vowels like taffy. "We are glad you've come to stay with us. Has Ura taken care of your needs?"

"Very well, yes," I said. Ura shot me a smile.

"She told you I have been working with Glenn to help our refugees?"

"She told me you were staying here. I didn't know it was a whole program." Arno frowned. If she expected the same skittish deference Ura showed her, she was not going to enjoy the interview. But I would.

"Oh, so you haven't heard of the work we've been doing? That isn't why you came to us?"

"I'm not from around here." Ura's mouth had dropped open, and I smirked, fighting the urge to wink at her.

"Ah, well, let me explain what's going to happen." Arno folded her hands over her belly. "First we will assign you a spot on the rotation for chores. Once you get used to a routine, we will see what responsibilities we can trust you with. Ura here is in charge of the library."

"Yes, I'm sure she's a whiz at dusting."

Arno narrowed her eyes. "You really ought to take things more seriously. Glenn is being very generous opening this place to you. I warn you not to take advantage of his hospitality."

"I don't plan to be here long enough to take advantage of anyone." I sat forward on the bed. "Don't get me wrong, I'm grateful for this place, and for Glenn. But you needn't worry about me. Once I'm rested up, I'll be on my way." At least I knew Ura had told me the truth about keeping Glenn's secret. If Arno knew I was his sister, she would have thrown that in my face by now.

"I'm sorry, am I mistaken that you have come here seeking sanctuary for a crime?" Arno sat forward as well, bringing her face close to mine. "Did you think we wouldn't have to turn you over to the city if you chose to leave?"

My face went cold. Glenn had never threatened to turn me in, mostly because despite my rowdy outbursts no one had been harmed in the past. But now an alarm blared through my mind. If the city was so afraid of Wild attacks now, and I had caused such a stir, and the city knew I had come to Glenn's church for sanctuary, would he be held responsible if I ran off? I jumped up, ready to run out right then, disguise or no, just so Glenn wouldn't be to blame for my escape, just some fat elf and a weightless sylph.

Arno jumped up as well, raised her hand, and uttered a command in the old tongue. A flame pulsed into life on her palm. Ura screamed and fell from her chair, and I threw myself in front of her. Both of us covered our faces with our arms trying to hide from that light, but I did my best to keep myself between Ura and Arno.

"That's enough." Glenn's clear voice sounded from the doorway. He rushed in and past Arno and was kneeling beside Ura and I an instant later. "It's gone, now, it's all right."

I lowered my arms enough to peek at Arno. She had turned away from us, both her hands clenched by her sides, and the strange purplish red fire was gone. I took a shaky breath and turned back to Ura. I thought, at first, she had fainted, she was so limp against the wall. I put my arms around her to help her up and she curled up against me, her eyes still covered.

"It's all right," I whispered to her. "You're safe now."

"Ura." Glenn said her name, and put his hand on her arm. Her name sounded sweet in his voice, like something he treasured. She turned her face to look at him, tears sprayed across her face. "Ura, come on." Between the two of us we got her to stand, but she still trembled. Then Glenn turned on Arno, but she turned back to him before he could speak.

"I'm sorry," she said. Her face and eyes were red. Her voice strained past her tightened jaw.

"Don't apologize to me," Glenn said. Arno turned to Ura and me and bowed her head.

"I'm sorry, Ura." Her voice was tender for those few words, but the strain returned again when she spoke to me. "I'm sorry Clara. I would not have hurt you. But I knew that would frighten you. And I didn't want you running away. It would reflect badly on us." Glenn pursed his lips, not happy about the qualifications attached. I was too floored at being apologized to by a cleric to be offended.

"I didn't know any of you could still do that." I kept glancing down at her hands. "I thought Ventor's blessings had all faded once the Wars ended."

"They were just out of practice," Arno said. She looked up at Glenn, puffing her chest out a bit. "Glenn is one of the few teaching how to use them again. We thought with the recent attacks it would be wise to be ready."

Glenn cleared his throat and waved his arms toward the door. "Yes, well, that's a discussion for another time. Clara and I have some things to discuss. Arno, we may be expecting some more company later, if you could check on dinner?" Arno nodded and left. He turned to Ura who was still leaning against us both, more on him than me. "Are you all right?"

Ura nodded. "Yes." He hugged her against him, and I felt her sigh.

"Do you want me to help you to your room?"

"No, I can get there just fine." She pulled away from us but paused in the door. "Thank you, Clara, for protecting me." Then she was gone.

"So," I said, glaring at Glenn. "Where would you like to start?"

"How are you feeling?" Glenn reached for my arm, but I stepped around him, He had set my pack by the door when he came in. I grabbed it and lugged it to the bed, digging through it for my disguise kit.

"Fine." I dumped the bag out onto the bed and shoved the camisa out of the way to uncover the kit and my purse. Glenn watched as I checked how much of the creams and powders I had left. His face had softened from the stern look he had given Arno, his gray eyes following my actions closely.

"You don't have to worry about doing that here," he said. "You should get some rest."

"Right, it's so peaceful here." I continued setting out what I would need to become Glade again.

"It can be." He leaned forward and put his hands over mine, stopping me from opening the jars. "She doesn't know about you being Glade."

"Ura does."

"And Ura has never told anyone." His voice remained even and confident, as did the look in his eyes. I plopped down onto the bed, then scrambled to keep the jars from my kit from spilling onto the floor. Glenn caught what I didn't.

"How bad is it?" I shoved the jars back into the kit and closed it. "I didn't mean to cause any trouble for you, too." Glenn sat down beside me and draped his arm over my shoulders. I stiffened and waited for the bad news.

"She's not pressing charges."

I squeezed my eyes shut and turned away from him. In some ways that hurt more than being prosecuted. I didn't deserve any measure of grace from Josie. I had trashed her place, thrown her at Otsoa, and shamed half of her customers. But of course, she wouldn't press charges. She probably wouldn't accept anything for the damages either. A slow pain spread out from my chest and into my arms, making my hands ball into fists. But she would never want to see me again.

"How much do I owe her?"

"She wouldn't give me a number." He tried to draw me around to look at him, but I stayed facing the head of the bed. I didn't want to turn back until I knew I wouldn't cry.

"And the others? Do you know if they reported me?" Josie had been my friend. Thromm and Otsoa had no such attachment to me. As Wardens it was their duty to report someone in such a breach of the rules.

"So far as I can tell, your identity as Glade is safe. You were not reported. It's being circulated as another Wild attack, and though the Hunters know that you've taken refuge here, they don't know that you're Glade." He squeezed my shoulder. "Give it a few days. The town will start talking about something else, and we can claim we took you back to the Wild. It's going to be all right."

"Oh, yes, it's going to be fine." I jumped from the bed and started pacing the small room, coming within inches of each wall before swinging back around. "That's why you've been training people to use Ventor's fire again? Because everything's going to be fine?"

"It was just a precaution," he said. His voice was still as a pool, but his eyes pleaded with me. "We wanted to help protect the town. I thought if more of the clerics were willing to step up, we could convince them to disband the Hunters."

"Have I ever told you I hate how sensible you are?" I stopped pacing and threw up my hands. "You always have an answer for everything. So, explain Ura to me."

"She came here for the same reason you did. She wanted refuge."

"And stayed for two years? Two years, Glenn? I can't stay here for two days without turning into an irritable wretch. She's still sweet as a summer breeze after two years?"

"She likes it here." His voice wavered and a hint of pink touched his pale cheeks.

"Oh Glenn." I came to stand in front of him and patted his cheek. "I'm glad you love her too. It would have been too much if she was pining after you and you hadn't even noticed. You can be so clueless sometimes."

"Don't tease me." He took my hand in his.

"Oh, come on, I never get to tease you about anything. You're too perfect."

"Yet you still manage to make me feel like a fool." He looked up at me, a smile warming his face, his eyes lit up from within. He was usually calm, content, cool when I had visited him before. Now he was merry.

"Only so I don't have to be one alone." I had to smile back. "I won't stay long, I promise. You're right, a day or two should do it."

"You can stay as long as you want. Ura would be happy to get to know you. She has a lot of questions."

"Don't we all." I huffed and let go of his hand. "She probably knows more than I do. Her father talks to her."

"Maybe she could answer some questions for you." He stood and straightened his robe. "Either way, she would appreciate the company. As you can imagine she doesn't exactly get along with Arno."

"I bet. How long has she been here?"

"Just a few months. She's almost completed her training though, so she'll be heading out again soon." He was about to say more when Ura appeared in the doorway.

"Glenn, come quickly, someone else has arrived." Without a question Glenn followed her out of the room, and I stayed close behind him. When we reached the top of a narrow set of stairs, I heard shouting echoing from within the sanctuary. Glenn hurried through the lobby and threw open the double doors. I followed more cautiously now, not sure if he had the main flame lit within. I peered around the door, but the brazier in the center of the room was empty. Ura stayed behind me.

"They said they know you," she whispered, pointing into the room. Thromm was standing with his back to us, struggling to hold on to Otsoa who was flailing around and shouting things in the old human language that made no sense.

"Keep the doors shut," Thromm shouted without turning around. I motioned for Ura to stay in the lobby and stepped into the sanctuary, closing the doors behind me.

CHAPTER FOURTEEN

Otsoa raved on about claws and trees and hangings, the guttural sounds bouncing through the empty sanctuary like drumbeats. Thromm was having trouble keeping him in one place as Otsoa kept waving his arms wildly, twisting and turning in Thromm's grip.

"Does Wild magic do something different to humans?" Thromm asked. He dragged Otsoa up toward the brazier in the center of the room, away from the pews. Then he gripped onto Otsoa's arms and did his best to look him directly in the face. "Stop." His voice thundered, making the windows shake, and Otsoa froze. He was still straining every muscle, and his eyes shot around like a frightened animal's, but he was still.

"You could've told me you were working with a paladin," Glenn said. He had come to stand beside me while I watched the struggle.

"A paladin? Thromm?" I pointed to the tall blond and looked at Glenn to be sure he meant that Thromm.

"Yes. Thromm." Glenn moved up the main aisle cautiously.

"It will not hold him long," Thromm said. He was actually out of breath. "Tell me if her magic did this."

I gulped. Glenn got as close to Otsoa as he dared and looked him over.

"I don't think so," he said.

"What I did last night should have worn off by now." I stayed in the back behind the pews. "Otsoa isn't like me, right?"

"No, he is not." Thromm looked down at him. "He is very different. I have seen him this way before, just not this fierce, and I am usually able to reverse it. Now I can barely keep him contained." He struck the hilt of his sword.

"I've never seen any Wild one's eyes do that," Glenn said as he peered into Otsoa's face.

"At least he has not changed completely yet," Thromm said. "But we do not have much time. Please, can you help me calm him?"

"She would be better at that than I am." Glenn pointed back at me. "Will you let her try?"

Thromm turned to look at me, his face drawn out by concern. "He needs to be quieted."

I nodded and started searching my mind for a song. I had no idea how strong it would need to be to work, since I had no idea what was wrong with him. Wild magic could induce violent frenzies, but that's not what I had made last night. That had been all pleasure and dance and revelry. Otsoa was staring back at me with a rage so intense I could see it in every muscle fighting against Thromm's spell. I took a deep breath and began to sing a lullaby.

At first it didn't seem that it was working. Otsoa was still tense and trembling. When Thromm's spell gave out he twisted and fell to all fours on the floor and scrambled away from the men and down the aisle toward me. Halfway he slowed, took a few more crawling steps and stopped. His breathing grew deeper, and he pulled himself up to his feet against a pew. When the last echo of the song faded from the room, he slumped forward across the polished wood and sighed. Thromm was by his side and helping him up. Otsoa was still shaking, his muscles recovering from whatever had gripped him. Thromm checked his eyes, and then nodded to me.

"That has done it," he said. "He is himself again."

I moved closer to them, my eyes shifting to Glenn, but he didn't seem to have any more idea what had happened than I did.

"Is she all right?" Otsoa asked. Glenn let out a questioning 'hm?' as Thromm tried to help Otsoa take a seat. Otsoa was ignoring him.

"I'm fine," I answered.

"Not you," Otsoa spat. "Josie."

"What? Why would you ask that?" My voice came out choked. Had she reacted like this too?

"She's fine," Glenn answered. "I spoke with her this morning. She's completely unharmed."

Otsoa sighed and his head flopped forward. He was relieved. He hadn't been worried that I hurt her, he had been worried that he hurt her.

"What did you do to her?" My eyes flared again. Downstairs it had tingled some, but here in the sanctuary they burned, a reminder that I was surrounded by Ventor's aura. I ignored it and tried to push past Thromm to Otsoa.

"What did I do to her? What did you do to us?" Otsoa looked up at me, and Thromm found himself stuck between us, one arm on each of our shoulders, holding us apart. "You stupid, fluff-headed pixie."

My arms flew up to claw at his face, but Thromm's arms were longer, and I couldn't reach him. "I swear if you hurt her, I will send you into a frenzy so fierce you will tear yourself apart from the inside."

"Enough, I told you she's fine." Glenn's arms clamped around my waist and he dragged me away from Otsoa. "You didn't hurt her; he didn't hurt her. She's fine." Thromm was whispering harshly into Otsoa's ear, probably something similar. Otsoa still glared at me, but he stopped struggling and sat in a pew. Glenn pushed me into a pew on the other side of the aisle, but he didn't back away. Instead he stared down at me and raised his brows, then waved his hand back at Otsoa. I rolled my eyes and tried to ignore him, but he cleared his throat and waved again, more emphatically this time.

"I'm sorry," I mumbled, not looking across the aisle. "I'm sorry for what I did to you all." I folded my hands on the back of the pew in front of me and bowed my head between them.

"So am I," Otsoa said. I looked across at him, not believing what I was hearing. "It doesn't usually get that bad. I'm glad no one was hurt. And I'm sorry I called you that." The last bit of fire in me died as I let out a laugh.

"I've been called worse." The tension in the room loosed, and Otsoa chuckled as well. Glenn patted my arm.

"So, this is your true appearance?" Thromm asked me. I expected disgust, but there was a shade of awe in his voice.

"Yeah. This is me." I pushed my hands through the fuzzy cloud of hair over my head, but it floated back up again. "I am half human, half nymph, and all crazy." Glenn said the last phrase with me, and we smiled at each other.

"I think, since we are confessing," Thromm said. He was looking down at Otsoa. "We may all have something to say. Would you prefer we stay here, or is there somewhere else we should go?"

"We could move to the kitchen," Glenn said.

"Will your apprentice be joining us?" My voice relayed just how excited I was by that prospect. Glenn shook his head.

"Arno takes meals around to some of the local families at dinner. It will just be us."

We were quiet setting up dinner. Glenn set out plates and ladled the stew into a large bowl. Ura mixed wine and water and filled a large pitcher, then set out two smaller pitchers. In one she made honey water, setting it beside my place at the table. In the other she mixed salt and something green for herself. The stew smelled thick and meaty, but Glenn also set out a bowl of mixed greens from the garden and more of the sweet bread.

Once we had settled, Glenn said the blessing, and I welcomed it. Ventor blessed food did more than nourish the body, it accelerated healing, and it also fortified the mind, even mine. The meal would do us all some much needed good.

"So, in order to alleviate any worry over our confessions," Thromm began as we all dug into our dinners. "I will go first." I exchanged a glance with Glenn, wondering what Thromm could have to confess. So far, he had been the only one of our party who hadn't lost control. Glenn shrugged. I looked at Otsoa, but he was focused on Thromm.

"You don't need to tell them anything," Otsoa said. "You haven't wronged anyone."

"I have been keeping secrets," Thromm replied. "And since Glade has revealed herself, and you are about to reveal yourself, I think it only fitting that I reveal mine." Otsoa shook his head but went back to eating. Thromm sat up straight in his chair, and looked around the table, meeting each of our gazes. "I am not from this plane. I am from a place called Redhawk. I was brought here by a mage who used strange objects, like the things on the sketches we found at the mansion, to summon creatures and cast spells. I had just fought a great battle and defeated hordes of evil that had infused all the elements. I was ready to return home to my princess when this mage approached me, opened a portal to this place, and pushed me through it."

"Another plane. Redhawk. Right." I flattened my hands on the table. "Next you'll be telling me the mages who live on the shore are real."

"I do not know anything about those. When I arrived here, I was in the middle of what you call the Wastes and was beset upon by a swarm of giant rat-like creatures. Otsoa rescued me. He used his own special magic, which as you have witnessed is difficult to control. I assisted him in regaining his senses. I am sure that is the only reason he has kept me with him so long. He probably thinks I am as mad as you do, but it does not matter. Roya believes me. He has let me know that the person we are pursuing has magic like the mage that sent me here." He paused and looked down at his bowl. "I would like to go home."

I had been ready to ignore his story and get on with whatever was wrong with Otsoa, but when Thromm mentioned Roya I focused again. If Roya believed him and knew that these many-sided objects could be used for magic like this, it was probably true. I looked at Otsoa.

"Is that possible? Could they use things like that to focus spells?"

Otsoa swallowed. "I'd have to look those pages over again, but if they found or learned how to make the right shape of faceted crystals, that might change the way the spells work. They would have to be completely perfect, though, or the results could be unpredictable."

"I hope you get home to your princess," Ura said. Thromm smiled at her.

"Thank you." He turned and watched Otsoa who was taking a drink.

"Oh, am I next?" Otsoa peered over his cup back at Thromm. When he set the cup down, he was smirking. "It's nowhere near as good a story as Thromm's. I have learned human magic."

Glenn dropped his spoon. I nearly spilled my drink trying to set my cup down. Ura simply stared with her wide blue eyes without blinking.

"So Wild magic is different for humans," Thromm said.

"I... I thought you were asking if my Wild magic would affect a human differently. I didn't know you meant Wild human magic. Are you...? Is that what all that was about? They didn't just throw you out into the Wastes?"

"Oh, they did. I was looking for a way to counteract the madness when I ran into Thromm. He can usually keep it from taking me over."

"You were looking for a way to fix it in the Wastes?" Glenn said. "That's like Glade looking for help in the woods."

"There are rumors of a temple to the old gods in the Wastes that wasn't ruined in the Breaking. I thought it was worth a try." He held our gaze, but only briefly, before looking down at his hands. "It was foolish, I know. I thought I could handle it, that I would be the one to figure out how to control it." Guilt pressed into his voice and weighed it down. Silence stretched out between us, and we ate some more.

"My turn. You know the big secret." I waved my arms, still honey colored, but no longer glowing. "But I wanted to make sure I had the blessing of the rest of you before revealing what we've found to Glenn and Ura." Otsoa and Thromm nodded. I launched into a description of what we had found in the mansion and in the woods, and the strange ways we had gotten there. When I described what happened to Meia, Glenn made a choking sound. Ura grabbed my sleeve when I finished.

"Do you think it could work?" Her eyes were wavering between me and Glenn. "Do you think they could find a way to fix us?"

I grabbed her hand. "That's not fixing us. She was dead to everything after, not just the Wild. I'm sorry. That's not a fix." Ura dropped her gaze back to her plate. I patted her hands and looked to Glenn. I wished that there was a fix, for their sake. No matter how much she loved him, she wouldn't be able to live here forever. The moment she left the building she'd want to run. "Rayul is a murderer. And he's going to start another war."

Glenn's face was red. "Yes. I agree. Perhaps not all, but a few of the clerics I've trained would be willing to help. Even if all we tell them is that we know who is responsible for the Wild attacks."

"That would be the best way to explain it to them. We're not under contract anymore, but we still aren't allowed to give out details of what we found." Otsoa's voice was back to its normal vibrant sound. "I'd rather not get on Roya's bad side."

"It would be best if we could confront him outside of the town." Thromm tapped his fingers on his chin. "He has many friends here. The Hunters at the least would be ready to defend him."

"And no one would believe us. We don't have any real proof. Especially now that Master Vonetti is dead. Not that he would have been a witness for us anyway." Otsoa arranged the silverware on his plate in various shapes.

"I will make him confess." Thromm ripped a roll in half.

"How would we even get him out of town, though. We can't throw a garden party for him," I said. Otsoa chuckled.

"We offer him something he wants." Ura's words were quiet, but steady. "You said he was doing this to attract the attention of someone in the Wild, and it didn't work. He will probably need another subject."

"No." Glenn and I said it at the same time. He reached over and grasped her hand.

"Don't even think about it," he said. "We will find another way to get to him." Glenn's voice was so gentle. He closed his eyes and leaned over to rest his forehead against hers. I kept my eyes on them, even as I felt the others staring at me. I swallowed, pushed my chair back and rushed from the room.

I blew through the hallways, only looking up to keep from bumping into walls or tripping up stairs. I ended up in the library, a wide arched room on the far side of the sanctuary. There was no dust, or any hint of dampness. Scrolls and books lined the walls and covered every spare inch of table or counter. A desk in the middle of the room had several books open on it. I swept around the desk and glanced over the pages without registering any of it. I crumpled into the chair and buried my head in my arms on the desk.

So many times during this job, the answer had come to stare me in the face, and I had hated it each and every time. I looked at it now, wishing I could claw its eyes out and run away. But that would mean they would have to use Ura as bait, and if anything went wrong Glenn would lose her. It was the surest way to draw Rayul out, and the most ridiculous and dangerous plan I had ever been a part of.

I felt someone enter the room, and recognized Glenn's steady footsteps. He stopped just inside the doorway and waited.

"It's the only way." I mumbled the words into my arms.

"No. I'm not using my sister as bait."

"Well we're not using your girlfriend either."

"No. We'll think of another way."

"There is no other way." I shoved up from the desk and looked at him, frowning down at me. "I'm the one he wants. It's perfect. You can tell him I'm too much for you to handle and you're releasing me outside of town."

"And if we can't protect you?" He crouched down next to the desk. "He's a strong artificer, capable of keeping the Wild at bay both in the city and in the forest. And he has no qualms about hurting people like you. I'm not risking that happening to you."

"You'll be there, and Otsoa and Thromm, and a few other clerics. I doubt he'll bring reinforcements to just collect a Changeling."

"And if he does? If he shows up with Hunters, it's going to be a hard fight."

"I don't know what else we can do, Glenn." I stared down at the books on the desk, sliding a few around. "It has to stop. And even if we don't overtake him, we just need evidence of what he's doing. The wand, maybe, or the witness of several clerics, to take before the council." I stopped at one book that showed a map of Casavera, criss-crossed with lines connecting various points. It was an old map, littered with temples to the old gods and fortified walls that had been overgrown long ago.

"If you truly choose to do this, I won't stop you. But don't only do it to keep Ura safe. That plan isn't an option at all." I had almost stopped listening to Glenn. Something about the map was troubling.

"What is this?" I tapped on the book.

"My research on the old Ventor gifts. It's how I learned to make the fire. It's accounts from the Iron Knights."

I shivered, remembering stories about the church warriors who had burned whole swaths of forest down before the Wild agreed to call truce. "No, what's this specifically."

He peered down at the map. "Those are the Ways. During the Wars the knights used them to travel quickly and gain access to the Wild. Each Way began and ended at shrines or sacred places of the gods. I was trying to figure out if they still worked, but I haven't made any progress."

I traced some of the lines with my fingers. First the one from Guild street out into the forest, then another from a spring that had once been outside the walls to another part of the forest, then another to a point at the edge of the woods north of town to something that looked like a fancy building. Each endpoint had a specific symbol written beside it in ornate calligraphy.

"And the symbols?"

"They correspond to the other pages." He pointed to the last symbol I had touched, and then flipped through the rest of the book until he found a page with the matching symbol in the top corner. "There is a page for each symbol. We have tried using the poetry there to open a Way, but it didn't work."

The page did have a few lines of poetry on it in the same curvy script, but there were lines of other markings between the lines of words. Small dark diamonds in rising and falling patterns placed along sets of green lines. I looked up at Glenn.

"Is there a Way that should open here? This used to be a temple to Ria, right?" Glenn nodded, turned back to the map for a moment, then flipped to a new page. "Where would it open? Or does it just open wherever I call it?"

"You should be able to choose where it goes.," he said. "What are you going to do?"

I looked over the page he had opened to and started humming. Ancient music notation was a strange thing, often not indicating things like rhythm or even the duration of notes, simply a basic record of the melody and what words were sung on which notes. This was no different, so I had to figure out what rhythm sounded right and worked with the lines of poetry. It took a few tries, but once I had something that worked, I began to sing.

I held the last note, letting it die out as I ran out of air. Glenn was still, and his eyes darted around. I was about to toss the book back onto the desk, when something popped in the air so loudly it made my ears ring, then a sucking sound filled the room, and a large hole appeared in the center of a bookshelf, spiraling open. The edges continued to swirl around the opening, even when it was no longer growing larger. It stayed about seven feet across and hovered a few inches off the ground. Glenn let out a puff of air that could have been a laugh.

"Where does it go?" I asked. I had to tap Glenn's arm to get him to answer. He was staring open mouthed at the swirling hole.

"You have to sing the song for the destination you want."

"He must have learned how to force them open." I stretched out my arm and pushed my hand through the hole. Glenn gasped. It was very cold, so I pulled my hand back quickly.

"What? Who?"

"Rayul. He's using them to get into the forest. He must have learned another way to open them. Unless you have copies of this in the library."

185

"No, this has been kept in the church archives for centuries. There are no other copies as far as I know." Glenn tilted his head. "But you think these are what Rayul is using? You didn't see something like this though."

"No, but if he isn't using them properly maybe they wouldn't look the same. Or maybe he has an illusion over those as well. He's very good at illusions." On a whim, I sang my short song for dispelling, and the portal shrank down to a small black dot that popped out of existence. "Give me a few hours, and I'll see if I can figure out how to hide one too."

Disguising one of the swirling portals was harder than I thought it would be. The first illusion I tried was fuzzy around the edges. The second one wasn't solid enough, and you could see the outline of the portal through the pretend image of a bookcase that I set before it. The only long-term solid illusion I had ever made had involved hours of makeup and artwork. I couldn't begin to guess how Rayul was hiding something this dynamic. He must have been a very skilled artist.

After three hours of trying, I scuffled out of Glenn's library. I noticed Arno at the far end of the hall, but she disappeared into another room and shut the door. I turned the opposite direction towards the lobby and the stairs back down to bed. Before I was halfway down the hall Glenn called to me.

"How's it going?" he asked. I just shrugged. "Do you think you're up for a visitor?"

"You're joking, right?" I waved my arm over my body. "I haven't had a chance to clean up yet. And who else would come here looking for me?" Glenn didn't answer. He just flattened his mouth and looked at me with genial eyes. "Flames, Glenn, is she here?"

"Language," he scolded. I rolled my eyes. "Yes, she showed up about an hour ago."

I curled into myself and leaned against the wall. Weariness pressed into me like wet clothes on a drowning man. I didn't want to do this now.

"I haven't told her anything other than admitting that you're here." He reached out to me but stopped just before touching my arm. "She'll understand." I shrank away from him and shook my head. "Should I tell her to go?"

"No." I choked on the word, held my breath and then let it out slowly. "Just, uh, give her a warning about..." Again, I waved my hand at my strange skin, my glowing green eyes, my fluffy hair.

"All right. She's in my office. Just give me a moment." He went back up the hall to a door a few feet away from the library. As soon as the door closed, I started hyperventilating. I gripped my stomach and bent over, squeezing my eyes shut against the stinging that filled them. I only allowed myself to the count of twenty, then I straightened up, took a long breath, and headed for the door. Glenn slipped out, nodded to me, and waited by the door.

I opened it just enough to push into the room. I heard Josie sigh like things were worse than she had expected and stand up.

"I didn't want to believe him," she said. She was using her performance voice, the supported deep voice they had taught us to use to be able to speak or sing, even when you were crying. "But, well, there you are." I kept perfectly still, so she could take in how Wild I looked. I heard her take a shaky breath and braced myself. Josie didn't cry in front of people when she was sad. If she started crying it was because she was about to tear into you.

"Here I am," I whispered.

"Why didn't you trust me? You don't think I would have kept this secret for you? Answer me!" Her last shout hurt. I don't think she intended to, but there was magic in it, and it hit me hard and sharp sure as if she slapped me. I looked up to see her standing with her fists at her side, her face red and twisted.

"I do trust you. I just didn't want to hurt you. I didn't want you to have to lie for me." I folded my arms across my chest.

"No, of course not. You never trusted me enough for that. You and that tramp friend of yours, sure, she could lie for you, and you for her, and you guys could go off and do the tricky jobs. Not me, no, I didn't care enough about you for that." I knew she was raging when she brought up Drinn. We had gotten over that particular sore spot a long time ago.

"I never told Drinn." I stated it as solidly as I could, hoping that she would believe me. "You wouldn't have wanted to be in on any of those jobs. You do what's best. It's what I love about you."

"Yeah, I do everything right. I come home to take care of mom, I don't take the risky jobs, don't hang out with the wrong people. You just want to keep me safe. I get it." She stomped up to me, short enough to look up into my face. "But you know what, that was my choice to make, not yours. I should have been able to stay in school if I wanted. I should have been able to come with you on those jobs. And you should have told me what you are and let me decide what was right."

She reached up and grabbed my face in her hands so that I had to look at her.

"And you know what? I don't care who your parents were. You are the best Warden and the best bard I have ever known. And there is no way I would have turned you in. Not even after what you did today."

"I'm so sorry, Josie." I put my hands on her shoulders. "Are you all right? I didn't hurt you, did I?"

"No, I'm fine." She patted my face. "I can't say the same for my bedroom." Her cheeks turned red and she turned away.

"What now?" I wasn't sure if I should be worried or happy for her.

"When I woke up the sheets were shredded, the floor was scratched, it was a complete wreck."

"But you're all right?" I tried to get a look at her neck or her arms, but she kept her back to me, her arms tucked in front of her.

"I told you, I'm fine."

"I'm sorry." I wondered if I should mention that he was here as well.

"I mean, I'd heard that Wild magic could make you do crazy things, but I didn't think..." She shrugged and wiped tears from her eyes. "Doesn't matter anyway. He was gone when I woke up. And it's not like it would have gone much differently even without magic. The job was over, and he'd head back up to the city and forget about me."

"He is not going to forget about you." I put my hand on her shoulder and tried to turn her around, but she resisted.

"I don't even remember what happened." She turned around but didn't look up at me. "Do you?"

I shook my head. "It's always like that for me. Can't remember much of anything, just a few dreamlike impressions."

"Well, good. He probably doesn't remember anything either. All for the best." She took my hand in both of hers. "And now Glenn says you're going on another job, a really dangerous one?" I nodded. "Be careful, Glade." She ran her hands over mine. "Funny, I don't remember what happened, but I remember how it felt. It was like being drunk but... so much better. Is it like that all the time for you?"

I nodded. "Pretty much. I don't feel it when I'm in here. But it pulls at me out there."

"What would happen if you go home?"

"Willingly? I don't think I'd be able to leave."

She reached around and hugged me. "I have to get back." On the way out she paused in the door as though to say something, and then changed her mind, and left me alone in the study.

CHAPTER FIFTEEN

I gave up trying to hide the portal in Glenn's study. There was little chance of it being in danger inside the church. Glenn gathered three more clerics with Arno, and they met with Thromm, Otsoa, and me in front of the portal. The song for the location Glenn had chosen took a little less time to get right, and as I finished singing the color of the portal changed from dark and smoky to something nearly transparent. I rolled my eyes, annoyed at how long I had tried to hide it, when it basically disappeared when it was working properly.

Glenn went through first, then Thromm. Otsoa and I followed after. We stepped out onto a raised marble circle cracked and uneven from years of roots growing under it. I hurried forward and stepped out of the columned arbor through a thin curtain of vines so the clerics following us had room to emerge. A few feet outside the arbor were seven lower pedestals in a circle around it. Each had held a statue ages ago, and some still remained in various states of decay. Just to our right was a worn but complete statue of Ulcan the patron god of smiths, his arm eternally raised over an anvil.

Behind us and the portal, stood a statue of Petos, still chiseled and perfect. There were dried flowers draped around his neck and glints of metal at his feet as though there had been worshipers there recently. Petos stood tall, a spear in his hand, dressed in the old classic fashion with yards of fabric pinned over his shoulder. Many believed that Petos was the father of Ventor the Breaker. I wondered if there was an equally well cared for shrine on the other side of town to Mosine, Ventor's mother, and maker of the muses.

"Well, you get points for irony," I said to Glenn as the last cleric arrived.

"Yes, well, it's remote, and there are plenty of places to hide around the shrine." Glenn made the sign of Ventor before the image of Petos, something meant to look like the breaking of bonds from around the wrists. The other clerics repeated the motion, crowding around the steps of the arbor. One of them lit a flame in the metal bowl at Petos's feet, and I hurried away. While they began chanting a prayer, I walked around the circle of statues trying to guess who each of them were. Most had either been worn by weather into little more than shapeless stone, some had been broken apart. I found one that had held Luther's statue, but all that was left were his legs and the lute at his feet. I sat down so his shadow hid me from the fire.

"Kindle our hearts again, O Breaker," Glenn said in old elvish.

"By your light we shall live," the others answered.

Thromm and Otsoa had followed me rather than stay and prepare with the clerics. I peered up at Thromm, unable to keep a smirk from my face.

"You're not going to pray with them?" I asked. "It's been a long time since we've had a paladin around. They'd be honored to include you."

"I do not know your gods," he answered. "I pray to mine at sunrise."

"What about you?" I turned to Otsoa. "Are you keeping an eye on me? Or do you hold to the old human gods?"

Otsoa chuckled. "What do you know about the old human gods?"

"I know I can't pronounce any of their names."

"Neither can I," Otsoa quipped. "Anyway, they seem to have a real brotherhood thing going on. I don't want to intrude."

Despite the fright of finding out my brother was a warrior against the Wild, I was glad he was part of something like this. Not only was he a part of it, he was their leader. I rested my head against the pillar, wondering where I would run to next time I messed up. I couldn't ask for sanctuary in the training center for Ventor's warriors.

Once the praying ended, the clerics took up positions in the bushes and behind the hills around the shrine. Otsoa and I tested their hiding places, looking from all along the path and around the shrine. Any way we approached left us vulnerable to at least one of them. Then Glenn stepped back through the portal to meet up with Rayul. I sat on the edge of the shrine and waited.

"They're here," Thromm said. Glenn and Rayul were coming down the path, Rayul a few inches taller than my brother. He was carrying a bag that he held out beside him so it didn't bounce against his body. I was surprised he had come alone.

As soon as Rayul saw me he stopped.

"Is there a problem?" Glenn asked, nearly running into him.

"I have never seen one so very... Wild," he said. His voice was smooth as glass. He started forward again, looking at me the way a jeweler examines a stone. "I can see how much a burden this must be for you. How much she resists being tamed."

"It has been difficult to manage," Glenn admitted. He was not trying to act sad, but kept a pitying look on his face as I had coached him.

"I have finally perfected the technique," Rayul said. He stopped at the outer circle of statues and stared down at me. Thromm and Otsoa were standing on either side of me, acting the part of my guards. He looked up at Otsoa. "Can you hold her still?" It didn't sound like a question. His tone conveyed command and that he was accustomed to being obeyed.

Otsoa's lensed wand passed over me and locked every muscle in my body. I fought the panic that sank my stomach to my toes, remembering that at any moment the clerics would burst from their hiding places and grab Rayul. I have no idea what they were waiting for. Rayul bent down and unrolled his bag to reveal a selection of glass wands. He chose a long green one and began to describe what he was about to do.

"The wand does not merely send a spell to the proper place in the mind that needs to be disconnected from the Wild. I must push the tip into the mind through the eye socket in order to properly work the magic."

Glenn looked ill. "What?"

"It's not lethal. There is some discomfort, obviously, but it usually heals within a few days." He pulled out a linen handkerchief and got into position over me.

"Wait!" Otsoa cried out.

"Wait? Oh, I'm sorry, am I to wait until your companions are able to jump out from their hiding places and stop me? I'm afraid we would be waiting for some time." The tone of Rayul's voice never changed, remaining smooth and polished.

"What have you done to them?" Thromm asked, grasping Rayul's arm. Otsoa released the spell holding me and I lunged for Rayul's hand and the wand. He flicked the wand he was holding. A shrill note rang out and it felt as though my head split open. Otsoa and Glenn shrank away too, and Thromm winced but managed to keep a hold of Rayul.

"Interesting," Rayul said. He pulled something from his belt and looped it over Thromm's arm. Thromm yelped and pulled his hand away, red welts appearing on his skin. Rayul twisted the band so it tightened around Thromm's arm and hung the other end on nothing in the air, but Thromm was frozen as though Rayul had tied him with metal bands.

The ringing of the glass faded and the pain in my head became bearable. I started to push up to my feet, fighting a wave of nausea, but Rayul took hold of my arm and pushed me back down to the ground.

"I knew what you were the moment you came to Casavera," he said pushing his face close to mine. He was slipping another strip of fabric from his belt, winding it around my arm as he spoke. "I hope you enjoyed my little welcome. I couldn't resist trying to trap a prize like you." Another spell began to take hold of me, not like Otsoa's that had locked me up but something slowing me down, making it feel like I was swimming through sand to try and pull my arm away.

Otsoa cried out, and I hoped that the clerics had arrived after all. Instead Navala's voice, hollow and shrill, was shouting commands. The Hunters had come with Rayul after all and were trying to get hold of Glenn and Otsoa. Thromm was straining against his bonds, but I kept limp, even while Rayul lifted me by the strap on my arm and reached up to hang me from another invisible hook. I peered over Rayul's shoulder. Glen was holding off one of the Hunters with a sword, and Otsoa keeping two at bay with his wand, a bluish glowing wall of energy between him and his attackers.

"I'll be right back," Rayul said, turning away to focus on Otsoa and my brother. He had slowed my body, but he hadn't thought to silence me. I closed my eyes and focused on the fabric on my arm until I could feel the one on Thromm as well, and then sang a disrupting tune full of sour notes. I stumbled to the ground. Thromm landed on his feet and lunged for Rayul calling out a warning to Glenn who was too busy with the Hunters to see Rayul coming up behind him.

Glenn panicked. I saw it in his face when he turned. He spotted Rayul approaching and shouted something in old elvish. His free hand burst into flames and several balls of fire spun out in all directions. All of the Hunters broke and dodged. Rayul had managed to retrieve the rest of his wands, and he pointed one at the fire rushing at him, making it swerve aside.

Thromm rolled out of the way as the flames passed over his head and crashed into the nearby brush, setting it ablaze.

"You take the Hunters. We'll surround Rayul," I barked at Thromm. He nodded and continued around Rayul and Glenn, drawing his sword. Three more Hunters had joined the fight but Thromm strode into the fray in front of Glenn, his long arms swinging his sword in easy strokes like he was warming up.

Glenn's hand was still aflame, but I had lost sight of Otsoa. As long as he hadn't been carried off by the enemy, it would be best for him to be out of the way. It would give him time to cast spells away from the most danger. While Rayul tried to surround Glenn with a similar shield to the one Otsoa had used, I began another song, this one low and menacing. If I sang it right it should cloud Rayul's mind enough to keep him from casting spells, or at least, from doing it so easily.

Before I finished the first phrase a sharp pain stabbed into the back of my mind, and Navala's voice slithered into my ears.

"Not so fast, Changeling, we're not done with you, yet." Images rose to my mind, glimpses of a crazed dance around an ancient tree, lying in carpets of leaves with the limbs of people I didn't recognize twisted with mine, running breathless and terrified through a forest at night chased by howling beasts. I wobbled and stumbled backwards, coming to rest against a marble pillar. Glenn screamed in pain, but it sounded far away. I tried to push against Navala's attack, but she was relentless, not only showing me the scenes but making me feel each memory like it was happening. So, I embraced it.

I reached as far down in me as I dared, and called on every feeling and desire the Wild had ever shined in me, gathering it up into one brilliant glowing orb and flung it at Navala with all I had. She squealed and fled my mind. When I opened my eyes again, I could feel that my eyes were brilliant, and my skin was glowing. All of the elation I had tamped down while in the church rose up in me, begging me to run away with it.

Glenn was kneeling on the ground in front of Rayul, his back arched and his face frozen in a scream, but there was no sound. Thromm was holding his own against the Hunters, but he was badly outnumbered, and was getting driven back towards us.

Then a spotted cat, the size of a mountain lion, pounced out of the brush and landed on Rayul, knocking him to the ground. Glenn slumped forward, but quickly started scrambling up and running towards me. Thromm had allowed the Hunters to push him backwards, and then swung his sword wide into the trees around us, dropping a massive burning branch between him and the attackers. Then he too hurried back to the shrine.

The wild cat let out a musical roar as Rayul threw him off. It landed and roared again, rising up on its hind legs to swat the wands from Rayul's hands. He grasped his bleeding hand, and then stomped on the wand. The shockwave from the sudden release of the magic knocked the cat away. It shook its head and pawed at its ears.

Thromm ran by and waved to the cat. "Come, Otsoa, we are retreating." The cat yowled and followed.

I called up another song as they all ran for the portal, a song driven by the desires roiling in me for the scent of earth and flowers and rotting leaves. I don't know why I was so certain it would work, but I knew it would, and I could picture the exact spot I was singing about.

"They're just going to follow us, you know," Glenn said as they rushed past me into the portal.

"Let them," I said.

"Is everyone all right?" I looked over them all, but mostly Glenn. He was still hunched, collapsed down to his knees after I dragged him away from the portal. The jaguar, which was apparently Otsoa, crouched near him watching the doorway for the first sign of the Hunters that were following us. Thromm was the only one that looked steady. He was cut in a few places, but gripped his sword and stood firm in front of both of them.

"I just need a minute," Glenn said, waving me away. "Watch your back." I looked over my shoulder, but nothing had come through yet. I looked to Thromm and grit my teeth.

"I really hate to ask this, but I don't have many options. Things might get out of hand. You might need to stop me." Thromm tilted his head. "You'll know when," I said. He nodded.

Five hunters stepped through the portal and into the glen, swords raised. Navala was leading them, but Tara emerged last. They spread out into a line and started sweeping forward thinking they could trap us against the trees.

"Where are you going to run now?" Navala asked, finishing with a little giggle. Her question echoed through the trees behind us in higher and higher pitches until it broke into squeaky laughter. Navala stopped and stepped back into the group of hunters. The only one not looking around in confusion was Tara. She was staring straight at me.

I hummed a quick dispelling tune, and the portal disappeared behind them. "Where are you going to run?" I asked. Navala laughed again, but with less menace and more hesitation. Again, her voice was echoed in the woods around us.

"We are hunters. We don't run. This isn't our first time in the Wild." This time the echo only repeated 'we don't run' over and over until the words were no longer recognizable.

"That's a choice. Don't know that it's the best one." While they had been distracted by the echoes, I had been opening up to the glen. It flooded through me in a rush of warmth and sweetness like taking a long gulp of mead and I bottled it up as well as I could, fighting the urge to just let it do what it wanted through me. I struggled to keep focused, especially when the words were echoed through the forest. Each one sent a shiver through me. I had to keep focused, I had to keep control over it, over them, or the heat of it would burn over everyone.

Navala rushed at me, trying to reach into my mind to stir my memories, but the memories only fed into the fire. I raised my head and smiled at her, my eyes glowing green stars in my face. I saw her shock, and then she disappeared in a cloud of bees, beetles, butterflies, dragonflies and all the other tiny creatures that had been in the surrounding trees. I heard Navala scream in my mind, but she had not time to make a sound before the cloud of insects dissipated and she was gone.

The other hunters stopped short, some even backing away from me, not only confused but disturbed by what they had just seen. My smile widened and the sunlight filtering into the glen brightened arounds us, casting sharp leafy shadows across the ground.

"It's not your first time out here, I know," I said. "But this time you aren't surrounded by a nice safe metal wall, with your master artificer keeping the monsters at bay. You had your fun bending the Wild to your will. Now it's our turn."

The three hunters I didn't know all rushed me at once, not wanting to wait for another swarm. So, I pulled the ground out from under them, calling the grassy floor to roll and split as they ran. Two of them tripped, one plunging into the muddy earth under the grass getting stuck to his knees. The third, a lanky elf, hopped gracefully over the splits and fired what looked like a sling at me. I almost laughed, focusing on entangling the two fallen hunters up in a cloud of ferns, until the projectile burst over my head. It was a small pouch of metal filings that burned into my face and eyes. Through a red haze I noticed Thromm moving forward to defend me, and I growled, wrapping the same vines around him that were strangling the hunters, and he tripped too, a shocked look on his face.

"They're mine," I said. I looked for the blur of the thin elf and tried to grab him with the vines, ferns, anything, but he kept slipping out of reach. He fired more filings at me. I ducked and rolled aside, trying to avoid the clouds of metal dust letting it burn through the leaves and vines that rose to my defense. I waited until he had run most of the way around the clearing and paused under an older, crusty barked tree. The others were starting to pull out of the vines, but they weren't close enough to worry me yet. I reached out to the dryad in the tree and woke her.

She was sleepy at first and shivered awake slowly. But when she heard the commotion and saw a mass of interlopers burning metal through the plants in her glen she swung into action, swooping her branches down and through the thin elf, dragging him up into the canopy. There was a short yelp and a few cracks, and then the whole of the tree swayed several times as though blown in a storm. She was waking the others.

The two in the vines hadn't seen what happened, too busy hacking through the plants. Thromm had pulled free before them, and was changing course, running at me instead of the hunters. He'd caught on a little too late. I pointed to the two hunters behind him and whispered in the speech of the dryads the word for what the Wild called them, *sfonias*, slayers. A pair of twin birches on the other side of the clearing leapt into action, their roots tearing from the ground and whipping around the waists of the hunters, dragging them beneath the earth with enough force to break their limbs to make them fit.

Thromm paused as he drew closer to me. His shining sword was drawn, and it seemed to be keeping the tender plants at bay. But a tree branch might not be as wary. He looked at me questioningly, just as the jaguar knocked me over and roared into my face loud enough to make my ears ring. His paws were heavy on my shoulders, but he didn't have his claws out. He was showing all of his teeth, and the heat of his breath made me gag.

"Right. OK. We need to get out of here," I said, struggling against Otsoa. Thromm swung around and caught Glenn up as easily as he had carried me, and ran out of the clearing, even the dryads pulling away as he passed. Otsoa needed to be more agile, but as a cat he leapt and bounded gracefully away and through the grasping branches. Tara was the most impressive. She pulled two swords from her belt and barrelled her way through the writhing tree limbs, slashing anything that came near her. There was no hesitation and no fear, only precision and determination. I hurried out while the dryads were focused on the others, waving them to keep going before the rest of the trees woke up.

I kept them running until we crossed a stream, and we all sat on the bank. Thromm set Glenn down beside him and went about healing him. The jaguar sat nearby, panting. Tara was the only one who didn't sit. At first, she moved to lean against a tree, then changed her mind and stood a few feet away from us.

"Why hasn't he changed back?" I asked Thromm, once my brother was breathing easier. I pointed to the jaguar who made a low singing growl and put his head down on his paws.

"We can straighten that out when we get back," Tara said. "We really need to get out of here."

"It's not supposed to work that way," Glenn said. His voice was raspy. "There's no shrine here."

"There was no shrine in that clearing either." Tara pointed at me. "She knows how to make them. Let her do it again."

I gulped, stood up, and stood on the bank of the stream, looking back the way we had come. The trees were quiet, and a lot of insects and rustling creatures were adding to the background noise, but there was something else under all of that. It was low and constant, a slow repetitive noise that I felt more than heard. I hadn't thought about what I was doing when I changed the other end of the portal, and Glenn was right, according to the books it should have required a shrine. But I could feel it, I could feel the song I would sing for this place, a slow quiet song with a droning harmony running underneath it all.

I started the song, easing into the sleepy melody, and the magic was working, I felt it working. A small smoky portal began to form at the center of the stream. And then fizzled out.

"What happened?" Thromm asked.

"Something's blocking it," I said. "We need to get out of its territory."

I was surprised no one argued with me, especially not Tara. She simply got in line with the rest of them, and we pressed on.

CHAPTER SIXTEEN

"You've been through this before," I said to Tara. She was keeping up beside me easily while the others trailed behind, afraid to come into contact with the brush or bushes around us. I cut through or pushed away as much as I could, but it was still rough going for them.

"Yes," she answered. She too was hacking at things as we walked, but she had a sword like mine, not made of metal but sharpened stone.

"The scars?"

She cracked through a thick branch with the sword, her mouth pressed into a hard line. "Yes." I was willing to let her leave it at that. Accidental encounters in the Wild never ended well, the idea that she had survived was enough. But she sighed and added, "Raishk."

"What? People don't survive those."

"I was lucky."

"That was more than luck." Raishk have six long claws and more teeth than anything else I'd ever seen. They never let go of their prey, not even if they somehow get killed. As they die, they clutch their prey tighter, slicing them to pieces. "Something saved you."

She shrugged. "And I've been hunting it ever since."

I almost told her to abandon that death wish, but she knew how to travel here, had shown no fear, and the world could always use one less Raishk. So, I bit my tongue and kept walking.

When I had traveled through Rhiandon Forest before, the call of Midsummer forced me on a long march to the Summer Tree. During those times, though, I was hardly in my right mind. Everything then seemed normal, natural. On this trip, there were times when we were moving through normal forest, birds chirping around us, with a bright blue sky above. Then suddenly it would be the dead of night, owl hoots and crickets, and a sky full of stars. Those were the easy transitions.

The hard ones involved being surrounded by trees made of crystals, or cloud, or hundreds of millions of insects crawling over each other. When I hear adventurers talk of brief treks into the Wild, they describe it like a dream, where nothing feels real. Maybe they had never been so far in, or there for so long. But this was not like a dream. Each version felt more real than the actual forest.

This was the natural way of things in the Wild. It's like a Venus fly trap, Wild places. They are designed to disorient and capture, no matter what sets off the trigger. But this felt different. It was growing worse, and I had to keep changing direction to keep going north. This was more than the typical trap, something was purposefully playing with us, trying to keep us from leaving. The sudden death Navala and the other Hunters had met with was beginning to sound like the less terrible trap.

After passing the same clearing for the third time, recognizable only because there was a squat gnarled tree there shaped like a crooked hand. No matter what version of the forest we were trekking through, it looked the same. I stopped us and took a deep breath.

"These people are my guests, guests of Nemus Clara, daughter of the Golden One, Mother of Flowers. To interfere with them, is to interfere with me."

I hadn't spoken my full name in some time, and it sounded so strange to me. Glade-Light was the closest I could come to it in the common tongue. As I spoke the clearing around us lightened, filled with the kind of light I was named after: Gentle, dappled summer sun. The others gawked at me with a mixture of fear and surprise. I preferred that look to the disgust I used to get as a Changeling girl, but I'd have traded all of it for the warm smiles of a happy, safe audience. The entire forest went silent, even the low sound that I had been trying to get us away from.

"I am taking my guests and leaving. Why are you keeping us here?" I shouted it to the trees around us.

"Why do you want to leave? Stay and play with me." The voice that answered was sweet, and innocent. There was no pretense to it; it sounded like a five-year-old saddened by the prospect of all her friends going home.

"Sacred flames," I whispered under my breath. "I am very sorry, but I don't think my guests can keep playing much longer. You can see they aren't well." Glenn was barely moving his left arm. Thromm had done what he could, but we were all worn out, and any kind of magic other than Wild took extra effort to cast here.

"Oh! Ok, so bedtime." The forest shifted into darkness again, and a clearing opened up before us, filled with large mounds of moss, like nests. I sighed, and shook my head, but Glenn crumpled down onto one of the nests. I turned my attention back to the disembodied voice but kept an eye on Glenn.

"No, I'm afraid we can't sleep here. There are too many things that would like to eat us if we stay here after dark."

"Oh, I can keep the dark things away easy." There was suddenly a ring of lights around the clearing, shining pillars of shimmering light, not red enough to be fire. "You can sleep nice and cozy and play when you wake."

"That's very kind of you," I said, taking a seat on another one of the nests. It was soft and springy. Such a shame. It would have made the most delightful bed. "And the lights are so pretty. Will we get to meet you? I would very much like to meet someone who can make such pretty things."

"Maybe." They drew out the first part of the word. "What will you give me if I show myself?" I did my best to not be disarmed by the voice. They sounded so young and spoke so kindly. But they had managed to alter the forest around us as a game and thought nothing of keeping us safe overnight in a forest that could eat you alive.

"Do you like songs? I could sing you a song."

In a sudden burst of dragonflies and flower petals, a small girl appeared before me, clapping her hands and hopping up and down.

"Oh yes a song! Sing us a song. I love songs," she said, their words tumbling together. She was small, her hair a tangled mess of moss and leaves, her clothes flower petals and tree bark, and her skin was a few shades darker than the shells of a milk-pod. And still, she was the most beautiful child I had ever laid eyes on. That was another trick of the Archons. Whichever one you were looking at for the moment was the fairest you've ever seen.

There were others around her, attendants, of all shapes and sizes. But they faded into the background around her.

So, I sang for her. I tried to sing something she would like, but you could never tell what that would be. I tried to take a cue from her looks, and sang butterflies feeding from flowers and honeybees buzzing and the marching of ants. She giggled, and started a little dance to my tune, spinning in place and setting the lights shaking. As I sang, thinking about bees and honey and flowers, I realized this one probably knew my mother. She might have even been related to me, somehow. I was unable to keep my thoughts and feelings about that out of my song, and the little person stopped twirling and grew very still.

"Oh, I know her." She tilted her head a bit, looking me over carefully. "I think you have her eyes." The words did not sound as kind as you'd think. It was almost mocking. "Do you want to see her?"

I shivered. Hope filled me for a brief moment, a sweet feeling. But then I remembered that no one commanded my mother but the Summer Queen, not even this beautiful one, and there was no way she would come just to see me. I tried to catch a glimpse of Glenn and the others, but my whole field of vision was filled with the Wild Ones. Some were Alettas, flitting and bright, some were Minims: dumpy little creatures that reminded me of toadstools. But one was a Changeling, like me.

"You're the one he's been after," I said. "You're Rahkel."

Everything froze then, absolutely everything. If we could have seen the clouds in the sky, they would have been still as stones.

"You can't have her. She's mine." The small one's voice was no longer sweet, or childlike. It sounded older than the creaking of hundred-year-old trees.

"Yes, of course she is," I answered quickly, trying to keep my voice calm and friendly. I glanced again at the Changeling. She was not very Wild, not as Wild as myself, anyway. Her eyes were large and cloudy hazel, and she was dressed much like the small one, but otherwise she looked like a normal elf. She seemed healthy, well fed and content. I had known Changelings that were under the "care" of Archons that were naked and near starving most of the year.

Rahkel stepped up a bit, and set her hand on the small one's head, and patted it softly.

"It's all right," she said. She had the most soothing voice, soft as a feather bed. "They haven't come to take me away. Even if they had, you know I wouldn't go." The little one sighed contentedly, and the world began moving again. "But you didn't come to take me, did you?"

"No, we didn't." My voice sounded harsh after Rahkel's speech. The small one looked skeptical, and looked around at the others in our group. Glenn was better, sitting up and not looking so pale, though he was still somewhat stiff. My stomach relaxed a bit.

"But this one," the little one's voice had returned to the sweet, young ring it had been before. "This one was working with the mean one." She stopped and pointed to Tara, who had been standing off to the side, away from the knot around my brother. The small one's attendants swarmed around Tara, picking at her hair and clothes. Tara barely moved, only blinking some, or keeping them from taking her weapons.

"She was, yes," I said, standing up. "But she is with me now."

"You? You that left all of the others in their cages? I should put you all in cages to make sure you stay with me." She didn't, however. At least not a cage that we could see. Despite the amount of power that she had, even this one wouldn't break the strict rules of hospitality the Wild kept.

"I saved her daughter," I said, gesturing to Rahkel. "I couldn't save them all."

209

"If you can even call that saving her." The small one was getting bored. Not upset or anything, just bored. "Well, I suppose we will have to see if I can keep you." The small one clapped her hands and vanished. Most of the attendants did as well, but Rahkel and a few of the toadstools remained.

"Follow us," Rahkel said, as the lights around us faded. She swept her arm behind her, and the forest parted like a curtain, opening onto a glowing cloudy nothing. I had never seen anyone do such a thing.

"Where are we going?" I asked, hoarsely.

"To court," she answered.

There are songs and stories that attempt to explain the splendor and shine that is a Wild Court, but they pale in comparison to reality. It is ten, or a hundred times more beautiful and perfect than any word could convey, being surrounded by so many Wild beings in one place. Even I couldn't describe it with any accuracy that wouldn't reflect badly on my poetic skills.

We stepped through the bright tear that Rahkel had made, and emerged in a lush green space, framed like a gazebo, but huge, with a roof so high it disappeared into the darkness overhead. The only way we could tell it was there were the flickering lights of small glowing creatures that were floating around, just below its crest.

There were seats, lounging couches, and tufts of moss set at random around the space, like they had grown there, and Wild people were draped across all of them, talking to each other in whispers that together sounded like the wind through the trees. Some of them were dryads, some were nymphs, all were shining and beautiful.

We were led through them along a strip of springy grass. Every step stirred up a scent of mint. No one looked at us as we passed. They just went on talking and drinking from flower shaped cups and eating from trays laden with all the fruits and nuts one can dream up.

At the end of the walkway, we neared a canopy that looked like a spider web sprinkled with dew drops. We must have gone farther from the center of the forest than I realized, since it was not the Queen of Summer who was seated beneath the canopy. The little one was there, seated beside her partner. Every Archon has a counterpart, an opposite. This one was large, almost shapeless, covered in fallen leaves. It moved sleepily, clumsily, and no wonder, as it was nearly the height of summer, and it was a creature of Winter. There was a heavy scent of earth and leaves and moss around them both.

"Wait here," Rahkel said, showing us to a long mound of grass off to the side of the thrones. "The judge has not arrived yet."

We sat where she told us. The others looked like they were dazed. They kept gazing around them like they were dreaming. Otsoa, however, did not sit. He stood behind us for a short while, and then started pacing. Every new thing that caught his sight made him start. I did the best I could to not look, to not breath it in, to not listen. Every tiny part of me wanted to burst into sunlight and dance in this place, and it terrified me.

Then everything fell still. It was not the disturbing stillness that had fallen around us before, when the small one had stopped the illusory world she had caught us in. This was a hushed, respectful silence. Not even the breeze wanted to interrupt what was happening.

We turned to see who had arrived, and I lost all of my breath. The woman—being—that stood at the far end of the space was the exact image of one I had studied for years. She was tall, dressed in long flowing white robes trimmed with gold, her dark hair fell loose over her shoulders. She carried a large sword, and her head was crowned with roses. I stood up before Rahkel commanded everyone present to stand for her entrance.

The Lady glided through the forms of the nymphs and stopped before the thrones. A seat made of twining branches grew beneath her and she seated herself, then nodded to the ones on the throne, signaling them to begin.

The two on the thrones did not speak for themselves. They simply pointed to various people around them who would step forward and present their testimony to the Lady. I barely heard them. All I could do was stare at her. She was so close, and so real. The roses at her head were perfectly formed, brilliant crimson and dripping with dew. The sword she carried was shining, straight, and clearly heavy, though she bore it as though it weighed no more than a flower. The only thing that brought me out of my study of her was Rahkel's soothing voice.

"They did rescue my daughter," she said, not raising her eyes to the Lady. "Though it was too late. All but that one. She was one of those that hunts us." She was pointing to Tara.

Tara had sat beside me for the proceedings, though it didn't seem that she was paying much attention either. She was staring at the ground, her scarred hands folded neatly in her lap. I fought the urge to touch her arm, to try and give her some sign that I was going to get us out of this. From the way she was holding herself, she would probably break my fingers.

There was a pause, and then the Lady turned to look at us. There were so many things I wanted to say to her, but they all clogged in my throat. Once I managed to get my thoughts straight, I realized who the Lady was looking at.

"They are giving you a chance to defend yourself," I said to Tara. She shrugged without looking up.

"What is there to say? They've told the truth." Our voices scraped like sandpaper after the musical sounds of Rahkel giving her testimony.

"But you have a reason," I argued. Even as a whisper my voice carried through the court. "You have every right to tell them."

"Let them do what they think is right." Tara kept her eyes down.

I took a deep breath and stood up. As they were my guests, I had the right to speak in their defense as well. I tried not to tremble as I looked up into the face of the Lady. She looked attentive and had been paying close attention through the whole proceeding, though her expression never changed in reaction to our words. She had a strong jaw, a long straight nose, and eyes that glittered gold in the twilight around us.

"I and most of my guests are guardians," I said, keeping my chin up as I spoke. "We admit this freely. If any of the Wild break the treaty, we capture or kill them. Just as you would do to any of the Free that wander your lands." The Lady nodded in understanding. "This one is, as you say, a hunter. But all of you can clearly see the scars on her arms. She doesn't hide them. She's proud of them."

Tara shook once. I barely heard her light laugh.

"As she should be," I continued. "All of you here know what leaves scars that way. But I doubt any of you here know one who bears such scars and still lives. She has been marked by a Reishk and has every right to hunt these lands until she takes her revenge on it, or it finishes its work."

"She was not the only Hunter in my lands." It was the first time the small one spoke up. Her voice was old again, and angry. "And they were hunting far more than Reishk."

"And they are dead now. Eaten by the Sylvans. But this one, this one has a right to hunt, and she is under my protection. So, if it is ruled that she is in the wrong, it is a ruling against me. I will pay the price."

Tara moved again, still not looking up, but her hands had moved. They were clenched fists over her knees.

"But before you make your ruling, Lady," my voice shook a bit at her name. "I would like to offer an exchange." That grabbed their attention. I used the word Roya had used to grab me just a few days ago. "You wish to have justice against this one, the hunter that captured so many of you. But if you will let her come with me, I will give you the one who started all of this. The one who goaded the hunters into entering the forest. The one who is trying to steal Rahkel from you. Let her leave with me, and I will give you Rayul."

The Lady turned to the little one and waited expectantly. What little instinctual understanding I had of how these things worked, she didn't have to deliver a decision, if an agreement was reached otherwise. She could just stand by and ensure that things went correctly. The small one could decide to take the deal, and I wouldn't have to watch them tear Tara apart.

"We have tried to capture him before. What assurance can you give us that we will be able to capture him?" It was disturbing to hear such a creaky old voice coming from such a small, adorable form.

"I can form a Way, I will guide it to his home."

There was a pattering of whispers from the audience, but one glance from the Lady and they fell silent again. There was a dry creak of laughter from the small one.

"No one controls the Ways," the little one scoffed.

"The Old Ones did," I argued, using a word that the Wild Ones used for the old gods. It meant something like ancestors, or origins. It was not something they spoke of lightly.

"And did they teach you their ways, Changeling?" It was not the little one that spoke, but one of the attendants. The word for

Changeling had multiple meanings too. None of them that I'd like to repeat.

"You are not the only ones with long memories." Rather than get caught arguing with those around me, I kept facing the Lady. "The hunters were using them to get into the forest, and into the city. And I used one to escape the city and come here. They can be used, and I will do what I can to take you as close to Rayul as possible."

I stopped there. No use muddying things with a long speech. It was a simple bargain, but a risky one. They may prefer expedient revenge to the promise of revenge in the future. They deliberated for minutes that seemed to last hours.

Rahkel crouched down beside the little one and began whispering to her. Slowly, a smile began to spread across the little one's face. It was not a pleasant smile.

"We accept," the little one said. "You may have this one, and you will bring us Rayul."

The little one and her attendants formed a knot around the thrones, whispering and planning. A screen of leaves and vines rose up between us. None of the Wild Ones in the audience paid us any mind after that. The arrangement had been struck, and there would be no further entertainment for them. I thought the Lady would be on her way as well, her job finished. But as the leaf curtain rose, she turned her attention to Otsoa.

He was lying on the ground, his head resting on his paws. He seemed much calmer than he had when we first arrived, and I worried maybe someone Wild had given him something to drink or eat while we were occupied. Several Alettas were dancing along his back, and he was quietly ignoring them.

The Lady looked at him with curiosity, and there was no fear in her gaze. I gulped and turned to look up at her. Though I had managed to speak for the trial, I couldn't find my words again.

"Speak, daughter," she said. I waited for the crowd to jeer, or grow quiet, or something. The Lady had not spoken before, and her voice was like the ringing of a steel sword being pulled from a sheath. But there was no reaction around me, not even from Thromm or Tara. "You spoke fair and honestly today. I will hear your request." I noticed then that her mouth didn't move as she spoke. She was only speaking to me.

"I am not worthy to be called daughter by you," I said, still trying to figure out how to make this request.

"Have you forgotten that you are Wild?" Her words stabbed into me.

"How can I forget? I am enslaved to it."

"So why not let them cut it out of you, if you hate it so?"

"They cut out more than just the Wild." My heart was throbbing, and a clog was forming in my throat. I hated it. And I feared what I would be without it. "You are not enslaved, but yet you are Wild." I dared to look up and meet the Lady's eyes.

"True. That is because I chose a higher master." She looked into my eyes, her golden gaze as hard as any gemstone. "What is your request."

Several images flashed through my mind. I saw myself with a strong, permanent illusion hiding my true form. I saw myself completely Wild, meeting my mother at the Summer Tree. I even had a glimpse of playing to a sold-out crowd at the largest concert hall in Rhiodeja. She had the power to grant me any of these things.

"Can you help him?" I asked, looking down at Otsoa. "I can't bring him back."

216

She did not smile, but her eyes lit up, and the roses around her head opened impossibly large.

"I can, but it will still only last until he changes himself again." She stretched out her hand, and Otsoa stood, shaking the dew and Aletta dust from his back, and lazily walked to her. He sat down just outside of her reach. "Cats," she said, and sighed visibly, though the words were still only in my mind.

"If you have a token, I could bless it for him." The word the Lady used for token was hard to translate. It meant something of value, but not necessarily monetary value. It had to have personal meaning, and the giving of it would have to be a sacrifice. I chewed my lip for a moment, and then reached into the pouch on my belt. I held up the silver charm that Roya had traded me to get me into this mess, the symbol of the woman before me.

"You may take this," I said.

"Oh, what lovely work." She reached down and took it from me. Her hand was much larger than mine, and the pendant looked tiny on her palm. "The elves have always been good with symbols. And this was made with great love and care. This will do nicely." She raised the pendant to her lips and kissed it. Then she lowered it back to me. It was warm and shining. "You must give it to him. It has been blessed by me, but it is your bond with him that makes it true."

I blinked and nodded. Otsoa stood as I drew close to him. I knelt down in front of him and, at first, he bared his teeth and growled, his head lowered, his front paws spread as he crouched. I stayed still, looking into his large green-brown eyes, looking for any sign that he knew me. He growled again, then sniffed, and sneezed, and I caught a glimpse of him. He closed his mouth but was still twitching, ready to run or pounce if needed.

I slowly spread out the chain and hung the pendant around his neck. He made an odd noise, too deep to be a meow, but it had the same feeling. Then he began to change back into the wiry, keen eyed mage I knew. The change was slow this time, not the same rapid, fluid motion it had been before. But when it was done, Otsoa was sitting on the ground in front of me, smiling.

"Thank you, Glade. You didn't have to do that." He picked up the pendant and peered down to look at it more closely.

"You ought to thank the Lady," I said.

"What lady?"

I turned to look for her, but she was gone, as were most of the audience. Tara and Thromm were sitting still in their places, and the little one was still conferring in her leafy shelter.

"The Lady was here and granted you this gift."

"And you too," he said, and pulled me into a hug. It surprised me, so it took me a moment to return it. It was a rough embrace, and he still smelled musky, but it was sincere. I patted his back a bit, and he pulled away.

"It was the least I could do."

The curtain of leaves parted, and Rahkel came out. The rest collapsed into nothing behind her, leaving a mound of leaves where the thrones had been.

"We are ready," she said.

CHAPTER SEVENTEEN

When the curtain fell behind her, everything was back to normal. We were standing in a copse of beech trees. A stream bubbled out of sight somewhere. There were a few things I was gambling on being true, and as I looked around at the peaceful forest scene I gulped and hoped I could get this right. One gamble was that the Ways were not responding because the Little One had been interfering with my magic, not because I was terrible at opening Ways. The other was that I could remember enough about Rayul's house to get us there, and not open a portal in the middle of the plaza or directly in front of his guards. Considering how little control I had over them, I tried to think of alternative places to connect to.

I stood up and moved around the clearing, slowly. I could feel the distance between us, and the ways change slightly, but I wasn't exactly sure how yet. It was something like how other strings on a lute would resonate when you plucked one.

Glenn stuck close beside me as I moved. "How are you?" I asked him.

"I'll live," he said, smiling. "I've never had a taste of a real magic battle before."

I narrowed my eyes at him. "You're not going to tell me you enjoyed that."

He shrugged, still smiling.

"I'm trying to concentrate," I said, nudging him away from me. He put his hands up in surrender and headed back to the group. I heard Thromm say something that sounded complimentary, followed by some masculine grunting approval from Otsoa. I ignored them and continued searching. I finally found the spot in the clearing that resonated most.

"I can tell you what to aim for." Tara's voice was soft. She was standing apart from the others, watching me. I nodded at her and she explained in impressive detail a part of the courtyard of Rayul's home hidden behind tall bushes in deep shadow.

"Will it work if you've never seen it yourself?" Glenn asked.

"I guess we'll find out," I said. I started the song that opened the portal in front of us, smiling when it appeared easily, but now came the hard part. I didn't even know what note to start on, or what words to say. After a few mediocre starts, I turned away from the portal and groaned in frustration. Otsoa was standing right behind me.

"What are they going to do to him when we turn him over?" Otsoa was looking at me, a strange expression on his face.

"You're feeling sorry for the monster that was killing people to get his sister's attention?" My words came out harsher than I intended, but he didn't flinch.

"No more than I'm feeling sorry for this one that was killing Wild ones for revenge," he said, waving his hand towards Tara. She also did not flinch, taking the accusation calmly. Like she had expected it. "I'm just asking if you think this is truly fair."

"I can stay here, if you prefer," Tara said, with a shrug. "I've fought my way out before. I can probably do it again."

We all stopped and stared at her then, mostly for the casualness with which she spoke.

"No," I said firmly. "Tara was fighting for something it was her right to seek. Rayul is bringing down danger not only on himself, but on all of Casavera, and eventually all of Cyfar. He doesn't care if he has to murder to do it, or sentence people to a fate worse than death, he is just trying to get what he wants. We are bringing him to the end he deserves. If you disagree, that's fine. You can go your own way when we get back."

"I just wanted to know you were certain." Otsoa still looked uncomfortable. To be fair, I was surprised Glenn hadn't objected as well. But Glenn had often surprised me with his choices. They weren't always what I expected. Otsoa set his hand on my shoulder and nodded toward the spot I had been working on.

"Try it again," he said. I shrugged and turned around. This time, as I started the song, I heard Otsoa begin the words of a spell. Something hummed between us that felt like the shock of rubbing a cat's fur the wrong way, and the portal connected to the other side in a rush, turning invisible and giving us a view of the very place Tara had described.

"What did you do?" I asked him.

"Improvised," he answered. "After you."

I nodded firmly and stepped through the Way.

Otsoa was the next one through, and he gasped a bit as we stepped into the courtyard of Rayul's house, in the dark of night. The others were surprised as well. I should have mentioned to them the fluidity of time in the Wild. It was day because that was convenient for them, but we had been there long enough for night to fall everywhere else.

The five of us emerged in a small space behind a tall stand of juniper trees. It was drowned in shadow being thrown from torches on the outside of the wall and along the back of the house. On the other side of the trees a fountain splashed into a wide marble basin, and glints of white glinted between dark leafy shapes, probably statues scattered around the garden.

"So, what's the plan, Wild Mistress?" Otsoa said. I could hear the smirk in his words.

"Just get him into the courtyard. The Wild will do the rest," I said, looking back towards the Way.

Thromm cleared his throat. "I will take Tara and we will search for what was promised to me."

"Tara?" Glenn said, quickly. "Why are you taking Tara?"

"So I may keep an eye on her." He didn't say it with any innuendo at all. It was a complete flat delivery. "Besides, she probably knows where he keeps such things."

"All right. You'll know once things have gotten started up here. How long do you think you need?" I said this to Tara. She thought for a moment and turned so she could look Thromm over.

"Eight minutes," she said.

"Great. That will give us time to get in place." They slipped off together, around the far side of the garden, and out of our view. I turned to Glenn and Otsoa, rather content that I was left the two magic users. This was going to require quite a few special effects. I drew them closer and began to outline the plan.

All of the torches in the courtyard blazed to a brilliant blue, jettisoning fireballs into the air. The guards left the gate to see what was happening, and they were joined by two more from inside the house. Otsoa was ready for them, and trapped them in a giant bubble, and sent them floating over the garden. Lights illuminated the windows, and I heard Rayul's perfect elvish demanding to know what was happening.

Getting him out of his house might be the easy part. convincing him to follow us into the Wild would be harder. Two more guards emerged and Otsoa tried to contain them as well, but they were ready for him. One dove aside, rolled and got back to his feet and charged at Otsoa. The other waved a wand and dispelled the bubble with a word.

Glenn drew the flame down from a torch on the wall trying to catch the wand in the guard's hand. The guard shouted in surprise but fended off the flames and searched through the bushes for Glenn. He was hidden almost exactly across the garden from me, manipulating fire around the courtyard rather than trying to create any of his own and give away his position. I whispered a song about darkness and tried to keep the shadows around my brother as thick and impenetrable as ink. I held my breath as the guard pushed into the thick hedges to the right of Glenn, and then a weird shock ran through me that made me nauseous.

I suppressed a gag and looked around wildly for another guard, but no one was near me. The first guard had reached Otsoa and was trying to strike him with his sword. Otsoa had raised a shield of stone that hovered between him and the guard. Why wasn't he changing? He crouched as though getting ready to pounce and the nausea hit me again. His eyes shot up and he actually looked straight at me, a pleading look in his eyes.

I gulped and looked away. We didn't have time to figure out what was happening, but it seemed the Lady's blessing was more

223

than a help for Otsoa. As much as I wanted him to change, I had no idea what it might take to change him back. Instead I picked my way through the shrubs closer to him and sang to make him stronger. The humming returned and Otsoa grunted, swinging his wand around his stone shield, and fired a series of darts at the guard. The darts sank through the guard's armor and he howled and backed away, leaning against the wall to stay on his feet. A window opened above us and Rayul peered down into the courtyard.

"What is going on? Have you caught the infiltrators?" The still searching guard came out from the hedges and shouted back.

"No, sir, they are covering with magic." Otsoa had disappeared into the darkness.

"Find them before they breach the house," Rayul growled.

Once the guard was back in the open, Otsoa fired another round of darts at him and he collapsed to the ground. This was my chance, and I thought we had given Thromm enough time, assuming Tara had held up her end. I stepped out of the shadows and looked up at Rayul, my eyes shining brilliant green in the darkness.

"We took care of your hunters even more easily," I said. He looked down in disgust.

"You? Well, you and your friends. I have a better stand now. You've invaded my home and the Watch will take care of you."

"We'll be long gone before they arrive, and we'll have our own stand to make." I made a show of pulling out a long glass wand and pointed it at him. "I may be thrown out of the city as a Changeling, but you will be run out as a murderer."

Rayul sat in the window, swung his legs over the edge and stepped out into the air walking down to me on invisible stairs. I didn't wait for him to reach me; I turned and ran for the portal.

"Not so fast, I'd like my wand back." I heard him reach the ground and the paving stones of the courtyard bucked beneath me, knocking me to the ground. I tried to scrabble up, but the stones turned to sand beneath me and I sunk into the ground.

I wasn't going to make it into the Way. I could feel the Wild on the other side, the deep burning that could shake through any defense hovering just out of reach. It wouldn't cross, not to save me, not even to grasp this man they hated. But they could, the minotaur had. All they needed was permission.

As my knees disappeared into the sand, I began to sing. It was an odd song. It was a song with a message, meant to particularly strike the interest of any fairy that heard it.

> *Hear the whispers on the breeze,*
> *they won't tell, they only tease,*
> *hinting where to find the door,*
> *but never leave the keys.*

> *Listen as the voices rise,*
> *thunder raging through the skies,*
> *seeking for the hunter's home,*
> *and drowning out his lies.*

> *But now my song will speak to you,*
> *giving you the clearest view,*
> *opening the hidden way,*
> *and bids you all come through.*

It spread out from me in soft undulating waves that I could feel echoing down the pathways spread before me. As I drew close to the end of my song, I felt a slight quiver in my knees.

Then I felt, and it was more felt than heard, them answer. First from Casavera, then from a few other pathways. It echoed around me, thickening the air the way it does before a summer thunderstorm. I grew warm, and my legs grew strong, and I surged out of the sand, when a rumble began, the rumble of far off thunder. Rhiandon was singing. Rhiandon was coming. And if I did not move quickly it would sweep over me and past me and pour into the house without me.

The earth shook and rippled through the courtyard. A roar sounded behind me, and I couldn't tell whether only I could hear it, or if the others heard it too. Rhiandon was barreling down the passage, and I would not be able to hold them back. I rolled out of the way and landed in a trimmed bush, the branches digging into my side.

Several dozen dervishes came spilling out of the Way and knocked Rayul back like leaves. Rayul responded to the whirlwind creatures with a flare of light that sent them hissing away, especially the minims and boletus that arrived next, who went rolling into the grass in the courtyard and covered their eyes.

The guards had broken free of the bubble trap and were trying to chase down the small ones, but the boletus could be slippery, and blended into the dark easily, their soft pink brown bodies shifting in shape. Several of the Wild creatures burrowed joyfully in the garden and uprooted every plant they touched and tossed them at the guards. Rayul was not distracted by them. He stood and stalked toward me, taking his time to build up a spell. I frowned. Considering how easily he had been tossing spells around before, anything that was taking time for him to cast would disintegrate me.

I could see Otsoa trying to work up something to counter him, but the wind I had summoned was keeping him from getting his ingredients together. And Glenn couldn't keep up the flames against whatever Rayul did before. Still, my brother moved to stand between Rayul and me.

"I won't let you do to her what you did to the others," he said, his voice firmer than I'd ever heard it.

"It won't only be me," Rayul replied. "Soon every town in Drakir will know how to free these poor souls from the Wild. It's not as though Ventor has deigned to free any of them in centuries. Get out of the way and let magic do what your god will not."

Glenn's fists clenched, but he didn't move, even as Rayul came within feet of us, his hands still making motions in the air. I heard a banging from inside the house. Thromm and Tara came bolting across the courtyard towards us, dodging the little Wild ones that were still blowing randomly around.

"Enough!" Rayul released the spell, and everything in the courtyard began sinking into the ground. Everything. Even his own guards. "The Watch will be here soon, and they will take all of you out of my home. All except for this one." He was stepping towards me, walking across the marshy ground on stones that rose under his feet with each step. "This one will stay here. I have a few other things I would like to try. And she is Wild enough to endure more than one trial."

And then the Archon of Rhiandon arrived.

She was a giantess and came flying out of the Way in a fury, bringing the breaking of a storm in her wake. She was cloaked in storm clouds, with a crown like lightning, and she rumbled thunder from her throat. I shielded Glenn the best I could from the sudden pelting rain. Thromm froze in wonder. I heard screams behind me, the guards running in terror. She flew through the courtyard until she reached the walls, and then bucked like a wild horse being bridled for the first time.

Rhiandon spun back and around, contained by the walls, creating a maelstrom in the courtyard. The Small Folk quailed away from her, or joined in the storm if they were able, contributing to the chaos of it all. Rayul was driven to his knees, as lightning

227

flashed around him, and the rain drove down on all of us. She dove at him, sweeping just over his head as he threw himself to the ground. The wind was her shrieking as she passed us, swerving again away from the wall.

Then, through all the wind, and the pounding rain, we heard a word ring out like a bell. "Peace," the voice said, and Rhiandon began to shrink. Slowly she grew smaller, with parts of her whisking away into the air like clouds. Eventually a woman stood in the courtyard: a giant of a woman, but the simple form of a woman, nonetheless.

Once the storm had ceased, and everything was still, I noticed the speaker. Rahkel had stepped through the Way and was surveying the shambles around us. The other Wild had stilled, and were watching her, as though for orders. The few guards that hadn't been beaten down by them or cut down by Thromm were standing soaked and shivering.

Rahkel went to Rayul and sat cross-legged next to him. He was on his hands and knees and she drew him to her, so he was nearly lying in her lap. She smoothed his hair with her hand, pulling the wet strands out of his eyes.

"You've done some terrible things, brother," she said, in that sweet lullaby voice.

"They took you away from me," Rayul said. "And you wouldn't come back, no matter what I tried. I tried to save you."

"Don't you remember, brother, when we were little, how sad I was here?"

I realized now how much younger than him she looked. He was only middle aged for an elf, which would put him at about 120. She looked like she was no more than a woman in her twenties.

"But I can make you better," he said. "I found a way to make you better, so you can be happy here with me."

"Oh sweetie... you have no idea. You have no idea how beautiful it is out there." As she spoke, Rayul's face went from twisted and sad to calm and wondering. His eyes glazed over, and I guessed that she was showing him something, some false wonderland promise of what the Wild was like.

"What is she waiting for?" Otsoa whispered, coming to stand beside me. "I thought they were going to kill him. The giant could have done that."

"They aren't going to kill him. They're going to take him," I said, watching her work. She was impressive, as good at persuasive words as her brother, but with a magical voice that could sooth, or delight, or deceive.

"Why don't you come with me, Rayul, and you can see. You can see how happy I am there?" She helped him sit up, and they stood together, Rayul completely under her charm, and going along as easily as Meia had obeyed us. But his face was blissful and calm, not flat and emotionless.

"They don't tell us about this part." Rayul was speaking in a sing-songy way, sleepily. "They don't tell you how perfect it is. Why do they want to keep us away from it? Are you sure I will be welcome there?"

"Hush, darling. Everything's going to be fine." Rahkel walked Rayul to the Way. She cast a glance at me and nodded. But as they were about to enter the Way, Rayul hesitated.

"I can't. I can't go there."

"Of course, you can." Rahkel put her hands on both sides of his face. "Open up, Rayul."

It looked as if his body jolted, and when he opened his eyes again, they looked like hers, bright and clear and focused. He laughed, shortly, then took her hand, turned her around, and nearly pushed her into the Way.

"Let's go Rahkel! I want to see it all." He was not charmed any longer. He was eager to be free, to be there. I knew that feeling. It made me shudder.

"Off we go!" Rahkel said, putting her hands over his. And then they were gone.

CHAPTER EIGHTEEN

The city guard arrived after the Way was closed and the servants of the house were busy cleaning up the yard. They had grown used to the hunters taking care of the Wild incursions, so they not only took their time getting there, but sent only two guards.

It was difficult for me to hide in one of the halls while Tara explained what had happened. She was a good liar, and I was still Wild looking as a dandelion and had to stay invisible. Initially there were cries of going into the Wild to save Rayul, but once the trove of forbidden magic in his basement was revealed, they changed their minds.

Tara cleared Thromm, Glenn and Otsoa and they helped me sneak out a side gate and get away from the house. It was quiet in the streets, only a few people peering through their windows as we passed. We made it back to Glenn's church without running into anyone.

"What happened to the others?" Glenn asked Tara. "Are they—"

"They're fine. Rayul had us put them to sleep. They are probably making their way back now."

Glenn nodded, and sat down gingerly at the table in the church kitchen. Tara stayed leaning against the door frame, and the rest of us settled down at the table.

"So, what did you find in Rayul's basement?" Otsoa asked Thromm. "From the way the guards were reacting you'd think they'd found a pond of mermaids or something. Did you get the contraband you were looking for?"

"You're one to talk," Tara said. "How long have you been working human magic?"

"How long have you been working for a villainous mage politician?" Otsoa responded. Thromm interrupted before they could start trading blows.

"I really had little time to do more than grab at a shelf and run." Thromm reached into his shirt and pulled out several papers and cards. There were sketches, and messy notes in elvish, and some pages that looked like they had been ripped from a book. There was a page with the drawings of several regular geometric shapes with numbers on each face, and notes about each one. Thromm pointed to one of the cards.

It didn't look like much. It was a regular sized card, decorated on the back with a long oval, and the five element colors spaced like the corners of a pentacle. To look at the thing you wouldn't think it magical at all. The front seemed to include instructions for how to open a portal between planes.

"It requires the presence of nature to draw power. Trees, in this case." He pointed to the notes in the corner. The symbol of a tree and a number.

"That's easy enough," Otsoa said, sifting through the papers.

There was a knock at the door. Glenn started to get up, but Otsoa waved him back into his seat. He opened the door and then stammered. Finally, he bowed and got out of the way.

Josie hurried in, nodding at Otsoa quickly before rushing for me. She didn't even react to my appearance, just hugged me.

"I am so glad you're alright." After hugging me she looked around. "All of you. Glenn, are you—" She noticed Tara last. "Oh, hello." She turned back to me quickly. "I won't stay, I just wanted to see you and be sure." She started back around the table, but Otsoa was in the way.

"Can we talk?" he asked her.

"Yeah, sure." She looked around, unfamiliar with the place. Glenn pointed to one of the doors and Josie disappeared into the hallway. Otsoa stopped on the way out and tapped Thromm on the shoulder.

"Oh, right." Thromm dug into another hidden pocket and handed a glinting bracelet to Otsoa. The bracelet he held in his palm was an intricate twist of several metals, engraved with symbols from all of the free races. I smiled up at Otsoa and had to work very hard not to bounce in excitement.

"She will love it."

"Wish me luck," he said, and ducked out into the hallway. I wanted to follow, but I took a deep breath and trusted that Otsoa could smooth things over, and that Josie would give him a chance.

"As charming as all of this is," Tara said. "I should be going. If the guard gives you any trouble, send them my way."

I fought the urge to scold Thromm as he stood and blocked the way out. Tara rolled her eyes and folded her arms.

"Do you still mean to find your revenge?" he asked.

"What difference does that make to you?"

"It will not bring you peace," Glenn chimed in.

"I'm not looking for peace," she answered. "I've been marked. And I'll fulfill my destiny one way or the other." When she looked up at Thromm again, his mouth flattened into a thin line, but he nodded and moved out of her way.

"Is it even possible for her to win against one of those things?" Glenn asked. Thromm moved to the window and watched Tara leave.

I shrugged. "She survived it once before."

We travelled outside the wall of Casavera. Josie came with us, mostly walking beside Otsoa and singing silly little melodies. Glenn stayed in town, as the clerics who had gone with us to the shrine had showed up at the church wanting to meet with him. We traveled to a nearby copse of trees that would shield us in case anyone was this far from the road.

"You don't know how to use any of the magic we found in that basement," Otsoa said as I laid out the papers Thromm had managed to get out before the Watch had arrived at Rayul's house.

"Nope." Most if it was just a jumble of diagrams of many-sided shapes, though this one included specific measurements and material suggestions.

"So, how is this going to work?" Otsoa picked up one of the pages and peered at it.

"We're going to improvise," I said. I turned to Thromm. "Tell me about your home."

"I have already told you, Redhawk."

"No." I sat down and patted the ground beside me. "Take your time. Tell me what it's like. How it feels to breathe the air there. Where you take that special someone for a night out." Thromm smiled and sat beside me. He closed his eyes for a few minutes in thought. When he opened them, they were bright and merry. With grand words and wide gestures, he described a land filled with magic and strange creatures. Some things sounded familiar, like elves and dwarves and fairy creatures, but he also spoke of dragons and monsters I had never heard of. Finally, he came to a woman. The woman he was meant to marry, and his voice grew so soft I could barely hear him.

Josie was almost crying when he finished. I thanked him, stood up and brushed the grass from my pants. I motioned to Otsoa.

"All right, spellcaster, your turn."

"What?"

"I need you to do whatever it was you did the last time. I doubt I can open Ways to other planes on just my own strength." I held my hand out to him, and he took it. In my other hand I held the portal card Thromm had discovered. I concentrated on Thromm's story, the feeling of being somewhere grand and terrifying all at once and sang a song of Redhawk. The humming energy between Otsoa and me crested in a visible current that ran between us. It rushed out in a swirling eddy that formed a massive portal before us.

This one felt different than the others. We could feel it pulling us toward it, pulling everything toward it. It seemed like the colors of the surrounding trees and grass were draining into it.

"I think we should wrap this up fast," I said, letting go of Otsoa's hand.

Otsoa and Thromm, rather than actually saying any goodbyes to each other, clasped their arms in an odd way, their hands almost at each other's elbows. Then he surprised the wind out of me by giving me a bone-crushing hug.

"You behave yourself, bard," he said, patting me on the head.

I dug out a small walnut shell from my purse and handed it to him. "It will play a song when you open it."

His brilliant smile was inspiring. Finally, he knelt down before Josie, gave her a gentle hug, and whispered something to her. She blushed and nodded.

Thromm turned to us all, smiled, and waved, and stepped into the portal. It closed up after him with a whump. It happened so fast, it was hard to feel sad. I was glad he made it home, and I wished him all the happiness in whatever realm, or 'plane' he lived in.

"I think we should burn that card," Glenn said. He plucked it from my hand and began to ready a fire spell.

"Burn this too," I said, handing the pages of geometric shapes to him.

"He was a good companion," Otsoa said, "But I'm glad he's home."

There was no clerk at the door this time at Roya's office. The door to his room was open, and when arrived, he called to me, and told me to come right in and have a seat. He was digging around in a closet in the back corner of his room. I could only see the edge of his robe peeking out of the door.

I plopped down into the chair. He eventually extricated himself from the closet, and came around the desk, leaning back against it. In his hands was a sizable bag full of coins. I could hear them clinking.

"Payment, for a job well done. I trust you will distribute this among the others?" He held the bag out to me, but I couldn't take it right away. It was a really big bag. Much larger than our original price, even if it was going to get split three ways.

"You knew, didn't you? You knew what was going on?"

"What was going on?"

"Oh, don't start that with me," I said, standing up. Even sitting on the desk, he was taller than me. "You knew someone was killing others like me, and you wanted me on this job because of that."

"I am not the highest paid questfinder in Cyfar for nothing." He hefted the bag of gold up a bit to make it jingle. "And really, can you complain if I happen to wish to take care of more than one job at a time? It's a very profitable endeavor."

"No, no I won't complain at all." I sighed. "It's not as though I have a choice."

"We all have a choice," he said, dropping the gold onto his desk with a loud thud. "I chose to put you on this job because I knew you would see it through. I know the way I hired you was unpleasant. I will not require that of you again. You need never listen to another job proposal from this office."

"Really?" I narrowed my eyes at him.

"Really. I'll swear to it before your brother if you wish. Though I have a feeling he is going to want to be in on these sorts of things with you."

"You might be right about that. Poor fool."

"But if you'd like the chance at these sorts of... important... jobs, shall I send around for you?"

I picked up the bag of gold, supporting a good amount of its weight against my stomach. "Yes, Roya. If you find more jobs like this one, I would be glad to hear you out."

About the Author

Melissa Matos is a creator of stories in many forms, including novels, games, art and music. Her love of fantasy began with Disney and The Last Unicorn. Since then fantasy stories have expanded her world with the likes of the Dresden Files and Name of the Wind. She enjoys creating complex characters having exciting adventures, usually with a bit of mystery thrown in. She lives in Philadelphia with her family and two grumpy cockatiels.

melissamatosauthor.com

LOCASTA, THE IRON SORCERER · MY WILL IS IRON · MY HEART IS ADAMANT · MY BODY IS STONE · I FEEL NO PAIN ·

In the realm of Gargantua, human's lives are dictated by the rulers of the four domains: Dragons, Giants, Rocs and Krakens. Locasta was raised by the dragons to further their brand of order. Her first mission is to find the missing Iron Champion who never returned from his quest to retrieve the sword Craven from the Giants who had stolen it. She is joined by Trax, a dragon descended humanoid, who is tracking down the survivors of a past tragedy. Locasta must decide whether to use her strength to conquer and destroy, as the dragons would want, or to find something deeper to believe in.

Join the author newsletter to receive this story and more free!
melissamatosauthor.com

MOMTOAST

PUBLISHING